FALLING FOR YOU...AGAIN

THE MURPHY CLAN—FALLING IN LOVE SERIES

KATHY COATNEY

Windtree
Press

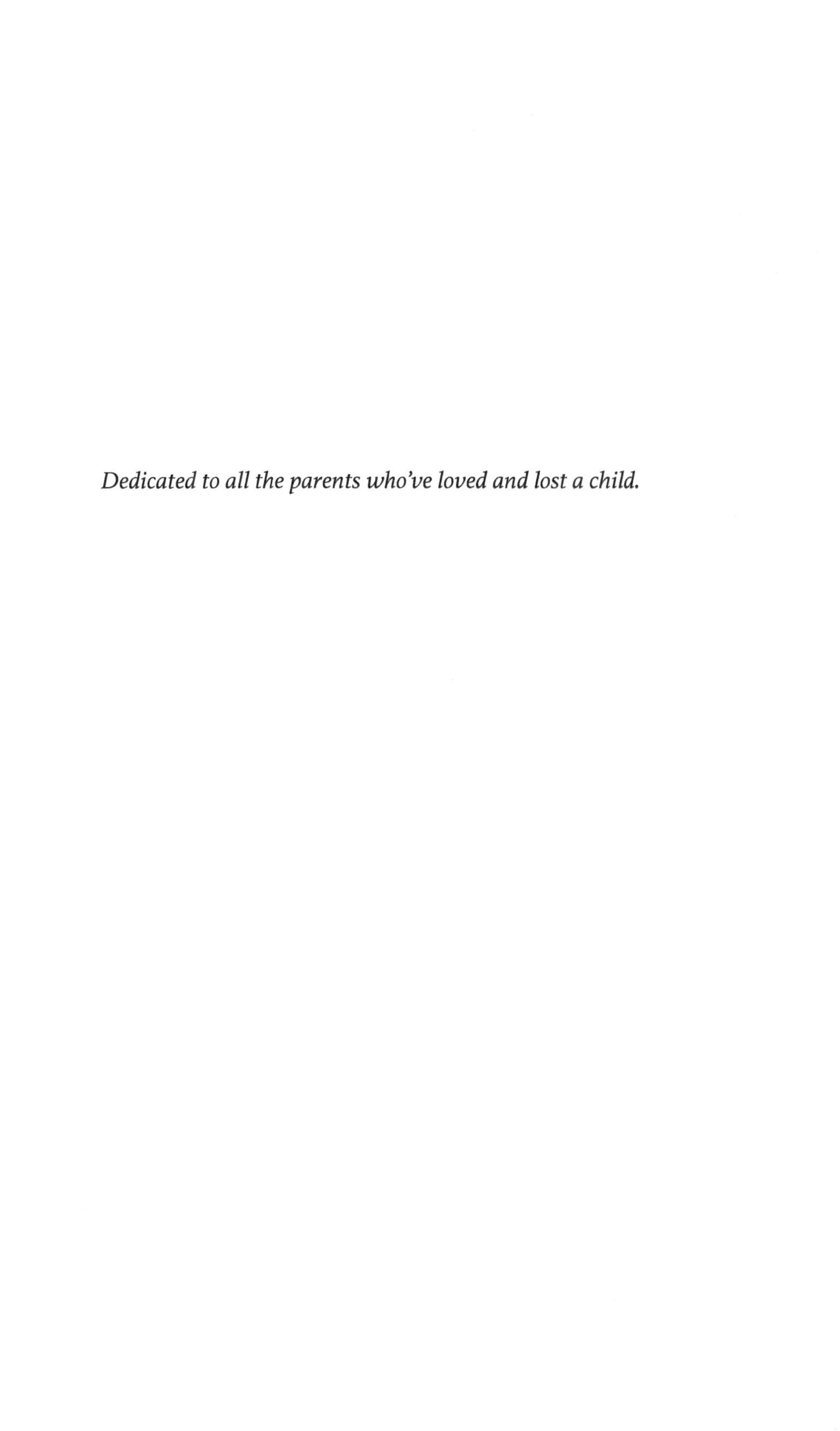

Dedicated to all the parents who've loved and lost a child.

ACKNOWLEDGMENTS

I've had a number of life-altering moments in my life, each special in their own way. The road to becoming a novelist has been smooth and rocky, but it has been an incredible journey because of those who have accompanied me.

My faithful email check-in pal, Jennifer Skullestad; my critique partners, Luann Erickson and Lisa Sorensen; my beta reader, Rebecca Clark—you are my GPS to finding the end. Friends and family made the journey memorable—Susan Crosby, Karol Black, Diana McCollum, Tammy Lambeth, Karen Duvall, Marie Hart, Alison Wells, Paty Jager, and my family—Nick, Wade, Devin, and Collin, Jake and Emily, and Allie and Russell. I'm blessed to have had you all beside me.

I've also had the pleasure to work with several talented businesswomen: Laura Shin, my editor, Yvonne Betancourt, my formatter, TINB Ink, and Tara, my cover designer.

ALSO BY KATHY COATNEY

Thank you for reading *Falling for You...Again,* part of *The Murphy Clan. The Murphy Clan* can all be read as stand alone books, but there are also three series within the Clan—*Falling in Love, Return to Hope's Crossing, Crooked Halo Christmas Chronicles,* and a *Vermont Christmas Romance.* If you enjoyed the characters of Paradise Falls, be sure and check out the Falling in Love series and the entire Murphy Clan.

If you liked this book, I'd love it if you'd leave a review at Goodreads and BookBub.

I love hearing from my fans. You can contact me through my website, newsletter, or join my Facebook group Kathy Coatney's The Beauty Bowl. I share information about my books, excerpts, and other fun information. If you like free books come join Kathy Coatney's Review Team by sending me an email kathy@kathycoatney.com.

All my books are small town, contemporary romances with uplifting stories of hope, a sprinkling of quirky characters and a happily ever after.

Contact me at:

Website

Kathy Coatney's The Beauty Bowl

The Murphy Clan

Falling in Love series

Falling For You...Again

Falling in Love With You

Falling in Love For The First Time

Falling in Love With Him

Return to Hope's Crossing series

Forever His

Forever Mine

Forever Yours

Crooked Halo Christmas Chronicles

Be My Santa Tonight

Her Christmas Wish

Under the Mistletoe

A Vermont Christmas Romance

Santa Comes to Snowside

Box Set

Falling in Love Box Set

Crooked Halo Christmas Chronicles Box Set

PRAISE FOR KATHY COATNEY

Praise for Kathy Coatney's second novel

"Kathy Coatney has written an achingly beautiful love story of survival in the face of heartbreaking tragedy. Make room in your bookshelf. This one is a keeper."

-- Georgia Bockoven, Author of the bestselling *Beach House* series

Falling For You Again: Life knocked her down, but she came up fighting.

When a small town teacher and a big city photographer meet, it's love at first sight—until tragedy shatters their fairytale romance.

It was a choice no father should ever have to make—save one child and the other dies. And Ethan can never forgive himself for making that choice. He loves his wife, Clare, beyond reason, but his guilt has put a wedge between them.

Two years have passed and Ethan and Clare's marriage is on life support. When Clare leaves on a photo shoot into the mountains and doesn't return, Ethan focuses on what really matters: his wife, and the love he never meant to lose. With a blizzard looming, he will risk everything, even his live, for a second chance at love.

Get your copy now because a second chance at love is always worth fighting for.

CONTENTS

1

Present day, Paradise Falls, Idaho...

Clare Burke bolted upright in bed.

The hazy light of dawn filtered through the French doors and sent a halo of light over the shimmering image at the foot of the bed.

"Grace." Two years and two days since her death, and her daughter still came to her, comforted her.

Questions overrode logical thought, but rather than sort through them she blurted out the one that continually weighed on her. "Are you happy?"

Grace smiled that smile that would drive a hermit in search of companionship, then vanished.

Had she been real or imaginary? The lines were as blurred as Grace's image.

Tears welled in Clare's eyes, and her heart absorbed a wave of grief. Why had Grace been taken from her? Why *her* child? All she had left of the daughter she loved were memories. Memories of pursed lips hiding braces, purple-streaked blonde hair and the snort of teenage sarcasm.

The faint light illuminated the sky blue walls. The room should have made her think of wide open spaces, but instead it had become her prison.

She stared at the stack of self-help books on her nightstand. She knew the titles as intimately as she did herself. *Learn to Grieve, Living Without Your Loved One* and her more recent pick, *The Top Three Reasons Marriages Fail: Finances, Communication, and Emotional Detachment.*

The knot wedged in her stomach wound tighter as she stared through a blur of tears at her husband, Ethan, sound asleep, twisted around the down comforter like a deranged pretzel.

When was the last time she'd felt truly connected to him?

Two years and two days.

They'd embraced life back then, now they tolerated it. They were shells of their former selves—colorless imitations of the vibrant couple they'd once been. Back then she would have told him about Grace's visits. Now they were barely civil to each other. Ethan was here physically. Emotionally, he had become as untouchable as Grace.

The faint shriek of their oldest son, Jack's, alarm filtered through the adjoining wall.

Tousled brown hair poked above the covers. A pair of matching brown eyes slowly opened and stared back at Clare.

"What time is it?"

Once upon a time that raspy voice had been her idea of a mating call. Now she felt a desperate ache that nothing filled. "Six."

His knuckles grazed her cheek. "Still a while until we have to get up."

Clare knew that tone, the darkening of his eyes, the wisp of a smile that had once held the promise of bliss. It would be impossibly easy to say yes, to curl into him and ignore the fact that sex for her had become as tempting as unflavored gelatin.

She pressed his hand to her cheek. "Could we just hold each other and talk instead?" Her words stripped the smile from his face.

He rolled onto his back and stared at the ceiling. "Honestly, Clare,

I'm all talked out."

"I'm not." She desperately wanted to recapture the closeness they'd shared, and the only way she knew how to do it was by talking.

He turned his head to look at her. "You never are."

Three simple words and their bedroom became a war zone.

Did she really want to pursue this? No, but an urgent need to connect with him drove her to press him. "What's that supposed to mean?"

He averted his eyes, but not before Clare saw a chill in them that left her hollow inside. Did saving one child only to have the other die take the joy out of living?

"Let's have it. Tell me whatever it is I've done wrong according to the latest self-help book you're reading on grieving."

His pointed stare at the nightstand had outrage overriding her good sense. "Why do you feel threatened by those books?"

His gaze cut to her. "Why do you feel a need to hide from life in those books?"

His criticism stung. They'd had a good marriage, a good life, until it all went horribly bad.

"There's no passion between us. There's *nothing* between us anymore. We don't talk, we don't touch, we don't make love, we have *sex*. I need to understand what changed."

"I don't need a book to tell me the obvious," he said.

"Which is?"

"It's damn hard to drum up passion with a ghost between us."

Had Ethan seen Grace too?

She sat up against the headboard. "What exactly does that mean?"

"It means Grace is always hovering over us. She's always on your mind."

He hadn't seen Grace. Disappointment settled over her, then anger. Of course Grace was on her mind. She was her daughter. Death wouldn't change that. "What do you want me to do, forget her?"

He swung his legs to the floor and sat with his back to her. He expelled a weary breath, then twisted around to look at her. "Can't we just sometimes not think about her?"

"You mean pretend she never existed?"

He grimaced. "I didn't say that. I just can't think about her every minute of every day."

Clare studied the photo of Grace on the dresser, her lips tightly sealed to hide her braces. She wished she could comply with his request. "I'm sorry. I can't turn myself on and off like that."

The very idea terrified her. What if she stopped thinking about Grace and she stopped appearing? Could she survive that?

Ethan shook his head. "I don't know how much longer I can go on like this."

The emotion clogged in her throat made it difficult to speak. "What are you saying?"

The silence between them had the same finality as their fourteen-year-old daughter's blue and lifeless body on that pristine steel table.

"I love you. I'll always love you, Clare, but I can't stay in the past. It's been two years since she died. I have to move forward."

"So do I."

The skepticism in his eyes was unmistakable. "You know, I think you really do believe that."

Was he right? Was *she* the one who couldn't move on?

Clare searched for the words that would convince him he was wrong, but nothing came.

He rose from the bed, and a moment later the bathroom door snicked closed.

Pain throbbed in Clare's heart like a knife buried shaft-deep in her chest. She slipped out of bed, opened the French doors, and stepped out onto the wood deck. The October wind tangled through her hair like the knotted emotions inside her. She crossed to the railing and leaned forward as if she stood on the deck of the Titanic. Peaceful one moment, disaster the next. The same as her life.

Golden leaves fluttered past like fat snowflakes onto the ruffled waters of Lake Serenity. A picture perfect scene. One that should have lifted her spirits, but instead it was littered with pieces of her heart.

JACK LAID in bed and listened to the shrill beep of his alarm clock. He preferred it to the muted sounds of his parent's argument that filtered through the adjoining wall. Finally, he reached over and switched it to the radio. "The Day That I Die" came out of the tinny speaker.

An image of Grace, eyebrows jutted, lips pressed tightly shut came to him. She'd hated this song, and he'd played it repeatedly just to torment her. Strange how hearing it now somehow eased the ache and the anger inside of him that her memory generated.

Why did she have to ruin everything by dying?

He shoved back the covers and kicked the pile of dirty laundry away from the bed. A crunchy gym sock bounced off the full length mirror. He paused to study his reflection, flexed his arm and saw the bicep jump. Not much, but enough to encourage him his weight lifting routine made a difference.

He sucked in a breath, and his chest stood out, scrawny and undefined. If he could just put on some muscle, he might look like a man instead of a gangly bean pole.

"Click, click."

Jack spun around to find Ben, his ten-year-old pest of a brother, in the doorway, camera in hand. "Get out of my room."

"Make me."

Jack lunged at him, but Ben was quicker. He sprinted down the hall to his bedroom, laughter trailing after him. Grace's laugh.

Jack stumbled, which gave his brother enough time to slam and lock the door. His fist pounded the wooden barrier. "If those pictures show up on your Facebook page, then the one of you running naked through the sprinklers goes up on mine."

Silence. "Okay, I won't put them up."

Too easy. "If I see those pictures anywhere, I'll make posters of your sprinkler ass and put them up all over town."

A noisy sigh came through the door.

"Is that a yes?"

Ben's door cracked open just wide enough for him to stick out his middle finger. "Okay, peckerhead."

Jack grabbed for his finger, but Ben quickly slammed the door. He pounded his fist against it a final time. "That's Mr. Peckerhead to you."

Jack went back to his room and slammed and locked his door. He never had any privacy. Eight more months and he'd be at college. Away from Ben. Away from the memories.

He turned back to the mirror, and scrubbed the handful of fuzzy blond hairs on his chin, and debated whether or not to shave. They were faint, but definitely there.

Before he came to a decision about whether or not to shave, his father's raised voice filtered through the wall.

Anger coiled deep inside him. Why couldn't Dad have just let Grace stay home? Why couldn't he have trusted her? The minute she'd stopped being his perfect little girl, he'd freaked.

What would he have done if she'd gotten a real tattoo instead of the wash-off, or if he'd seen the real piercing Grace's friend Amanda did to her bellybutton?

Eight more months and he'd be out from under his parents' authority. And he wouldn't be around when they called it quits on their sad excuse of a marriage.

His mother's angry retort sent Jack to the closet in search of another Jack. One that provided him with a hell of a lot more comfort than his parents did these days. He emerged with the bottle of Jack Daniels and took a swig. What would Grace think about her perfect, straight-A-valedictorian-bound oldest brother now?

More harsh words came through the wall and Jack washed away his pain with the numbing warmth of Tennessee's finest.

∽

THE EARLY MORNING light angled through the big, sunny yellow country kitchen. It was the kind of morning that used to make Ethan wish for the weekend. But not today. Today his mood remained gray-sky angry, and work would be his escape from Clare and their problems.

The bacon popped and sizzled along with Ethan's temper as he expertly flipped the pancakes.

Clare opened the cupboard door and accidentally bumped into him. She shot him a wary glance, then gave him a mumbled apology, and went back to fixing lunches and sneaking sips of his coffee when she thought he wasn't looking.

He wished he knew how to fix what was wrong between them. She was right that the passion between them was gone—or at least her passion for him. She never said it, but he knew making love had become a chore, a duty. Something she did for him, not because she desired him. And that knowledge stung. He wanted her to want him.

His temper skipped a notch when he spotted yet another self-help book on the counter. What they never told you in those damn books is nothing makes it hurt any less or brings your child back.

Ethan cursed and pushed aside the latest gem, *Grieving Over a Loved One*, she'd left open. No doubt for him to see and have some great epiphany. Just how many books did you have to read to get that they all had the same theme—that there were steps to grieving, but even so, everyone grieved in their own way. For some reason Clare missed that point. All she came away with was he wasn't doing it right.

He broke several eggs into the bowl and vigorously whisked them into a froth that kept time with his temper.

His attention moved from the book to Jack and Ben's squabbling. It was their usual start to the day and one he generally dealt with in good humor, but today it grated on his already frazzled nerves.

Ben picked at the center of his pancake with his fork. "This is raw in the middle."

What was it about ten-year-olds and their food? Ethan could make Ben's favorite meal and there would be something wrong with it.

Jack doused his pancakes in syrup. "You're too picky. It's fine."

Ben's fork banged against his plate. "What would you know about it? You'll eat anything. Even live fish on a dare!"

"Shut up," Jack said.

"You shut up."

"No, you."

"You wanna make me?" Ben's chair clattered to the floor when he leapt to his feet, fists balled. He charged his older brother.

Jack threw up his hand, and with his palm pressed to Ben's forehead, he easily fended him off. Whistling off key, he held Ben at bay while he sipped his orange juice.

Ethan yelled over Ben's howl of fury. "Hey."

No response.

He tried again. "Knock it off, sit down and eat your breakfast."

Still no response.

Ben's howling reached an ear-piercing level. Grabbing the frying pan he'd used to cook the pancakes, he slammed it down on the counter with enough force to crack the ceramic tile he'd so painstakingly laid.

Jack and Ben froze. Clare gaped at him as if he'd announced he was an alien. He was not a man known for a short fuse.

"Every day it's the same damn thing." He focused on Jack. "Finish your breakfast."

He turned to Ben. "You sit down and don't leave until you've eaten every last bite of that pancake. I don't care if you slurp the middle of it through a straw. And both of you do it in silence."

Without another word, he stormed out of the room, leaving them in stunned silence. Good. It was about time they realized their even-tempered husband and father had his limits.

CLARE LOADED her photography gear into the back of her SUV. Even though she was running late, she did a quick check of the survival gear and the food she always carried for her and the animals. Only someone with a death wish went into the wilderness unprepared, and Clare had had one too many close encounters not to appreciate the necessity of being ready for anything. It was the reason they'd adopted Bailey, a Siberian Husky mix, and trained her to go into the mountains as protection.

Clare whistled. "Load up."

The dog bounded around the side of the house and leapt into the rear of the car in one smooth motion, settling into her customary spot next to the side window.

Ballistic released a pitiful meow that was hardly befitting of his name. The mangy, one-eyed, smoke-colored cat had done his fair share of rough living before Bailey had found him on one of their trips into the mountains. And once Bailey had taken the malnourished creature under her wing, there had been no leaving him behind. So, they'd inherited a crazy feline who strutted around as if he were a five-hundred-pound Bengal tiger.

Clare picked up the cat, who'd only really liked being handled by Grace, but tolerated Clare's touch out of necessity, and deposited him in the car. He promptly curled up next to Bailey.

Slamming the rear hatch shut, Clare climbed into the driver's seat and cruised into town an hour behind schedule. Taking Warner Street, she drove through old town where "grand opening" flashed on the marquee of the refurbished Paradise Falls theater.

Her chest tightened, and a slow, steady ache threaded its way through her heart as she recalled the line of kids she'd seen buying tickets to opening night two days ago.

Grace should have been there, damn it!

Her phone beeped, indicating someone had left her a voice mail just as she was on the verge of losing cell phone service. With a grateful sigh, she pushed the painful memories aside and pulled onto the shoulder, then called for her messages.

"Clare."

Simultaneously she experienced warmth and misery at the sound of Ethan's voice. Why did love have to be so complicated? Why couldn't life have been one big happily-ever-after from the moment she and Ethan had said I do?

"I'm sorry about this morning. Be careful, and I'll see you tonight." A long pause, then, "I love you."

Clare pressed end and blinked back tears. She stared out the window. He loved her. After all they'd been through she'd wondered if they'd lost that, too. But even with his hesitation just now, she knew the words had come from the heart. Was it enough to save their marriage and heal their family? She wished she knew.

She brushed away a tear that had escaped and quickly dialed Ethan's cell phone. He would be in class, but she didn't care. She wanted to leave him a message.

The computerized voice announced she'd reached Ethan Burke's voice mail.

"Ethan, it's Clare. I got your message. I just wanted to—"

Wanted to what? Say she was sorry? Yes, but what she really wanted was to undo the damage she'd done after the accident. Shame kept her silent. You couldn't steal a man's dignity and not have consequences for those actions.

Her voice thick with tears, she continued, "I just wanted to tell you I love you, too, and I'll see you tonight."

Before she could put the phone down, it rang. She answered it without checking the Caller ID and immediately regretted it when her mother's voice came over the line.

"Clare, I'm so glad I caught you. I called earlier. Didn't you get the message?"

The barely veiled note of censure hung between them. "Yes, Mom, I got it, but I haven't had a chance to call you back."

"Well, it's fortunate I caught you now."

"Actually, I'm working—"

"Oh good, then we'll be able to talk."

Clare sucked in a sharp breath and an equally sharp retort. Explaining her job to her mother was useless. Alexandria Benton dismissed Clare's work as an outdoor photographer as a frivolous hobby, no matter what Clare said to the contrary.

Acknowledging defeat, Clare closed her eyes and prayed the call would be over soon. "I'm headed into a heavily wooded area, and I'll lose phone service, Mom, so we'll have to make it quick."

"You're going into the forest alone?"

Clare rubbed her forehead as pain throbbed behind her right eye. "You know perfectly well that is where I do most of my work. Don't worry, I take every precaution."

Her mother sniffed. "Yes, well, we know how effective that protection worked in the past."

Exceptionally well. Clare's gaze shifted to Bailey. She'd be dead right now, if not for Bailey's protection.

"Mom, tick-tock. What did you call me for?"

"Must you always be so rude?"

"Must you always chastise me before getting to the purpose of your call?"

Her mother's voice went whisper quiet. "Some daughters actually enjoy speaking with their mothers."

Guilt. Her mother could spread it like icing on a birthday cake. The thing was, if she'd been wrong, Clare wouldn't feel guilty. Why couldn't she look forward to, anticipate even, talking to her mother? She longed to be close to her, but every effort she'd made had been rebuffed, so Clare shielded herself from rejection by erecting an emotional wall between them—a wall eerily similar to the one Ethan had constructed.

Putting on her best conciliatory voice, she said, "I'm sorry. I've got a lot on my mind. What did you need to discuss?"

The huffed sigh indicated her ruffled feathers had been placated. "I needed to let you know we won't be able to fly out until Thursday. Your father has a business emergency he has to attend to."

No big surprise there. Her father's work always took precedence over everything and everyone. They'd barely made it out for Grace's funeral, and they certainly hadn't been available for Clare to lean on when she'd needed them most. If there was one thing she and Ethan had gotten right, it was putting their family before their careers.

That wasn't to say there weren't times she didn't long for the financial security of her childhood. But growing up with wealth and privilege carried a burden, and it was one she'd walked away from with no regrets. Still, after more than two decades of struggle, she'd come to appreciate how much easier life was when you had money.

"That's not a problem, Mom. Just let me know when your flight arrives and either Ethan or I will pick you up."

"I thought Jack was picking us up?"

"That was when you were coming in tomorrow. He has a test on Thursday he needs to study for." Fear threaded its way through her. That was also before Clare had learned about her son's drinking and driving incident.

A disappointed "oh" drifted over the line.

"You'll have all weekend to see him."

"Well—"

Here it came. Reason number five thousand, three hundred and thirty-six why they'd have to leave immediately after they set Grace's headstone.

"I'm afraid we won't be able to stay as long as we'd planned."

Clare's silence spoke for her.

"Clare, are you there?"

"I'm here, Mom."

"Don't you have anything to say?"

"What is there to say? You can't get here until the last minute, and you have to leave right away. Doesn't that pretty much sum it up?"

They'd abandoned her after Grace's death, so why should she expect them to support her when they set the headstone? Why couldn't they see how much she needed them, how hard this was for her? It had taken a year to get Ethan to agree to the simple ceremony, and she wanted her parents here, needed their support. An unrealistic expectation she knew, but she still hoped her parents would change.

Her mother's affirmative response sounded defeated, and Clare experienced another wave of guilt.

"I'd better let you get to work. I'll see you Thursday."

Clare said goodbye, and tossed the phone onto the passenger seat. She started the car, and another wave of tears threatened. Ruthlessly, she pushed them aside and focused on work—the one thing in her life she could control. The one thing that gave her some semblance of comfort.

If a problem arose, she could fix it, unlike the strained relationship with her parents. Unlike her marriage. Those were far more complicated than photography.

The road narrowed and made a series of sharp turns as Clare ascended into the mountains. She maneuvered the curves with practiced competency. She climbed to Parker Pass, a stunning elevation of over six thousand feet.

A narrow shaft of sunlight slanted through the heavy canopy of cedar, fir and tamarack trees and reflected off the windshield. Her breath caught as she recalled the first time Ethan brought her up here. These mountains had always been a magical place for her. A place where she'd made love to Ethan the first time, told him she loved him, conceived Grace here. They held the happiest moments of her life and she craved their solitude and peace now when her world was shattered. Maybe it was even a place to heal and why she continued to return.

She pushed aside the past and focused on the photo shoot. She hoped she hadn't missed out on what Galen Rowell, the famed outdoor photographer, called that unexpected convergence of light and form.

Over the years, Clare had discovered that her mantra "follow the light" had resulted in some of her finest work.

She envisioned this same ray of glowing yellow light angling through the trees at the photo shoot she was headed to as it cut through fluffy white clouds to a faint mist rising off the Serenity River.

The blast of an air horn snapped Clare's attention back to the road. A logging truck bore down on her. She slammed on the brakes and swerved hard to the right.

The SUV skidded on the graveled shoulder.

Clare's scream echoed across the mountain as the car spun out of control and followed the light into the canyon.

2
———

B e-e-e-ep.

Ethan lounged against the scarred yellow doorway as the second-period bell announced the end of his science class. Laughter filled the air as the students elbowed and jostled past him out the door to their lockers.

Turning away from the commotion, bone-weary emptiness settled over him. He crossed over to his desk and sat down.

A locker door slammed, followed by the squawk of rubber-soled shoes on worn linoleum. Ethan ignored the sound, dropped his chin onto his upturned palms, and closed his eyes. Warmth whispered over his shoulder as if his daughter sat beside him, bubbling with excitement and vitality.

He opened his eyes to assure himself she hadn't materialized, and stared at the stool in front of him. A smile replaced his fatigue when he recalled how Grace would straddle that stool, toss her head back, hold out her arms and legs and spin the seat like a Tilt-A-Whirl. A *weeeeeee* followed each revolution. So much like her mother. Both embraced life at that same breakneck speed as if they feared there wouldn't be enough time to experience it all.

The memory eased the pain within him, but when it faded, the silence of the empty room mocked him. A blatant reminder he was completely and utterly alone.

Truth be told, there were far too many times he believed Grace was alive, even with overwhelming evidence to the contrary. Ever since he awoke in that hospital room and learned Grace hadn't survived the boat accident a sliver of hope, a niggling doubt, festered inside him that this was a hoax. That Clare and everyone else was mistaken. That Grace hadn't died. That she hid from him. Waited for him to find her. Rescue her.

It was beyond crazy, he knew, but there just the same, and the reason he'd presented Clare with one excuse after another not to set the headstone. It was also the reason he tried so hard not to think about Grace.

A high-pitched giggle drew his attention to the hallway where Jeremy Muldoon snatched Shelly Givens' backpack. Shelly was the youngest sister of Amanda Givens, one of Grace's friends.

The dull ache that never truly subsided jabbed him, needled him yet again about the unfairness of it all. Why couldn't Grace have lived? Why couldn't she be dating? Getting her driver's license like Amanda? Just the other day he'd seen Amanda pick Shelly up in her parents' car. That could have been, *should* have been, Grace picking Ben up, but that would never happen.

Never.

He repeated the word hoping the finality would settle into him.

Grace was dead. He had to accept it and move on or become a useless waste of a man who could only think about the daughter he'd failed to save. He couldn't wallow in the past like Clare. He couldn't keep thinking about Grace or he would go fucking nuts.

Shelly's delighted screech echoed back to him. Jeremy held her backpack above her head as she grabbed for it. Their antics were all fun and games right now, but it could easily turn to hysterics and tears in the blink of an eye. No one had warned Ethan that comforting a stressed-out, tearful eighth grader was part of his job description. The female mind and its operation continued to baffle him. There was absolutely nothing scientific about it, and for a man committed to science, it remained as great a mystery as the magnetic field of the earth.

As Jeremy and Shelly shuffled off to class, Ethan's gaze circled the cluttered classroom. A Bunsen burner sat in the corner next to tilting stacks of science texts in desperate need of replacement, much like the rest of the school.

Regardless, he loved the three-story brick-and-mortar structure with its creaky wood floors and semi-reliable plumbing—loved all the memories it evoked, good and bad. Most of all, he loved that he had a job he enjoyed and the respect of his colleagues.

And respect was something he'd cultivated, strived for, longed for all of his life. Something Clare had grown up with and discarded without a second thought.

The bell rang and the students rushed off to class, their energy pulsing up and down the corridor.

He glanced at the wall clock as it clicked past eleven. Pulling his cell phone from his pants pocket, he looked to see if Clare had returned his call. No messages, which could mean one of two things. She either hadn't checked her voicemail, or she was still angry with at him and was ignoring his call. Either was a likely scenario.

He started to dial Clare's cell, then stopped when a single, swift rap on his open door announced the entry of his friend, Noah Murphy.

"Hey Ethan." Noah's rumbling bass voice ricocheted off the metal lockers in the empty hallway.

Noah was the eighth grade P.E./math teacher and one of those guys that everyone loved. While he had a voice that rang with authority, it was all bluster. Beneath that booming voice was an all-around nice guy. Perhaps too nice because there were those who took advantage of his good nature.

Noah slumped down onto Grace's stool at the table closest to Ethan's desk and scrubbed a hand over his face.

"Rough morning?" Ethan asked.

Noah lifted his head. Deep circles ringed bloodshot eyes.

"Or rather a rough night?" Ethan amended.

"Yeah, but not from tying one on, if that's what you're implying. Sarah threw me out."

Again, Ethan silently added. Their battles were becoming more and more frequent.

"Oh hell, I'm sorry."

"Yeah, me, too."

"Do you want to get some coffee?"

"This is your prep period. I don't want you to waste it listening to the boring details of my failed marriage, especially since you've got a perfect marriage."

Perfect? Where had Noah gotten that idea? He and Clare were hanging by a thread.

"I have nothing to prep for. I'm free."

Even if he'd had something pressing, he still would have given up his prep period. Ethan wanted, desperately *needed* to understand what had happened to a couple who'd seemed happy and content not that long ago.

He'd thought Noah and Sarah could work out their differences. It had given him hope he and Clare stood a chance of holding their fragile union together, but he was beginning to wonder.

Grabbing coffee from the teacher's lounge, they exited the side door and sat at one of the few picnic tables that wasn't shaded. Fluffy white clouds drifted overhead, shadowing the baseball field where Charlie Cooper, head of maintenance, drove the riding mower.

The innocuous white clouds were gradually replaced with deepening gray ones. They didn't look threatening enough for the full winter storm being predicted, but anyone who'd lived in northern Idaho as long as Ethan had knew anything was possible. And snow in October wasn't that uncommon.

The wind whipped through Ethan's hair, and a shiver, not entirely from the cold, consumed him. A sense that trouble was brewing slipped over him. He ignored the sensation and focused on his friend. "So, are you going to tell me what happened?"

Hunched forward with his elbows braced on his thighs, Noah

stared down into his coffee as if the answer to all his problems lay hidden in the murky brown depths.

"Same old shit. Sarah thinks I'm still in love with Abby."

Noah had never even hinted he had feelings for Abby. He'd always been committed to Sarah and the kids.

"What happened?"

"She's upset that Abby and Jon are building a house on the lake. She wants us to move."

Ethan studied his friend. "And you don't want to I assume?"

"I love our house." Noah paused and swallowed, then looked at the sky. "Jon's dying. I want to spend time with him while I can."

Noah, Jon and Abby had been best friends growing up, and they'd remained close.

Noah jammed the toe of his shoe into the grass. "I love Sarah, and I'd do anything for her and the kids, but not this. She doesn't want me to see Jon and Abby, but that's nothing new. Every time they came home from their travels, she comes up with one excuse after another not to see them."

Noah released a bitter laugh. "It was so hard when we first got married. We were so young and all we did was work to support the kids. I kept thinking it will be easier after we finish college and have a stable income. And it was easier, financially speaking, but now that we have time for each other, all we do is fight. I think we were happier in those early days when all we did was struggle. Any more I dread going home, dread spending time with her. It's an effort to find anything to talk about that won't end in an argument."

Ethan remembered those earlier times as well and wondered how they'd slipped away so quickly. He used to be Clare's sounding board for her work, but not since the accident. Not since he'd shut her out. Not since she'd lost faith in him.

Noah took a taste of his coffee and shuddered as he swallowed the stale brew. "That's bad stuff," he said, but took another sip anyway before he continued. "Suddenly the kids are off doing their own thing, and we're alone with nothing to talk about, so instead we fight. It's entertainment to relieve the boredom, I think. One minute we're talking about some mundane thing that happened that day, and then we're yelling and screaming about whose turn it is to feed the dog, which eventually turns into you don't respect me, you never listen to what I say and I can't take it anymore. The next thing I know, I'm stomping out the door, relieved to be away from the hell my life has become. But at the same time, I'm scared shitless my marriage is over."

He and Clare hadn't reached that point, yet, but the sudden jab of fear that tightened his gut left Ethan wondering if he wouldn't be crying on Noah's shoulder in the very near future.

The piercing honk from a flock of Canadian geese drew Ethan's attention skyward. He watched as they dropped down in front of the gymnasium and settled onto the lawn. "Where did you stay last night?"

"In my truck."

"Why didn't you stay at your parents' or come to our place?"

Noah's chuckle was humorless. "And be the center of gossip, again. No thank you."

It was true. Whenever he and Sarah had a fight it went through the teacher's lounge faster than fresh donuts. The tight-knit community of teachers knew everyone and their business. And that was rarely a good thing.

"What are you going to do?"

"I don't know. Sarah wants us to go to counseling."

Once upon a time Ethan had believed in counseling. But after three different counselors and feeling worse after each visit instead of better, he'd given up on them. They'd tried emotionally focused, insight-oriented, behavioral, integrative behavioral counseling, and he'd even read some of Clare's damn books. The truth was, there were just things he couldn't talk about with anyone. Not even Clare. He could live with the distance between them, but never her loathing. So he chose silence.

But just because counseling hadn't worked for him didn't mean he'd discourage his friend. After all, it could just be him and not the counselor that was at fault.

"Are you going to go?"

Noah gave him a blank look. "I don't know."

They watched the geese methodically feed on the grass, inching closer and closer to the picnic table. Ethan envied geese. They mated for life, remained together throughout the years and had extremely low "divorce rates," unlike humans who forfeited their vows at the first sign of trouble.

"You know, it seems like just yesterday—and forever—since Sarah and I danced at the prom." Noah laughed, a real laugh for the first time that morning. "She was funny and she smelled amazing."

Ethan chuckled as he recalled his first meeting with Clare, and the gloom that had hovered over him lifted.

"Hey, are you laughing at me?"

Still grinning, Ethan shook his head. "No, just remembering the first time I saw Clare."

"Knowing Clare, it's got to be memorable."

"Definitely."

When Ethan didn't elaborate, Noah pressed him. "Well, are you going to tell me or leave me hanging here?"

"Funny you should mention hanging because that's exactly what she was doing the first time I laid eyes on her—she was hanging upside down from a tree."

"No way."

"I swear. It was my second year of teaching, mid-May, and you know how the kids are toward the end of the school year."

"Boy, don't I. They're all going ape-shit-crazy. Don't know what I'd do without summer."

"Exactly. Everyone was ready for vacation, especially me, so rather than keep them cooped up in the classroom, I scraped together enough money to take them to the Serenity River for the day. I think the kids were as excited as I was to be out of the classroom. We were studying the different types of rocks along the river and the insects that lived under them. I looked up, and there was this woman hanging upside down, a good twenty-five feet up a pine tree in a rock climbing harness that she'd attached to the trunk, snapping pictures."

In truth, she'd scared ten years off of him. Clare embraced life, he survived it and he'd been grateful when she'd tamed her wilder side.

"What was she taking pictures of?"

"Damned if I know. My attention was focused elsewhere."

Noah's eyes sparkled with humor. "And exactly what part of her anatomy was your attention riveted to?"

"None of your damn business." Every detail, from the form-fitting shirt that inched up just enough to expose a smooth expanse of her belly to her body hugging jeans, was burned into his memory. And male that he was, he'd waited, and watched, and hoped for a glimpse of more.

"I had twenty eleven-year-olds acting as chaperones," Ethan reminded him.

"And they always think we're here to keep the kids in line. If they only knew the truth—the kids are here to keep us in line."

Ethan grinned. "For sure."

"So, did you at least talk to her?"

"Oh yeah. When she finished taking pictures from the tree, she came over and asked what we were doing, then she started taking pictures of my class, things the kids found and all that. She asked if she could bring the photos to school for the kids, and that was, in a way, our first date."

"And a wedding ring and three kids later, here you are." Noah winced. "Oh man, I'm sorry. I didn't mean to bring up Grace."

Ethan waved off his apology. "You didn't say anything wrong. Grace was my daughter. I can't ignore that, and I don't want to." He just couldn't dwell on it the way Clare did, couldn't constantly talk about her, constantly search for answers when the truth was he, and he alone, was responsible for his daughter's death.

"Time goes by fast, doesn't it?" Noah's voice held a hint of wistfulness.

Ethan nodded his agreement. It seemed like just yesterday he and Clare had been head-over-heels in love. From the first moment he'd laid eyes on her all those years ago, he'd known she was the only woman for him. The perfect woman, in fact. The woman he'd dreamed of. Beautiful, elegant and respectable—all the things he wasn't, and all the things he'd never be.

But that hadn't stopped him from pursuing her and making her his. It had been selfish, no question, but he didn't care. He'd wanted her the instant he'd seen her, and after she'd brought the photos to school for the kids to see, he'd been determined to have her. Once he discovered Clare was looking for a simple life, he courted her with nature walks and camping trips.

Noah didn't comment on his sudden silence, and Ethan was grateful because he didn't want to discuss his marriage. He was too raw, too terrified that someday soon he'd be sleeping in *his* truck, lost and confused and alone.

Ethan's phone vibrated. He took it from his pocket hoping it was Clare, hoping the sound of her voice would chase away the demons inside of him that left him tense and edgy. But it wasn't Clare's number on the screen, it was his father's.

Noah pushed to his feet. "I'll give you some privacy."

Ethan shook his head as he tucked the phone back in his pocket. "I don't have time to talk."

The bell rang on the heels of his comment. Ethan breathed a sigh of relief. He didn't have the time or the mental fortitude to deal with his father. He sometimes thought it had been easier to handle him when he'd been a twelve-pack-a-day-drinker rather than after he found sobriety. Ethan couldn't just forget the past. Bitterness clung to him, unforgiving and unforgettable. And he didn't miss the irony that while he clung to that part of his past, he desperately sought to move beyond Grace's death.

"Back to work."

Noah tossed the last of his coffee in the grass. "Thanks for letting me spill my guts. It helped."

"Good."

As Ethan walked back to class, a longing for those early days with Clare consumed him. He missed the way they used to talk late into the night even when they both had to get up early to work the next day. He missed the closeness they'd shared physically, too, and he was petrified they'd never recapture what they'd lost. And if they couldn't, would either of them be satisfied living out their lives in this shell of a marriage they'd created?

3

Twenty-three years ago...

The sun tilted low in the sky and a single ray of sunlight slanted over Clare and Ethan sitting side by side at the scarred picnic table at George's Diner. Knees bumping, they sipped wine as the Serenity River meandered past.

Bryan Adams, "Everything I do, I do for you," drifted out of the tinny speakers mounted above the diner's open window. A shiver of delight swept over Clare when she looked down at the brochure to the Coeur d'Alene resort where Ethan had made reservations for their first romantic getaway.

"This is so sweet, but I can't go."

"Why not?"

"I have to work." Clare's fingers trembled as she pulled an envelope from her purse. "I got my first assignment."

"What! Seriously?" Ethan jumped up, pulled Clare to her feet and swung her high into the air. Her surprised squeal echoed across the river.

When they sat back down, Clare handed him the letter she'd

received. "It's from *Sunset* magazine. They liked the samples I sent them, and they want a whole series of photos from McKenzie Meadow. But I only have two weeks to get them done. So that means I'll be working all weekend taking pictures. I'm sorry. I really would have liked to go away with you. Would you give me a rain check?"

Ethan shook his head. "I can't do that."

Clare stared at him, speechless. Ethan had always been so easy going, she never expected this response from him. "What do you mean, no?"

"Well, it's like this. I made plans to spend the weekend with you, and I'm not giving them up."

"But, but, I can't go away with you."

Ethan shrugged. "So we'll stay here together."

"But I'll be in the mountains taking pictures all weekend. You'll be bored."

Ethan was a distraction she couldn't afford. She needed to focus on work, but she didn't want to hurt his feelings either.

He slipped an arm around her shoulder and leaned in to whisper in her ear. "If there's one thing I never am around you, it's bored. Besides, you can't work twenty-four/seven, right? And I figure a girl's gotta eat, so I'll come along as the official cook and housekeeper and take care of all the details while you work. And just so you know, I'm an excellent cook."

Warmth flooded through Clare. She studied Ethan's lean face. A major distraction. "But you planned a romantic getaway, and I've spoiled it."

His fingertips gently brushed over her cheek and a shiver reached clear to Clare's soul.

"You haven't spoiled anything. And what makes you think camping can't be romantic?"

"Well, probably because it's dusty and dirty and there aren't any showers and—"

Ethan pressed a finger to her lips. "I think you need to look at this from another perspective. We will be alone, in the mountains, with plenty of fresh air and sunshine, alongside a breathtakingly beautiful river. Did I mention we'd be alone?"

He wiggled his eyebrows and laughter bubbled up from inside her. "I believe you did mention that at least once, but I still don't see it as romantic as a weekend at the Coeur d'Alene resort."

"That's only because you aren't thinking outside the box."

"And a science teacher whose world consists of formulas and scientific equations is more capable than a photographer of thinking creatively?" she teased.

"In this instance, yes."

"You do realize romance and sex are not the same thing, don't you?"

"Who said anything about sex?"

Clare laughed again and shook her head. The man thought he understood discretion, but clearly he was clueless. His intentions were unmistakable—from that barely restrained twinkle in his eye, to the slight tilt of his lips he couldn't quite conceal. Not that Clare objected. She was more than ready to take their relationship to the next level.

"I just can't picture a sleeping bag in the middle of nowhere as romantic as candles, soft music, and a bottle of chilled chardonnay at a five-star hotel."

Ethan brushed aside her concern. "Leave the details to me. I'll take care of everything."

It doesn't have to be perfect to be right, she reminded herself.

Clare looked deep into Ethan's eyes, and all thoughts of going it alone vanished. Her heart expanded and warmth spread over her.

"Okay."

IT WAS STILL DARK the next day when they left Ethan's truck. The crisp hint of fall air nipped at Clare's nose and chilled her arms. A full harvest moon guided them up the narrow dirt trail to McKenzie Meadow.

As planned, they made it to the meadow before sunrise, and while Clare set up her tripod and unloaded her gear, Ethan set up camp. She began shooting as the hazy light of predawn painted the water in the faintest shades of violet and richest, ripest plum. A thin mist descended as dawn broke and swirled around her while she moved along the grassy riverbank.

She continued shooting until well after sunrise, forgetting everything but her work. Where was the best light? What angle captured it best? Which aperture setting and shutter speed should she use for the available light? Did she want to slow the motion of the water or speed it up? She changed lenses and filters. She scrambled over boulders and waded into the icy water. It wasn't until the sun was well overhead that she paused long enough to discover that Ethan had set up camp, had a fire going, and bacon frying.

Clare's stomach rumbled, reminding her she hadn't eaten since the night before. She gathered up her gear and lugged it over to camp.

Her step faltered when she came upon the tent Ethan had set up close enough to the river to hear it gurgle. She ducked inside and a long shudder traveled through her when she discovered a cozy bed made from two sleeping bags zipped together.

The fragrant aroma of fresh brewed coffee drew Clare away from the tent and to the fire that crackled and popped in unison with the bacon Ethan was cooking.

He looked up and smiled. The steady throb of her pulse kicked into double time. He handed her a cup of coffee, and she accepted it, cupping it between her hands while she worked to control the desire that quickly turned to full-force lust.

Sinking down in one of the two folding camp chairs set in front of the fire, she sipped the coffee and sighed. "This is as good as George's Diner."

She took another drink, scanning the camp. Ethan had created a mini-paradise for them. How in the world had he managed to haul all this in on his back?

She was about to ask, when he took a pair of eggs from his back-pack and cracked them into the pan with the bacon.

"What else do you have in that Mary Poppins bag of tricks?"

Ethan grinned, his brown eyes twinkling and set fire to more than her pulse. "I'll never tell. Did you get some good pictures?"

"I think so, but I won't know until I develop them."

"If they don't turn out, we'll just have to keep coming back until you get what you're looking for."

The subtle arch of his eyebrow made her wonder if he was talking about something more than her photography. Before she could ask, he turned his attention to their breakfast.

"Hope you're hungry."

"Starving."

"A woman who's not afraid to admit she's got an appetite. That's certainly a novelty. You just keep surprising me."

"Good. I'd hate to think I'm predictable."

Ethan set the pan aside and squatted in front of her. His dark eyes smoldered with passion. "Never." He kissed her, and he tasted of sweet cinnamon and fresh-brewed java.

Distraction, distraction, distraction.

Her fingers shook when she threaded them through his hair and pressed herself against him. "I want you so much I'm shaking." She took his hand and pressed it to her heart. "Do you feel that? It's what you do to me."

He pressed their clasped hands over his chest. "You do the same to me."

Clare pulled in a shuddering breath. "I want you, right here, right now, but I can't. I've got to get back to work before I lose the light."

His hands slid around her waist, and he lifted her to her feet, cradling her in his arms. "I know. Besides, I'm not finished yet."

Her gaze circled their camp. "What more could you possibly do out here in the middle of nowhere? It's not like you could bring in a band to play romantic music for us."

"I could." The seriousness of his tone sent her pulse rat-tap-tapping and convinced her anything was possible with this man.

Ethan's fingers gently smoothed her bangs. He pressed his lips to her forehead. "I love you, Clare. I want this to be special."

Emotion swirled within her. "Oh Ethan, I love you, too, and just being here with you makes it special."

His erection pressed solidly against her belly. The man was a distraction beyond measure! Even without the physical evidence of his desire for her, one look into his eyes said everything. He wanted her as desperately as she wanted him.

"You're making it damn hard for me to hold back when you stare at me like that."

Clare managed a dry laugh. "It's not any easier for me."

Ethan released her. "We should eat before the food gets cold."

Like she could eat now.

Somehow she managed, and somehow she banked the desire that Ethan's touch had ignited and went back to finish her assignment. Within the hour she was lost in her work. She scaled boulders, climbed trees, traipsed up and down the river, while she searched for unique and different angles that would set her work apart. By evening, mud and grime covered her clothes and perspiration clung to her like cheap cologne. The last thing on her mind was a romantic evening, and yet when she got back to camp, her heart leapt.

How he'd done it, Clare didn't have a clue, but Ethan had transformed their campsite into an elegant restaurant on the river. Soft music played, the campfire light flickered and cast an amber glow over a folding table set with a linen tablecloth and napkins, and real plates and glasses. And she smelled like a locker room full of sweaty athletes.

She glanced at the river and a shiver, not of desire, but at the thought of the temperature of the water, stilled her urge to dive in.

Ethan came up behind her and swept her into his arms. "How was your day?"

Clare twisted out of his hold to prevent him from getting a whiff of her, particularly when he carried the heavenly scent of sun-dried sheets. "I stink."

He raised a brow at her. "I don't care."

"I do."

Ethan's grin was infectious. "Then maybe you'd like a nice warm shower."

"We have a shower here?"

"We do."

He took her hand and led her around to the side of the tent where he'd erected a portable shower. Neatly folded on a camp stool was a towel and clean clothes. Never had anything looked more wonderful. She wanted to hug him, but decided she'd wait until after she showered.

"Shower and then we'll eat." He kissed her before he walked away.

Clare quickly showered with the limited water, then dressed. No makeup, no fancy clothes, but at least she was clean.

She headed for the table, then paused to peek inside the tent and gasped when she saw rose petals scattered over their bed. The man had thought of everything, but what was even more surprising was he'd never struck her as a romantic. Tonight, however, he'd made an all-out effort to make their first time special, and it touched her more than any over-priced resort.

"Are you hungry?"

The sound of his voice sent a renewed yearning for him through her.

"No."

"Dance with me then?" He held out his hand, and she stepped into his embrace.

They slowly swayed on the grassy bank of the river, the recorded music and the crickets serenading them. The flickering light from the fire reflected over the water. A log shifted and sparks ignited the velvet sky in a spray of color much like the fireworks shooting off inside of Clare.

"Ethan."

"Yes."

"Thank you."

"For what?"

"For this. It couldn't be more perfect."

They danced in silence a few moments longer, then Clare raised up on tiptoe and whispered in his ear. "Make love to me."

His eyes drank her in as if she were his last drop of water. Finally, he kissed her and kept on kissing her while he danced her backwards to the tent. A trail of clothing fell in their wake, and by the time Ethan lowered her to the sleeping bag, they were both naked and on the brink of spontaneous combustion.

Ethan started to shift his body off of her, but Clare held him firmly in place. "What are you doing?"

"Last time I checked it was called foreplay."

"Next time. This time I want fast and hard."

Ethan's eyes darkened as he reached over the side of the sleeping bag for a condom.

Clare took it from him and glided it on, then nudged him onto his back and slid down onto him. "Are you ready for a ride on the wild side, cowboy?"

PRESENT DAY...

Clare sighed. The dream filled her with a warmth and contentment she hadn't felt in a long, long time. Why couldn't they go back to those days? The magic of early love when Ethan had been a succulent dessert she'd wanted to devour.

She inhaled and pain exploded in her lungs. Her eyes flew open, panic settling in her chest when the air bag threatened to smother her.

Suddenly the SUV tilted sharply forward, and Clare's pulse went from a gallop to a dead run when she stared out the windshield. She wished she could go back to being unconscious because reality was scaring the shit out of her.

Her car swayed on the rock ledge like a possessed seesaw from a horror novel. The only thing preventing it from plunging to the bottom of the sheer thousand-foot drop were a pair of scrawny pine trees.

Every move she made sent the car inching forward. Bailey's whine from the rear forced Clare into action. She had to get out of the car and rescue the animals.

She released her seatbelt and eased open her door. The SUV groaned and lurched forward. Clare froze, then exhaled heavily when the car ceased its movement.

Forcing air into her lungs to calm the frantic beat of her heart, she placed her left foot on the ground. When the car didn't move, she slowly shifted her body toward the door.

Bailey jumped at the netting separating the rear hold from the backseat. Clare and the animals let out a screech when the car lurched forward again. Wood snapped, metal shrieked like a banshee as the SUV rocked forward.

"Bailey, sit, stay."

The dog immediately stopped its frantic movements and stared at her with panic-glazed eyes.

"I'm going to get us all out of here." White-knuckled, she clutched the steering wheel and sent up a prayer that she could indeed follow through on her promise.

She'd barely finished the prayer when the car stopped moving. Clare reached into the passenger seat, picked up her backpack and dropped it onto the ground, then inched out of the SUV. The minute both feet were on the ground, she raced to the rear door.

Slowly she eased open the back door. "Bailey, come."

The dog stared back at her through wide frightened eyes, but didn't move.

Clare lifted the door higher to grab her collar and drag her out. The SUV begin skidding.

"Bailey, Ballistic, come."

The SUV groaned as the metal undercarriage ground against the rock ledge. The rear door ripped out of Clare's hand. She stumbled and her feet skidded as the rock crumbled beneath her. The car shot forward, crashing through the trees.

Clare hit the ground hard. Gravel, rock and pine needles scraped her forearms and knees as she slid after her car. She frantically grabbed for a lone bush growing out of the sheer wall of rock. Her fingers raked across the brush as she sailed over the cliff and followed the SUV into the canyon.

4

The clock at Citizen's Bank struck noon as Ethan drove through downtown Paradise Falls. Ben bounced on the seat beside him, excited because of a short school day and the story he was telling.

"Dad, it was way cool. You should have been there." Ben's face lit up like Rockefeller Center at Christmas. "Jimmy Kimball started turning green, and Mr. Thornton kept yelling, and ya just knew he was gonna puke, but Mr. Thornton didn't see it coming. But Jimmy puking wasn't the best part. It was how it nailed Mr. Thornton in front of nearly the whole school."

"But what about Mr. Thornton? I don't like you finding humor at someone else's expense, even if he's a difficult person. And don't you think a little sympathy for Jimmy is in order here?"

The sparkle in Ben's eyes flickered then faded away, and he shot him an exaggerated eye roll. "Dad, you don't get it. Jimmy is the most popular kid in school because of this. And Mr. Thornton's a whole lot more than difficult. He's mean."

Ethan couldn't deny David Thornton was a lousy teacher. There were just some people who didn't belong in teaching or working with kids in general, and David was one of those people.

So knowing this, why did Ethan feel compelled to defend the man?

Because respect begat respect. And people who least deserved it were the very ones that needed it most. He needed Ben to understand that. Still, he couldn't deny the fact that standing up for David when he didn't have any real sympathy for the man made him appear insincere.

"Yes, he is mean, and the truth is that teaching is not a good fit for him, but have you ever considered why he behaves as he does?"

From the scowl Ben leveled at him there was no question he'd overreacted. Yes, he had a tendency to always make sure his kids weren't cruel. Maybe he went overboard sometimes, and maybe he came off as sanctimonious on occasion. So string him up for making every effort not to be like his father. And wasn't it better to err on the side of being overly responsible than irresponsible?

Ethan parked the truck in the Little League parking lot and faced his son. Ben quickly turned to stare out the window. "Please don't turn away from me. I listen to you, and I expect the same courtesy in return."

Ben glared at him. "I'm listening. You're the one that's not. You pretend like you do, but you don't. Why do you always have to ruin a good story by being a grownup? You take the fun out of everything."

Ben got out of the truck and slammed the door. He stomped to the back, grabbed an armload of baseball gear, and headed for the dugout.

Ethan pushed open his door, grabbed the rest of the gear and followed Ben to the dugout. He heard the tail end of the same story his son had told him on the way over, only Tommy Jensen told it this time and had everyone in fits of laughter.

He caught Ben's I-told-you-you're-overreacting look and silently conceded he could have a point. The fact that he was standing up for David when he didn't have any real sympathy for the man made him look like a hypocrite. Kind of hard to teach compassion when he was running short on it where David was concerned.

A burst of laughter echoed through the dugout when Tommy finished his version of the David Thornton story.

Ethan's phone vibrated in his pocket. He took it out hoping it was Clare. He couldn't shake the feeling she was in trouble. The problem was, every time she went into the mountains he thought that, especially after her encounter with the mountain lion.

Of course, she hadn't needed him then or when Grace died. She'd handled it all with effortless efficiency. That fact festered inside him, too.

Ethan noted the incoming number, silenced the phone, and shoved it back in his pocket. He still wasn't ready to deal with his dad.

Was it possible his father had actually known what he was talking about when he'd told Ethan that Clare would eventually become dissatisfied with him? The idea his father could have been right didn't settle well with him. It implied he wasn't enough for Clare, and he didn't believe that. Not for a minute. That day returned unbidden and unwelcome, the baseball field fading away, and suddenly he was back in his house on Eagle Lane.

TWENTY-THREE YEARS AGO...

Clare flitted around the cozy living room fluffing pillows and straightening pictures. She'd been nervous and jumpy since his parents had agreed to come to dinner.

Ethan wished he could reassure her, but it was nearly impossible to do since he never knew what to expect. His father could arrive stone-cold sober or falling-down drunk. It was always a crap shoot. And the level of his intoxication would be the telling factor in how well the evening went. The more his father drank, the worse it would be, and Ethan had no control over his drinking or his behavior.

He sat down on the plaid sofa and stretched out his legs on the scarred maple coffee table in an attempt to be the picture of confidence when in truth his gut churned and turned in apprehension.

He patted the lumpy cushion beside him. "Clare, everything looks great. Sit down and relax."

"I can't. I'm too nervous."

He snagged her hand when she paced past him and gently tugged her down beside him. "Let's see if I can't find a way to take your mind off of things."

Pressing his face into her hair, he inhaled the sweet scent of apple blossoms. He nibbled his way down her neck.

Clare giggled and pulled back from him. "That tickles. Stop."

Ethan ignored her girlish shriek and continued to nibble, eliciting another delighted screech.

She twisted away from him, her blue eyes vibrant and sparkling with retribution.

Before he realized her intent, she pounced and straddled his waist, then began tickling his ribs bringing forth a rush of laughter.

"So you want to play, do you?"

"You started it," Clare was quick to remind him.

He had, and he'd accomplished his mission of taking her mind and his off of dinner with his parents. Quickly twisting his body, he reversed their positions so he had her pinned beneath him.

"Ethan Burke, don't you dare mess up my hair."

Ethan smiled and leaned down to stroke his hand over the side of her cheek. "I wouldn't dream of it." He dropped his hand to cup her breast.

Her gasp of surprise pleased him as he lowered his mouth to steal a kiss. The chime of the doorbell stopped him.

He groaned, his lips hovering above hers. "Maybe they'll go away."

Clare's eyes darkened with rebuke, making it clear he would not escape tonight.

"You can't blame me for trying."

She planted her hands on his chest and raised up all sass and attitude. "And you can't be upset that it didn't work."

"Why not?"

Clare didn't respond to his question. Instead, she swung her legs to the floor. For a moment he kept his arm around her waist. Finally, he blew out a breath, accepted the inevitable, and released her.

Tugging her sweater into place, she checked her hair and makeup in the mirror, then clasped his hand, pulled him to his feet and led him to the door. The soft press of her skin was reassuring, and he needed that before he faced his parents.

Bracing himself, he opened the door. Most dinner guests came bearing a bottle of wine. Not his father. He came with a twelve pack cradled under his arm—make that an eleven pack since he'd already popped open one.

Clare opened the door wide and ushered them in.

Ben shoved the beer into his son's arms and turned to Clare. "Well, let me get a look at the woman who has my son all tied up in knots."

He spun Clare around and nodded his approval. "Son, you've got yourself one fine looking woman here." He jerked a thumb at Ethan. "You sure you want to hang out with this guy?"

Clare's laughter bubbled up and over like champagne spurting from a freshly opened bottle.

"That's where you're wrong, Mr. Burke. I'm the fortunate one. I don't know how I managed to find such a sweet, caring man."

Clare's response soothed Ethan's ruffled feathers, and sent a rush of happiness through him that replaced the emptiness he'd felt moments before.

His father's brows shot up. "Are we talking about Ethan Burke?"

Clare's smile turned radiant as she slipped her arm through Ethan's. "We most definitely are. Why don't we go into the living room."

If Ethan hadn't already been head-over-heels in love with her, Clare's easy handling of his father captured his heart forever and always.

"Would you like a glass of wine, Mrs. Burke?"

"I would love some, and please call me Dot. And this lovable but overbearing dolt is Ben."

Tension coiled through Ethan. He wished he could come to

terms with his childhood, but every time he tried, his father's behavior reminded him he'd been the one to support his parents financially from the moment he was old enough to hold a job. They had failed him, and it was a burden no child should have to bear.

Finding blame and pointing fingers didn't resolve those issues. In truth, Ethan really wanted to let go of his bitterness because he wasn't blind to the fact it hurt him the most.

"I'll get the drinks and be right back," Clare said.

Ethan rose to follow her. "I'd better check on dinner."

The scorn in his father's voice rekindled his resentment. "You're cooking?"

"Yes."

"You aren't going to poison us are you?"

"Ethan's an excellent cook," Clare chimed in before Ethan could voice the sharp retort that he'd been about to give.

As the evening wore on, Clare continued to divert the conversation and avert an altercation between him and his father. But as Ben had another beer and another, it became an even greater challenge that even Clare couldn't overcome.

They lingered over dinner. Finally, Clare rose and began gathering up the dishes.

Ethan started to help, but Clare shooed him away. "You cooked, I'll clean. Why don't you take your parents into the living room while I put the coffee on to go with dessert?"

His mother picked up a platter. "I'll help you."

After Ethan added wood to the fire, he sat opposite his father.

Ben's voice cut through the uncomfortable silence. "This is a mistake, and you know it, Ethan."

"What is a mistake?

"You and Clare."

Ethan's temper flared. He reined it in. "You don't know what you're talking about."

"Don't I? I married a woman who wasn't from here, remember? At first she was happy living up here away from everything and everyone she knew. But then times got a little lean and what did she do? She ran to her parents begging for money."

"Mom got tired of starving. There's a big difference between wanting things and necessity."

Ben shook a finger at him. "You mark my words, Clare's no different. Sooner or later she'll get tired of doing without, and then she'll go to her parents the same as your mother did."

"Aren't you getting a little ahead of yourself? Clare and I are only dating."

"I'm not blind. I can see she's the one."

"Isn't it a little late for fatherly advice?"

"Honestly, I didn't think you two would last more than a couple of dates. I mean the girl is clearly out of your league, besides which, you would have told me to mind my own business."

"So why aren't you?"

His father's eyes darkened as if he could predict Ethan's future. "It's my duty to warn you."

"Why is this the only parental duty you've decided to take seriously?" Ethan muttered.

Ben gulped down the last of his beer, then slammed the empty can on the coffee table. His gaze bore into Ethan's. "I like Clare, but she's no different than your mother."

For once he was correct. In this regard Clare and his mother were quite similar. Neither cared about monetary things.

The two came out just then with the coffee and dessert chatting like old friends, totally unaware of the drama that had unfolded in their absence.

Ben shot a dark look between him and Clare.

"He's wrong, Ethan," a voice whispered inside his head. "Clare loves you. You know she would never hurt you like that—never."

PRESENT DAY...

Ethan blinked. The memory faded when a chorus of voices demanded, "Coach, are we gonna practice?"

Fifteen expectant faces stared up at him. "Yeah, everybody out on the field."

Cleats clattered over the concrete floor as the players grabbed their gloves and headed out onto the field.

Ethan focused on Ben, lagging behind the rest of his teammates. His silence signaled his irritation with him. That even temperament Ethan counted on had disappeared like sunlight behind darkening clouds, and Ethan was to blame.

He waited until the rest of the team had gone out to the field to warm up before he spoke. "Okay, I'll concede you may have a point about Mr. Thornton."

"No maybe about it."

"Hey, give me a break. I'm a parent *and* a teacher, and it can be a real burden sometimes." He ruffled Ben's hair.

Ben shoved his hand away, but he couldn't hide the grin that threatened. It told Ethan all had been forgiven. That sunny disposition that never failed to brighten his day was back in place, and all was right with the world.

Ben walked out to the field, and Ethan's thoughts returned to the past as they did far too frequently these days. Was it possible his father's words all those years ago had been a prophecy?

Impossible. Ethan was a man of science, not voodoo.

He collected his glove and a bat from the equipment bag. His father couldn't predict the future. It had just been a lucky guess that Clare would go to her parents and ask for money. Or perhaps the more scientifically accurate explanation was, his father had seen what Ethan had blinded himself to—that Clare was committed to their life until the going got tough.

5

Clare's arm hooked over a thick pine branch. The sudden halt swung her body hard into solid rock wall and gave her already bruised ribs another thwack. She groaned and started to heave herself onto the ledge when her SUV slammed into the bottom of the canyon.

Shockwaves raced up the canyon wall and through her arms. The branch cracked, dropping her farther over the ledge. She scrambled for a foothold. Grunting out a breath of air, she pulled herself up the rest of the way, just as the branch snapped off completely.

Clare flopped onto the narrow outcropping where her SUV had been perched moments before. She gulped in great lungfuls of air, her ribs protesting the inhalation. Slowly, she rolled onto her back and a shadow fell over her accompanied by a loud, very welcome bark followed by a series of slobbery kisses.

"Bailey, you got out!" She looped her arms around the thick, furry neck and squeezed. Bailey responded by poking her nose in Clare's ear. Laughing, she drew back, scanning the ledge for Ballistic.

"Ballistic," she called hoping against hope the feline that had spent all nine of his lives before coming to live with them had pulled a Houdini and escaped as well.

Clare's gut clenched as the echo of her voice faded away. She couldn't bear the thought of losing that maniac cat.

Rising on shaky limbs, she called out again. She searched the narrow ledge, but there was no sign of him.

She slid back down to the ground. A tear splattered onto her leather hiking boot. She swiped her hand over her face and pulled herself together. Why was she crying over a cat who hadn't cared about anyone other than himself?

Because after all he'd survived, he deserved a dignified end.

Bailey's wet nose pressed against her cheek. Slowly Clare raised her head to find a pair of sorrowful eyes staring at her.

As she stroked Bailey, the last trace of sunshine disappeared behind heavy black clouds. The gentle breeze shifted to a biting wind and carried with it the nip of the snow storm brewing.

Inhaling a steadying breath, Clare took stock of her situation. The road was always the best option for rescue. Tilting her head, she stared up at the sheer vertical cliff. Climbing out wasn't an option.

She stared down the canyon where her car had gone, and debated hiking down. Chances were her SUV was mangled, but her tent and some of her gear could probably be salvaged. Cars exploding were Hollywood stunts, not real life.

Clare pushed to her feet and hissed out a breath. Every breath was a reminder she'd been hit by an airbag deploying at two hundred and thirty miles an hour. Her chest ached, and she'd bet a doozy of a bruise was forming over her left eye where she'd taken the brunt of the impact. And now she sported a pair of scraped knees from her latest fall.

An irate meow cut through the air.

Clare froze. She looked at Bailey, but the dog only stared up at her with a puzzled expression as if she couldn't believe what she'd just heard either.

Another infuriated meow sounded, louder and more shrill.

"Ballistic."

A get-me-the-hell-out-of-here yowl answered her call.

Clare dropped back to the ground, laid flat on her belly and inched forward until she could see over the side of the ledge.

Directly below, Ballistic clung to the root of the tree.

Clare wrapped her legs around what was left of the tree trunk and slowly inched forward. She leaned down to grab the cat, but when her fingers brushed his neck, he flinched away from her.

"I'm trying to save you, you mangy cat," Clare muttered.

He hissed and glared at her. His green eyes snapped with fury.

"Dammit, now is not the time to be persnickety."

The cat let out another incensed howl before taking a very careful, very deliberate step toward her. The root wobbled and Ballistic dug his claws in and froze. He eyed the yawning canyon, then Clare's outstretched arm. Finally, with a toss of his head, he leapt into the air and seconds later landed on Clare's shoulder.

She grunted, then hugged the cat to her chest, and quickly rolled back to safety, grateful Ballistic had scrounged up another life. No question, he was a pain in the keister most of the time, but he was her pain in the keister, and she was thankful he was alive and well.

Releasing him, she whistled at Bailey. The dog came to attention and Ballistic leapt to his customary position, the middle of Bailey's back. "We're going down."

Clare scooped up her backpack, and with Bailey in the lead, the dog cut a trail through the twisted, tangled mess of trees and vines. A rain drop slapped against Clare's forehead as a frigid gust of wind rattled the crispy golden leaves of a group of Aspen trees. It reminded her of the time she and Ethan had been stranded in the mountains in a full winter storm.

Clare had wanted to get pictures of the leaves turning, so Ethan had suggested they go up and stay at his friend's cabin for the weekend. It became a weekend of firsts. Their first trip into the mountains that wasn't camping, and Clare's first lesson in just how swiftly northern Idaho weather could change. And it was a lesson she'd never forgotten.

~

Clare spun in a circle in the tiny living room. "Ohmygod, it's perfect, Ethan. We're really staying here?"

"We are. It's hardly a mansion, though."

"It's better. It's cozy and warm." She placed a hand on her hip and arched a brow at him. "And very romantic."

"Romantic? You've got to be kidding. It's barely a step above camping."

Clare rolled her eyes and shook her head. "Oh, p-l-l-lease. This is the Taj Mahal in comparison. We have running water, a fireplace, a kitchen with a stove and refrigerator, electricity, a shower, and an honest-to-goodness bed. There is no comparison."

Clare burst out laughing at the look of utter disbelief on Ethan's face.

"What the hell is so damn funny?"

He was so darn cute when she baffled him that Clare laughed harder.

"Why is it you always prefer austere to extravagant? It's as if you think you're unworthy of nice things."

His insight immediately squelched her delight.

"That's ridiculous." She crossed over to the door. "I need to get my gear and set up."

"It's convenient how you always have an excuse not to discuss this subject whenever it comes up." His dark eyes probed hers, not in censure, but in genuine curiosity and concern.

Even with as much as they'd shared over the past several months, Clare still hadn't bared her innermost secrets to him. It was one thing to tell a man you loved him, to make love to him, but to share the most painful, intimate parts of your life, that wasn't something you did without careful forethought. So she would hide behind her work a little while longer until she dredged up the courage to tell him about her childhood, her family, and the fortune she'd walked away from.

She went out to Ethan's car and grabbed an armload of gear, anxious to put some distance between them so she could collect her scattered emotions. She also needed to get set up for her photo shoot of the sunset, which was just a few hours away.

Ethan trailed after her and scooped their suitcases from the backseat. The door slammed, and when she heard him retreat, she blew out a sigh of relief. It was short-lived, though. When she closed the trunk, she found him standing on the porch waiting for her.

"I love you, Clare, and whatever it is you're afraid to tell me won't change how I feel about you."

She so wanted to tell him everything right then and there, but she couldn't. Telling him about her family, the kind of privilege in which she'd been raised, embarrassed her, especially after she'd learned their extravagant lifestyle was funded at the expense of employee benefits and living wages. Once she told him the truth, things would be different between them. She wouldn't be plain old Clare any more. She'd be Clare Benton of the Connecticut Bentons. No, she wanted her anonymity for just a little while longer.

Hitching her camera bag higher on her shoulder, she waved and hurried off. Clare positioned the tripod so it framed a group of Quaking Aspen, their leaves a deep, russet gold as the last rays of the fading orange sun fell over them. The leaves trembled in the breeze, the same as Clare's heart when she considered telling Ethan everything.

She paused, the polarizing filter in her hand as she stared into the cabin window. Ethan's off-key singing boomed from inside. A smile inched up her lips. How could you not cherish a man who found you a place in the mountains and cooked while you worked?

Ethan was her man. She liked the sound of that, liked everything about him. So if that was the case, why was she holding back from him?

Fear. It pursued her as persistently as the mosquitoes buzzing past her head. She'd made a break from her parents, claimed her independence. A commitment to Ethan meant giving up some of that hard won independence.

Clare winced when Ethan reached for a high note and missed. The man certainly couldn't sing worth a damn.

So, he wouldn't serenade her. Big deal. Then again, knowing Ethan, he just might, and wouldn't that be a memory to treasure?

She repositioned the tripod so that it faced the cabin. The fading sunlight cast Ethan in silhouette. She snapped a series of pictures of him as he worked at the kitchen sink.

Perhaps giving up a bit of her independence was worth it in trade for a kind, loving man like Ethan.

Full darkness and a horde of ravenous mosquitoes finally convinced Clare to call it a night and resume shooting in the morning. Even with the jacket Ethan had brought out to her earlier, she was freezing. The white puffy clouds that had transformed into black, low-level clouds, or Nimbostratus as Ethan would call them, were perfect for sunset pictures. "Not necessarily ideal for comfort, though," she muttered.

A snowflake landed on her eyelash while she folded up her tripod.

She blinked it away and looked up into the dark sky as the swirling white flakes descended on her. The sudden swift change in temperature had an ominous feel. Goosebumps rose up on her arms —not from the cold, but rather from premonition.

Clare shouldered her gear and went to the cabin where warmth and light and love waited for her.

By the time they finished dinner and settled down in front of the fire with their wine, the light dusting of snow had turned icy and transformed into an all out blizzard, complete with howling wind.

Ethan added another log to the fire, then sat down beside her, his arm draped over her shoulder. Snuggled together they were cozy, intimate, and it was the perfect end to a long day.

"Clare."

"Hmmm."

She closed her eyes and snuggled deeper, his soft wool sweater warming her cheek. The slow, steady thump of his heart thudded in her ear.

"Why is it we never talk about our childhoods?"

Make that an *almost* perfect day. She should have known he'd circle back to this subject. He might appear casual and relaxed on the surface, but underneath that façade the man was a pit bull when it came to getting what he wanted. What he wanted at this moment was information, and he wouldn't stop until he got it.

She stalled the inevitable. "It was so long ago, what difference does it make now?"

He sipped his wine and contemplated her words. "When you say it analytically like that it sounds reasonable, but when two people are in a relationship, it's different. I need to be able to share my past with you."

"You can. I want to know everything about you."

"But you don't want to reciprocate, do you?"

She looked away, unable to meet his piercing gaze. Sharing that part of her past had always ended relationships rather than deepened them.

His fingers caressed her shoulder. "You don't have any doubt I love you, do you?"

Clare rallied against her fear. "None."

"Then why can't you trust me?"

"It's complicated."

"Complicated how?"

The hard light in his eyes made it clear he wouldn't be satisfied with partial answers. Things between them would be different.

"I've never had a good outcome after sharing this information."

"Then maybe it's time for a change."

The sincerity and the love shining in his eyes almost made her believe his words, but past experiences told a different story.

"My family," she began, "isn't what you'd call ordinary."

Ethan shrugged. "Whose is?"

"My family is Rockefeller rich, Ethan."

He leaned back against the sofa and whistled as he absorbed the information, then shifted his head to look over at her. "Okay, so they're rich. Big deal. Why all the drama?"

She almost smiled at his naïve response, but didn't because of how sad the truth really was, and how far from ordinary her family was. Ordinary. She'd have given anything to be just that.

How to explain? She cringed recalling how Peter, her college boyfriend, had told her in front of his cronies at the Alliance for a New Economy that her father's chain of hotels and spas underpaid and overworked the employees. She'd expected a psychology major to be more compassionate than that, but maybe the truth was he hadn't cared enough about her and used her father's behavior as an excuse to end their relationship.

"My family hasn't always had the most ethical business practices. And once people learn about it, their feelings toward me have changed," Clare said.

The storm outside didn't look nearly as threatening as Ethan's expression. "Are you implying that how your family behaves will change how I feel about you?" His voice rose with every word he spoke.

Clare didn't back down from his fury. "You may not realize it, but yes, I believe it will."

Ethan's hands cupped her face, the storm in his eyes was tempered with love. "I thought you, of all people, the woman I love and who I thought loved me, would have more faith in me than that."

"I haven't told you what they've done."

He tenderly cradled her against his chest. "Why would you think I would hold you accountable for your family's behavior?"

Peter had, but Ethan wasn't Peter. He had depth of character Peter hadn't possessed.

As she told Ethan what Peter had done, her embarrassment and humiliation returned as if it happened yesterday. She'd read the scorn on the groups' expression. They'd seen her as an elitist, the girl with the silver spoon in her mouth who had never worked a day in her life. And in truth, they'd been right.

Ethan's expression darkened when she finished. "I wish the bastard was here so I could punch him." His hands tightened around hers. "Are you sure he told you the truth?"

She nodded. "I confronted my father, but he didn't see anything wrong with his practices. He called it 'just part of doing business'."

"But you did."

"Yes."

He paused a beat, a teasing glint entering his dark eyes. "So, I'm dating a wealthy woman."

She laughed, and the tension expelled from her body. "The truth is I'm flat broke."

"Ah, a woman who can't manage her finances. A dream come true."

"Well, not exactly. I turned down my trust fund when my father refused to change the company policy."

"Good to know I've chosen a woman of principle."

Clare flashed him a wobbly smile and snuggled closer to him.

Ethan's fingers traced her cheek and sent a shiver over her. "I love you, Clare."

Tears trembled on her eyelashes. "I love you, too."

He buried his face in her neck and squeezed her to him. "Let's continue this discussion in the bedroom."

CLARE YAWNED and stretched her arms above her head the next morning. She reached for Ethan only to discover his side of the bed cold and empty. Disappointed, she quickly pulled on her clothes and went in search of him, hoping he had the coffee brewing.

When she opened the bedroom door, a rush of cold air greeted her.

"Ethan."

No fire. No coffee. No Ethan.

The wind howled, an eerie sound as it hurled snow against the front window. A sea of white blotted out the landscape. It was at once beautiful and terrifying, and only served to remind her of the emptiness within her without Ethan standing beside her.

She turned away from the window to check the bathroom and the second bedroom, but didn't find him.

Where was he?

Clare pulled on her coat. The fear she'd kept tightly in check took possession when she stepped into the mass of swirling white.

"Ethan."

The wind swallowed her voice. She searched for any sign of him.

Nothing.

"Ethan!"

She inched her way toward the woodpile unable to see more than a few feet in front of her.

Nothing.

Clare retraced her footsteps. Gripping the porch railing, she carefully descended the icy steps and moved to the car.

She shoveled the snow aside and opened the driver's door.

Empty.

Clare slammed the door and started for the trunk. She nearly tripped over a boulder.

Boulders didn't grunt, did they?

Reaching down, she found Ethan buried beneath the snow.

"Ethan, Ethan. Wake up. We've got to get inside."

He mumbled something garbled. Clare ignored him and tugged on his arm. She got him up after considerable struggle, and hauled him into the bathroom. He came around enough to help her get his clothes off and step into the shower. She propped him under the water, and breathed a sigh of relief until the water running down his body turned pink.

Blood!

It streamed from the back of his head.

With gentle fingers she smoothed his hair aside and found an inch long gash. What had happened to him?

The head injury explained his incoherency, but also terrified her. He needed medical attention, and Clare's expertise ended at applying Band-aids.

When the hot water ran out, she helped him dry off then

wrapped him in a blanket and led him to the sofa. She found bandages in the cabinet. Three tries later, with a wastebasket full of wadded up tape and cotton, she managed to wrap up the cut on his head. As soon as she finished, he was asleep.

Clare rebuilt the fire, then curled up next to him on the sofa. She kept her arms wrapped tightly around him to provide warmth, but mostly to hear the steady beat of his heart as it thumped against her ear reassuring her that he was alive and breathing.

Ethan slept while the storm raged and showed no sign of letting up. Clare did the only thing she could think to do. Keep them warm and fed, or at least she tried to. She kept the fire blazing, but did little more than dribble a few spoonfuls of broth into him.

Finally, late that afternoon, he woke up. "What happened?"

Clare rushed over from where she'd been adding wood to the fire. "I don't know. I woke up this morning and you were gone. I found you outside next to the car. I was hoping you could tell me. How do you feel?"

Ethan frowned as he eased to a sitting position. "I remember getting out of bed to get something out of the car before the storm got any worse. I stepped off the porch and heard a noise. I spun around and my foot slipped. The last thing I remember is going down."

"What were you getting out of the car?"

"I don't remember."

"Do you think it was important? Should I go look?"

Ethan shrugged. "I don't know."

"I'll go look just in case it's something we might need." She pulled on her coat and was out the door before he could object. It had to have been something important to get him out of bed at that time of day, and she didn't want to wait for the weather to worsen.

She found two paper bags in the truck, grabbed them, and hurried back inside. She set the bags next to Ethan, then went back out to get more wood.

By the time she finished hauling in the wood and adding some to the fire, Ethan had gone through the bags.

"Is that what you were looking for?" Clare asked.

"Yeah."

She crossed over to see what was so important, but the moment she approached, he closed them.

"Hey, what's the deal? I go out in subzero weather to haul in this stuff and you won't let me see what I risked my neck for."

"It's a surprise."

"I think I've had enough surprises for one day. Just show me what you've got." She reached for the bag, but he stuffed it behind his back.

Clare stiffened. Worry, compounded by stress, fear and a healthy dose of anger caught up with her. The adrenaline that had kept her functioning throughout the day evaporated.

"Show me what's in the bag, Ethan."

He shook his head. "I want to do it right."

"Do what right?" She sounded childish and unreasonable, but she was beyond caring.

"I can't tell you."

"I want to know what's in that bag, Ethan Burke, and you are going to tell me right this instant." Her voice was shrill, and shaky, and she felt as if she were about to explode.

Ethan's expression turned serious. "Clare, it's just a surprise I put together for you. I want to get everything set up before you see it, just like I did when we went camping that first time."

She gave him a hard stare. "I don't want or need any more surprises. I've been worried about you for hours."

Ethan took her hand and tugged her down beside him. She resisted when he tried to pull her close.

"Clare, I'm okay. It's just a little bump on the head."

Clare faced him, her pulse pumping, and her body clammy and trembling all over. While her voice remained calm, inside she shouted out the words. "It was not a little bump on the head. You were unconscious for hours and hours. You could have died. I could have lost you. Do you understand how scared I was?"

Tears burned her eyes, but she held them in check just as she'd held the fear inside since she'd woken up alone.

"Clare, I'm not trying to make light of what happened or how frightened you were. I'm trying to say, I'm okay. I'm here, and I will do everything in my power to never leave your side."

She gave him a wobbly nod, then said, "What the fuck is in the bag?"

An itsy bitsy smile inched over his lips. "I've been a bad influence on you."

"If you're referring to the language, I'll have you know I'm no saint."

Ethan tapped the end of her nose. "Maybe not, but you're the closest thing to one I've ever known."

"Are you going to make me ask again?"

Ethan blew out a breath. "You're not going to give up are you?"

"No."

"Okay, but just remember, I wanted to make it romantic, and special, and you wouldn't let me."

"Show me."

Ethan took out a white linen tablecloth and matching napkins, a pair of wineglasses, a bottle of Chardonnay, a box of Godiva Chocolate, and lastly a black velvet box.

Clare began to tremble again, this time with giddy anticipation and a healthy dose of embarrassment. This was the very last thing she'd expected. Tears suddenly clouded her vision. "Oh Ethan, I'm so sorry."

His joyous expression turned bleak. "Are you saying you don't love me, or that you don't want to marry me?"

"Neither," she hastened to assure him. "I meant I'm sorry I spoiled your plans."

His face relaxed. Carefully, he eased onto the floor and he kneeled before her. The fire popped, and crackled, and sizzled like the blood flowing through her body.

"I love you, Clare Benton. I've loved you from the first moment I saw you hanging upside down in that tree. Will you marry me?"

Tears spilled down her cheeks. "On one condition."

"Anything."

"We don't go back into the mountains until we've had survival training."

Ethan grinned. "Now, I remember the other reason I want to marry you."

"Why?"

"Because you're smart and wise. How about we take our honeymoon at a survival camp?"

Clare smiled through her tears. "How about we don't? I love camping as much as the next girl, but for my honeymoon I want luxury—running water and electricity."

"Okay, then the survival camp will be our engagement gift to each other."

"Agreed."

Ethan tugged her down beside him on the floor. Her heart fluttered when he kissed her, sealing their love and their future.

~

Present day...

A drop of rain slapped Clare in the face, washing the memory away. "I'm here, and I will do everything in my power to never leave your side." Ethan had made her that promise and kept it. Now, she was the one in the precarious situation.

A pang of longing struck her. She missed Ethan, wanted to fix things between them. She tipped her face to the sky. The clouds had grown heavier and thicker since she'd started down the narrow path. Sore knees and painful breaths accompanied her descent down the canyon. And she wasn't ruling out the possibility of a bruised rib or two from the accident. But injuries were the least of her worries. Getting to the car before it got dark took priority.

She paused to rest a moment and watched the soft misty rain drift down from the heavens. Automatically she reached for her cameras, but they weren't slung around her neck.

Reality slapped her hard and fast. Her cameras were gone, the loss a reminder of just how close she'd come to dying. How precarious her situation remained.

She'd survived the crash and so had the animals. That was what she needed to focus on. And she would stay alive until Ethan found her, because she had a hell of a lot to live for.

The bushes rustled.

Bailey froze. A growl rumbled low in her chest.

The hair on Clare's neck bristled.

The bushes thrashed again.

Clare's heart hammered when Bailey's growl deepened.

Bailey shook Ballistic off her back and tore down the trail, spewing dirt and rocks over Clare.

She dove into the heavy undergrowth. A howl of pain rang out.

Clare raced forward. Her foot caught on a root. She went down hard. She raised her head and through the haze of dust, a pair of gleaming green eyes stared down at her.

6

Long puffs of dust trailed Ethan and Ben as they turned off the main road and followed the narrow dirt drive carved between fir and quaking aspen to their house. Ethan sighed recalling how a much younger Ben had demanded to know the scientific name for plants and trees rather than the common ones, despite the sometimes unkind ribbing of his siblings. But those days, as many others, were gone. Life was speeding past, and far too often Ethan felt left in the dust.

Ethan parked his pickup in front of the garage.

"Dad, where's Mom?"

Ethan's attention moved to the spot Clare always parked her SUV. The vacant space sent a stir of unease through him. Because of his childish display of temper that morning, he'd left without asking her destination. He always knew where she was working. Always.

It was only two, but she should have been home by now. Clare definitely wouldn't stay in the mountains with a storm brewing. They'd both learned that lesson the hard way.

"I don't know." He managed to keep his voice steady even though he felt shaky inside.

The dark, silent house loomed before him, taunting him,

reminding him she wasn't inside burning dinner. She also wasn't there to demand conversation, to analyze their relationship.

"She's probably at the grocery store." Even as the perfectly logical explanation slipped out of his mouth, Ethan knew it wasn't true.

A voice that sounded an awful lot like Grace's echoed in his head. *She needs you.*

Clare was fine. He couldn't let his imagination run wild every time she was late.

The rumble of a car engine drew his attention from thoughts of Clare to the driveway. His father's battered truck pulled up.

Oh holy hell. Dealing with his father was the last thing he needed.

The rusty-hinged door of the old Chevy squawked as an equally battered, but stone-cold-sober Benjamin Burke crawled out of the cab. If it was possible for something good to have come out of Grace's death, it was his father's sobriety. That of course hadn't magically changed all that was wrong between father and son. Too many years of neglect prevented an instantaneous repair to their fractured relationship.

"Grandpa." Ben ran over, threw his arms around his grandfather and squeezed. He'd been too young to differentiate between the twelve-pack-a-day drunk his grandfather had been and the sober grandpa. Both had been fun in Ben's opinion.

Too bad his father had become a grandfather before he could figure out how to be fun and sober. Sure would have been an improvement on Ethan's childhood.

His father looked over at him. "Hey, son."

"Dad." Ethan propped a foot on the bumper. "What are you doing here? I thought you were working today."

With sobriety came steady work as a grocery store clerk. It certainly wasn't exciting or glamorous, but Ethan had to admit it fit him. A natural extrovert, this job allowed him to chat the day away and collect a steady paycheck.

"I do, but I have the late shift tonight, so I don't have to be there until three." His expression turned serious. "Have you got a minute we could talk—in private?"

"Sure." His agreement lacked enthusiasm. "Ben, haul your stuff inside and see if there's a message from Mom."

"Okay." He gave his grandfather a parting hug. "Are you going to be at my game Saturday, Grandpa?"

"Wouldn't miss it."

As selfish as it sounded, there was a part of Ethan that resented the relationship between his son and his father. It was the relationship he'd hungered for as a child. And that little boy still longed for his father's love and approval. Even after the two years of sobriety, Ethan was reluctant to believe this was real. That his father would stay sober this time. And until Ethan was certain, he wasn't risking more disappointment.

Ben trotted to the truck, grabbed his gear and went inside.

"What's up, Dad?"

"Mind if we walk down to the lake?" He started walking without waiting.

The serious expression his father wore was out of character. "Is everything okay with Mom?"

"Yes, she's fine."

"And you're doing okay?"

"Yes." He stopped when they reached the graveled shore. He picked up a rock and flung toward the lake, watching it skip across the water.

He blew out a breath and faced Ethan. "I've been debating all day whether to discuss this with you. I don't think there's any question I haven't been much of a father. I wasn't there for you when you needed me, and I'm sorry. I don't think an apology is anywhere near enough to make up for how I've failed you, but that's not why I'm here."

"Why are you here, Dad?"

"Before I get into that I want you to know how proud I am of you. You're the husband and father I never was."

His father's praise made Ethan squirm. He was more of a failure as a husband and a father than Benjamin Burke had ever been. At least he'd had drinking as an excuse for poor parenting. Ethan, on the other hand, had been sober, lost his daughter and fucked up his marriage.

His father reached out to squeeze his shoulder, but his hand fell away before he made contact.

Ethan didn't need to see his reflection to know his body language flashed "hands off" like a giant neon sign.

"I overheard something at the grocery store yesterday that I think you should know about."

Ethan couldn't imagine what gossip his father had heard that he deemed important enough to share with him. "What?"

He shifted his feet before he looked Ethan in the eye. "Two of Jack's friends were discussing a party they went to last week, and how they and Jack had gotten drunk. Jack apparently took them all home from McKenzie Meadow and nearly drove off the road into the canyon. They were laughing about it and talking about another party they're attending this weekend."

Mangled bodies, late night phone calls, frantic race to the hospital—all a parent's nightmare, and Ethan's deepest fear. He'd worked hard to be a good parent, to instill the dangers of drugs and alcohol to his children, especially drinking and driving. How could this have happened?

"Who were the boys?"

"Pete Danby and Joe Kerr."

Jack's best friends. His father had overheard the truth.

"Kids drink, Ethan."

Anger burst from him. "This isn't a boys-will-be-boys moment, Dad. Jack could have been killed, killed his friends, and let's not forget his grandfather is an alcoholic, which predisposes him to being one as well."

His father raised a hand to placate him. "I wasn't trying to make light, Ethan. If I hadn't thought this was serious, I wouldn't have come to you."

Ethan reined in his temper. "I'm sorry. I don't mean to take my anger out on you. You did the right thing coming to me."

This was his responsibility, and he would deal with it.

"I need to get to work."

Ethan walked his father to his truck.

He climbed inside the cab and rolled down the window. "Jack's still a good kid, and you're still a good father," he said, then drove off.

Not that long ago Ethan's first reaction would have been to consult Clare. Together they would formulate a plan, but no more. Not since Grace's death. Why couldn't things be different between them? Why couldn't they lean on each other?

He grabbed his briefcase from the truck, then froze when the voice spoke again.

Find Mom.

Something was wrong, really wrong. Clare should be home.

He hurried inside and dropped his briefcase next to the back door. His apprehension ratcheted up a notch when he found no signs of Clare's presence. No charred meat smoldering in the sink. No fire in the wood stove. No glass of wine next to the stove. No silly laughter at her mistakes.

"Ben, did you find a note?"

His son turned from the open refrigerator where he was rummaging for food and shook his head.

Ethan picked up the telephone and dialed her cell. It immediately went to voice mail.

"Clare, where are you? Call me."

He hung up the phone. He called Sarah and Tammy and his mother, but no one had seen her. He stared out at the dark clouds that blotted out the sun, the same way Clare's absence extracted the sunshine from his heart.

"Where do you think Mom is?"

"I'm not sure. She probably just got delayed, or she stopped in town for some groceries. Why don't you go put your things away and wash up?"

Ethan waited until he heard Ben clump up the stairs before he dialed the sheriff.

"Sheriff's department, please hold."

A twangy country western song grated in his ear. He waited a moment, then disconnected the call and dialed the emergency room at the hospital.

"Paradise General, how may I direct your call?"

"Have you had any accident victims come into the ER in the last few hours?"

"What is the name of the person you're looking for?"

"Clare Burke."

The keyboard clattered as the receptionist typed Clare's name into the computer. The seconds ticked off like hours.

"No sir."

"You're certain?"

"The ER has been empty all afternoon."

Ethan sank down on the stool, his knees rubbery with relief. "Thank you."

But the fact that Clare hadn't been admitted to the hospital didn't mean she wasn't in trouble.

He redialed the sheriff's department and after several rings the dispatcher picked up. "Sheriff's department, please—"

"No, I won't hold. My wife is missing, and I need to know if you've had any accident reports."

A long pause, then, "Let me check."

The seconds ticked by like years of his life as he waited yet again. Finally, the dispatcher came back on the line. "No accidents have been reported."

"Then I need to file a missing person's report." He was connected with Randy Tompkins, a deputy sheriff he'd worked with on search and rescue.

Randy's voice came on the line moments later. "Ethan, how have you been?"

"Better."

"What's wrong?"

"Clare's late and she's not answering her cell."

"Is she on a photo shoot?"

"Yes, and with a major storm brewing. She wouldn't stay late."

"Have you called her friends?"

"No one's seen her." Ethan's mind raced with all kinds of scenarios.

He answered the rest of Randy's questions on autopilot. Ten minutes later he hung up the phone and dialed the leader of the search and rescue team he belonged to and simultaneously took out a pad of paper. He began listing all the possible areas Clare could have gone.

The search and rescue leader answered. Ethan quickly explained the situation, they set a meeting place, then hung up.

"Dad, is Mom okay?" There was just enough of a tremor in Ben's voice to tell Ethan that an-everything-is-fine line wouldn't wash.

"I don't know. One thing's for certain, though, your mom knows how to handle herself in the wilderness. And don't forget she has Bailey and Ballistic with her."

Ben stared out the kitchen window as raindrops began to patter against the glass. "But it's cold out there."

"I know, but your mom never leaves here without her gear. She'll find shelter or make it." So long as she's able to, he silently added. "And besides that, Noah and Rudy and I are going out to find her and bring her home."

"I want to come."

"There isn't room."

Ben's eyes shone with youthful belligerence. "You're just saying that because you think I'm a little kid."

That was exactly the reason, but he didn't say that. "We'll barely have room for the three of us with all our gear. Besides, I need you and Jack here in case your mom calls in with her location. That is a critical job."

"So, I'll be in charge of answering the phone?"

"You know the procedure, right?"

Ben scrambled over to the phone, yanked open the drawer below it, and pulled out the message pad and a pencil. "Name, location, phone number and injuries."

As if on cue, the phone rang, and Ethan's pulse skittered as hope surged.

Ben grabbed the receiver eager to show off his skills.

"Burke residence."

"It's Jack. He's going to pizza," Ben mouthed to him a moment later.

Ethan took the receiver. "Noah is going to pick you up. I need you home ASAP. Your mother is missing."

"I don't need a ride. I have my truck, and besides a bunch of us are going to pizza."

"Pizza will have to be another time, and as of this minute your driving privileges are suspended. Leave the truck there and I'll pick it up later."

"You can't take my truck away."

"I can and I have. Until I'm certain you aren't drinking, you're not driving."

"Why?"

"You know exactly why. You almost wrecked your truck coming back from McKenzie Meadow because you were drunk."

"But Mom said—"

"Mom said what?"

Clare had known about this and didn't tell him? He pounded a fist against the counter. How could she do that? Had their relationship deteriorated to the point that she treated something this serious so casually? He would demand answers for all his questions when he found her.

"I don't have time to discuss this. Here are the facts. Your mother isn't home. She isn't answering her cell phone. Noah is picking you up."

The bigger picture finally penetrated Jack's consciousness. "Mom's always home by now."

"I know."

"Are you going to look for her?"

"I am."

"I want to come."

"Like I just told Ben, there won't be room."

"I can drive my truck."

"We just had this discussion. But just so we're clear, you won't be doing any driving for the immediate future."

Even if he hadn't been drinking and driving there was no way in hell Ethan would let him drive. This was dangerous enough with experienced search and rescue members. Jack had had some limited training, but that didn't qualify him as experienced. And the last thing he needed was another worry. He needed his entire focus on finding Clare.

"I could ride with someone else on search and rescue."

Any other search and rescue Ethan might have agreed, but not when it was Clare, and especially when he didn't know if she was injured or how seriously. He wouldn't allow either of his children out there with so much uncertainty about her condition.

"If Jack goes, I'm going," Ben said.

Ethan held up a hand to silence him. "No, I need you here."

Ethan hung up the phone and grabbed his list, then went upstairs to change.

JACK ENDED THE CALL, and slammed his fist into the gym wall. The wood creaked and his hand immediately began to throb.

Why did his dad always have to treat him like a kid? When Grace was alive she'd been the one he focused on. Now that she was gone, he'd taken her place. At times, Jack couldn't breathe he felt so constricted by his parents.

Pete leaned around the corner of the building. "Hey, Numb Nuts, if you're done beating up the building let's go get some pizza."

"I can't. My dad found out about last weekend. I'm grounded for —" Jack shrugged. "Until I'm fifty or move out, I guess."

Pete sucked in a breath. "Ouch. Sorry man. My dad promised he'd slip us some brewskis, too."

A beer sounded damn good. Too bad his dad wasn't like Pete's. He gave them beer and let them drink with him. Treated them like adults. He was seventeen, but his dad still treated him like a little kid.

Fat raindrops splashed on the ground between him and Pete and doused Jack's anger like water to a campfire. Mom was missing. Lost in the woods with a big storm headed in.

"Yeah, it sucks. But even if he hadn't found out, I'd still have to go. Mom didn't come home."

Pete absorbed the information as if he'd just been told they had a pop quiz tomorrow. "Sorry, man. Her car's probably just stalled somewhere."

There had been a day Jack would have shrugged it off too. But since Grace, life had become serious. Bad shit happened. People died. People he loved died, and his friends didn't get it. Except for Matty. Only he wasn't here to talk to. He'd left for college six weeks ago.

Pete and the others didn't know anyone that died and none of them wanted to talk about Grace, which was just fine with Jack. He partied with them to keep from thinking. To forget the emptiness inside him that never went away.

He might have managed without Matt if Grace hadn't died, but losing Grace and then Matt had been too much.

He fisted his hand into a ball wanting to punch the wall again, but didn't. First, because he could barely bend his fingers, and second, because it hadn't made him feel any better.

Pete looked at him as if he'd grown horns. "Are you okay?"

"I'm fine."

"Do you need a ride?"

Jack shook his head. "Coach is picking me up. See you tomorrow."

"Okay."

Jack picked up his gym bag and headed to the front of the school to wait for Noah. He leaned against the brick wall and stared at the street light that had turned on several hours early because of the dark sky. Mesmerized by the rain streaming through the fuzzy light, it looked the same as his brain felt since the accident. The only thing he'd managed to maintain was his grades and that was mostly a point of pride, plus he forgot about Grace when he studied.

His friends left and loneliness enveloped him. He stood alone in front of the school. Everyone else had left for the pizza parlor. He was an island. An outcast. No one understood him or what he was going through. His friends didn't get it. His parents were unreachable.

Jack Daniels listened. It also got him into the trouble.

He used to care about school, about his peers, about what his parents thought. What did any of it matter now?

A truck appeared in the distance and moved closer until Matt's dad, Noah, pulled up. Jack climbed into the cab of the pickup. He snapped on his seatbelt and Noah set off.

"Has there been any word about Mom?"

"Nothing."

Jack dug his fingers into his gym bag. "Any accidents?"

"No."

Jack sagged back against the seat. What would he do if something happened to Mom?

He lived without Grace. Sort of. But he couldn't live without both of them. The idea of going on without his mom sent adrenaline rushing through him. He wound his fingers around the door handle, whitening the knuckles.

"She's okay, Jack. We're going to find her." Noah's voice was strong and reassuring, but it didn't stop Jack from lashing out.

"Like we found Grace."

In the intervening silence the isolation Jack felt earlier intensified.

"I'm not going to sit here and blow sunshine up your ass. It's true, your mom is missing." Noah stopped when the light turned red and faced him. "But there's one thing I know for an absolute fact. Your mom is a fighter. She's smart. She knows how to handle herself, and she's not alone. Her odds of surviving in the wilderness are a hundred times better than almost anyone else's."

Noah and Matt were a lot alike, both in looks and how easy they were to talk to. They had a way of laying out a situation, whether it was sports or life and death, that calmed him. They made him laugh when he felt like crying. They just made things better.

He wished Matt were here. They'd been friends for as long as he could remember from bike riding to baseball. Matt had always been there, but he was gone and right at this moment Noah was the next best thing.

"Yeah, I guess you're right."

"I am right. I don't know why she isn't part of the search and rescue team because she's a hell of a lot better at it than most of us. She knows those woods like her own backyard. She will find a place to hunker down and wait."

Jack smiled for the first time since talking to his dad. His mom was smart, and she would find a way to survive until they found her. And he didn't care what his dad said. He was going to search for her with or without his approval.

7

———

Ethan yanked on cold weather gear—field pants and a wool shirt —and silently vented his frustration. What was going on with Jack? Of all their children, he'd always been the most level-headed and conscientious.

Sitting on the edge of the bed, he tugged on a pair of nylon socks followed by wool. His anger fizzled to worry about Clare.

Was she was warm and dry? Was she hurt?

No! He refused to consider she was injured and unable to take care of herself. He would find her. She would be okay, and maybe if he kept telling himself that, he'd believe it.

He pulled on his boots, then grabbed his gloves and jacket. He headed out to the garage, leaving Ben to man the phone.

Ten minutes later the crunch of gravel alerted Ethan someone had arrived.

Rudy's truck pulled in, followed by Noah and Jack.

"Dad, I want to come with you," Jack said, bypassing a greeting.

"We went over this on the phone. We barely have enough room for the three of us and the gear. You and Ben are staying here to answer the phone."

"That's kid's stuff."

"Since you've been behaving like a kid, I'd say it's an appropriate assignment, wouldn't you?"

Jack's face flamed red. He shot a sideways glance at Noah and Rudy who had moved away to give them privacy. "So this is punishment."

Ethan inhaled and brought his temper under control. "No. I need someone here who has a clear head in case your mom calls. I know I can count on you to relay that information to me."

He squeezed Jack's shoulder.

Jack shrugged off his hand.

Ethan was losing the battle of wills between them. If he had more time he could come up with a better way to handle the situation, but he didn't. He had to get moving.

"I'll find her and bring her home," he promised.

Jack gave him a stiff nod and went to the house without another word. Clearly he didn't like being left with Ben, but that was how it had to be.

Ethan went over to help Noah and Rudy load their gear and prayed he'd be able to keep his word and find Clare.

Noah opened the truck door. "Which way are we headed, Ethan?"

Ethan stuffed his bag in the back of the truck. "Tony said they're setting up the base camp near Parsons Meadows."

"I know that. What I meant was, where did Clare go today?"

Rather than admit he didn't have a clue, he pulled a quarter from his pocket. "Call it, Rudy."

Noah groaned. "Shit. Tell me you have more information than that. You always know where she's gone."

"Not this time."

ETHAN DIDN'T PROTEST when Noah insisted on driving them back to the base camp several hours later. They'd found no sign of Clare. He stared out the windshield, the wipers slapping back and forth to keep up with the rain.

He'd let Clare down. It wasn't the first time he'd done that, but this time it wasn't just Clare's respect at stake. It was her life.

Ethan stared at the glowing green dial on the stereo as he went over every word he and Clare had exchanged that morning searching for a clue, anything that would lead him to her, but he came up empty.

That familiar sensation of apprehension filled him just as it had the first time he met Clare's parents.

Twenty-two years ago...

Ethan straightened his tie yet again as he and Clare climbed the steps to her parents' home. She'd warned him they were rich, but this was beyond comprehension. Acres of perfectly manicured lawn accompanied them up the half-mile-long driveway to the two-story colonial. The mansion was solid, and that in itself spoke of permanence, of stability, of belonging. In comparison, Ethan's childhood homes had consisted of a series of crumbling apartments and pay-by-the-week motels that shouted transient.

More acres of lawn circled the estate and rolled out to meet the Atlantic ocean. Her parents must have a whole team of gardeners to keep up with it all.

Ethan reached for his tie again.

Clare clasped his hands and pulled them away from it. "You look fine. Quit worrying."

If only she knew he'd really been debating strangulation. That sounded a hell of a lot more enjoyable than a weekend with Clare's parents.

"I don't know why you wore a tie. I told you to be yourself."

Oh hell yeah. Confirm what they already suspected. Their daughter had agreed to marry a backwoods lumberjack whose pastimes included banjo playing and hunting for Bambi. No sir, he wasn't about to give them any more reasons to dislike him than they already had—his heritage, his lack of refinement, and most of all his empty bank account after buying Clare's engagement ring.

"I want to make a good impression."

"The only impression that counts is mine." She raised up on tiptoe to kiss him. "And just so you know, no one, and I mean no one, could make me happier than you do."

Her words made him focus on what was important—he loved Clare, and she loved him. Her parents could believe whatever they wanted. What mattered was that Clare knew the truth—he didn't give a damn about her money. He loved her. He could support her, perhaps not in the style she was accustomed to, but they could lead a comfortable middle-class life, which was what she'd assured him she wanted.

Ethan dipped his head and returned her kiss, then deliberately loosened his tie and stuffed it in his pocket.

Clare's smile turned radiant. "I swear there is nothing sexier then a man who takes his tie off just for me."

Relaxing for the first time since they'd left Idaho, he said, "Just wait until later. I've got a whole lot more to show you."

Her eyes warmed at his words. "Why don't we just skip this altogether and go back to our hotel room?"

Ethan shook his head. "Anticipation will only make it sweeter."

Clare frowned at him. "Anticipation is highly overrated."

Before she could object further, he pressed the bell and sealed their fate.

❧

Ethan joined his soon-to-be father-in-law, William Benton, for a stroll on the beach after dinner that evening. Winston, a purebred golden retriever, romped in and out of the surf chasing the stick William threw for him.

Clare's parents had been nothing short of gracious from the moment he and Clare arrived, but Ethan sensed all that was about to change now that he was alone with Clare's father.

"So," William began, "you and Clare are engaged."

"We are."

"And you plan to stay in Paradise Falls, is that correct?"

"Yes, it is."

"Pretty isolated there, I imagine."

"It is, but very beautiful, too, and perfect for Clare's work."

William nodded. "Yes, she's built herself a nice hobby."

"It's an even better career."

William pursed his lips. "I don't think you can call poverty level income a career. It's a job."

Ethan stopped and faced the older man. "Then I guess that's what I have, too, since Clare makes more money than I do."

William picked up the stick Winston had dropped at his feet and met Ethan's unwavering stare. "Maybe it's time we spoke man to man."

Tension vibrated through Ethan while he waited for William to continue.

"You seem like a good man, a decent man, Ethan."

"Thank you."

"Which is why I don't want to see you get hurt."

Of all the things Ethan had expected from Clare's father this wasn't it.

"Don't misunderstand. I love my daughter. I would do anything for her, but we've been at odds for years. Whatever I suggest, she does the exact opposite."

Ethan didn't doubt he loved his daughter, but the man had no confidence in her abilities. For an intelligent man, he didn't know his daughter. "And you think I'm the opposite?"

"I think she's dabbling with you the same as she's dabbling with her photography. Someday she'll come to the realization that she wants more from life, and she'll regret her decision."

"And regret marrying me?"

William stepped back to avoid a breaking wave. "There's no question she loves you—deeply, but what if she decides she wants this life back? What if she discovers she wants her inheritance and all it entails?"

Ethan studied Clare's father a long moment. "Meaning I'm not the type of man you picture living a *civilized* lifestyle?"

Her father didn't shy away from his question. "You strike me as a man who wants to provide for his family."

Bingo. He'd nailed Ethan to his core.

"I think you would do anything to make my daughter happy. What I fear is you will eventually become unhappy and regret marrying her."

"What are you suggesting? That I should step aside so she'll come to her senses?"

"It would be best for both of you. Divorces are messy and very public."

"What if you're wrong? What if this is what she really wants?"

"How can it be? This is the life she's always known. The world she was groomed to live in. She's taking pretty pictures in Idaho and defying me. Eventually she'll tire of her childish behavior and come home."

Ethan watched Winston leap into the surf after the stick. The wave crested and broke washing over him and sent him tumbling. He rolled, once, twice, gained his footing, then shook the sand from his coat before retrieving his stick and loping back to his master. The same response Clare's father expected from Ethan—unquestioning obedience.

The man was about to be disappointed. "I think you underestimate her talent, Mr. Benton. Her work may seem frivolous to you, but what Clare does is important. She makes people smile. She brings beauty and color into their world, and that's a rare gift."

No question William Benton loved his daughter, but equally obvious was the fact he didn't really know her. Didn't know what a wonderful, talented person she was.

"Just so we're clear, if Clare should decide she wants to reclaim her position here, I will support her one hundred percent," Ethan said.

"But what about your career?"

"What about it? I can teach anywhere. It's not where I teach that matters to me, it's that I teach. What I want is Clare. Everything else we'll work out, if and when the time comes."

The waves broke against the shore as predictable and steadfast as Ethan's belief in his relationship with Clare. He would be a man Clare could depend on through good times and bad.

"I've said my piece. I won't bring it up again." William held out his hand. "Welcome to the family."

Ethan shook his hand.

While Clare's father might appear cordial, Ethan knew he would never really be truly welcomed into the family. He would forever and always be the man who kept Clare from living up to her potential.

Present day...

Had he held Clare back, kept her from her dreams as her father intimated he would? Ethan didn't think so, but he certainly wasn't making her happy. He slumped back against the seat as Noah parked the truck at the base camp.

Helplessness, frustration, and guilt swelled within him, but only one question spun through his mind like an out-of-control Ferris wheel.

Where was Clare?

8

Clare raised her head and peered through the thick layer of dust. She breathed a sigh of relief when she recognized Bailey's green eyes staring back at her and not a wild animal. The dog whined and plopped down beside her, her whiskers brushing Clare's cheek.

Rubbing the grit from her eyes, she frowned at Bailey. "I deserve more than a repentant whine of apology."

Bailey pressed her wet nose against her cheek, and Clare cracked an eye open. She released another pitiful whine that Clare recognized as pain, rather than a bid for sympathy.

She started to roll to her knees, then groaned when the movement sent pain rocketing through her. She eased to her knees, cradling her ribs then reached for Bailey's collar and pulled her close. She counted ten to twelve porcupine quills imbedded in her nose.

Clare forced Bailey's mouth open. She went weak with relief when there weren't any inside her mouth or throat—definitely good news. The bad news, she would have to take out the quills herself—a job Ethan generally handled.

But Ethan wasn't here.

Clare remained motionless for another moment, her body trembling. Finally, she straightened her shoulders and rummaged through her backpack until she found her fold-up pliers.

She opened them and had Bailey lie down.

Ballistic stood beside Clare and watched closely as she put a hand over Bailey's eyes to keep the dog from panicking.

Bailey jerked when Clare pulled out the first quill. She leaned down and whispered in the dog's ear. "You have to stay completely still so I can get these out, then you'll feel better, I promise."

Bailey leaned against her as Clare removed more quills. "Silly girl. I thought you would have learned not to go running willy-nilly into the brush after the last time."

Ballistic arched his back, his gaze narrowing when Bailey flinched again.

"I'd like to see you do better," Clare told the haughty feline when he shot her a narrow-eyed glare.

When the last quill came out, Clare hugged Bailey. "All done. I'll bet you feel better now."

Bailey nudged her hand, and Clare reached out to pet her, her hands shaking and nausea churning in her stomach. The tension slowly eased out of her as she stroked the dog.

She smiled when Ballistic rubbed up against Bailey, the most he'd ever offered in the way of comfort. Bailey in return nudged the cat with her nose, then flicked her tongue over his head and down his flank.

Ballistic shook, glared at the dog, then with a huffy tilt of his chin turned up his nose as if to say, "You've stepped over the line."

A second later, the feline arched his back, then hopped onto Bailey's back, circled once and laid down.

Clare laughed at the cat's antics, then picked up her backpack, feeling a sudden, urgent need to get moving. She winced when her ribs protested the movement. Ignoring the pain she eased the backpack over her shoulder.

Raindrops splattered against the dusty trail and left huge round circles in the dust. Clare glanced up to study the sky. Fat, pregnant clouds hung low, sunlight angling through them. She studied their continuous motion. One in particular stood out. It was as if someone had sculpted Grace's face into the cloud. The cleft of her chin, the sloped tip of her nose, the perfectly spaced eyes, all Grace's.

Clare pushed her whimsical thoughts aside. She didn't have time to be thinking about Grace. Daylight was fading fast, and she needed to get moving before it did more than sprinkle.

Whistling to Bailey, they resumed their trek down the narrow path. Clare estimated they had another solid hour of hiking before they reached the river.

An hour later, exhausted, dusty and hungry, they reached the river. Clare took a long drink of water as she studied the demolished SUV. No way it would serve as shelter. It was smashed too flat. Her shoulders slumped and she momentarily sagged against the car as she regrouped. So, she wouldn't use the car. She'd get her gear and set up her tent. It took several tries before she managed to pry open the rear door.

She immediately pulled on her jacket and gloves, then searched for her cell phone or the tiny pieces that were left of it. Even if it had survived the crash it was doubtful she'd have service. She blew out a breath and pulled out the pup tent. She set it up next to the car using the SUV as a barrier from the wind and rain.

Once she had shelter, she began collecting firewood—enough to last the night or more if need be. After she started the fire, she searched the car for any other usable items. She grabbed an extra flashlight from under the driver's seat, a stash of nutritional bars, bottled water and a bag of treats for the animals. She bumped her camera bag when she reached for the flashlight in the backseat. Broken plastic and glass jingled from inside like a macabre wind chime.

Clare sifted through the remains of her cameras, and it hit her how fortunate she and the animals were to have gotten out of the car before it went over the ledge. They could have ended up a bunch of broken body parts, but by some miracle they'd been spared that fate, and Clare was determined to get them home.

Ethan would search all of her regular haunts, and eventually someone would come here, she hoped. She had to believe they would find her. And she could and would survive until then.

Clare added more wood to the fire, then whistled for Bailey and Ballistic. As soon as both animals were inside the tent, she crawled in and zipped the tent closed.

Clare took out the food she kept in her backpack for Bailey and Ballistic, then unwrapped a nutrition bar for herself. It wasn't a five-course meal by any means, but it quieted the growling in her stomach.

When she finished her meal, she added more wood to the fire, then shivering, squirmed into the sleeping bag and snuggled up against Bailey wishing for the first time in a long time it was Ethan she snuggled against.

Bailey smelled of musty dog, and it was the most wonderful scent right now. She smiled picturing her mother's horrified gasp. Dogs, even clean dogs, which Bailey was not at the moment, was something her mother avoided. But Clare had to admit Alexandria Benton's annoyingly compulsive drive for perfection had its moments, and it had saved Ethan public humiliation on their wedding day.

Mesmerized by the flickering firelight, her mind slipped back to her and Ethan's wedding day. For the first time all day a smile lifted her lips and her spirits, and the heaviness in her chest eased.

Twenty years ago...

Clare's pulse fluttered as she tossed back the pristine white comforter and threw open the curtains. Sunlight flooded the room. She stepped out onto the balcony, the frigid January air penetrating her blue flannel pajamas, but the cold couldn't dampen the joy in her heart.

Today was her wedding day!

Sunlight glinted off deep snow banks circling lake Coeur d'Alene, the backdrop to the small, simple wedding she and Ethan had planned.

Rubbing her arms to dispel the chill, she closed the door, and crossed over to the closet. She took out her wedding dress and held it against her, spinning in circles before collapsing onto the bed.

Her mother dashed past the long window opposite her bed in full neurotic-party-planner mode.

The only mar on her perfect day—her parents. They'd arrived late, as usual, and barely made it to the rehearsal dinner last night. Not that Clare had been surprised by their last minute appearance, since her father lived for his work and it took priority, even over his only daughter's wedding. But just once, she'd hoped her wants and needs would rank number one with them.

A tap on the door was followed by her mother's appearance. "Clare, this simply won't do."

Nothing, not even her detail-oriented mother, would ruin her day. "What won't do, Mom?"

"Your soon to be father-in-law. He's drunk and loud and making a spectacle of himself."

Clare's happiness dimmed. The one thing she'd dreaded, not Benjamin Burke's behavior, per se, but his drinking and its impact on Ethan. She'd hoped for his son's sake he would curtail his alcohol consumption, but obviously he hadn't.

"What happened?"

Her mother perched on the edge of her unmade bed. "He's fallen twice, and the last time he knocked over a table."

Clare stared out at the pristine water so calm and unruffled. In comparison, anxiety rushed through her. "Has he hurt himself or anyone else?"

Her mother calmly folded her hands in her lap. "No."

"Then we'll just have to work around him the best we can."

"You can't just let him behave this way. He'll ruin the wedding."

"What exactly should I do about it?"

"I think Ethan should talk to him."

Asking Ethan to talk to his drunk father was the last thing she would do. His father's behavior was not something he could control, and she did not want to upset him today of all days. She stepped away from the window and moved to the closet.

"Ethan has talked to him. He's tried to convince him to stop drinking, but you can't force an alcoholic to stop or limit his drinking. He has to want to do that on his own."

Clare watched her mother stand and walk over to the mirror above the dresser. Their eyes met as she patted her hair into place. "That doesn't mean you tolerate rude behavior. You're doing him a disservice by condoning his conduct with your silence. It implies tolerance."

"I'm not condoning it. I'm making the best of a bad situation."

"I still think you should have someone as quietly as possible remove him."

Clare gave an indelicate snort. "He would only come right back and make an even louder and more embarrassing scene. I won't upset Ethan or his mother by doing that."

That cool blue gaze sliced through Clare the same as her words. "Call the police and let him suffer the consequences of his actions."

"No! Absolutely not."

"Don't you think Ethan will be distressed by his father's behavior?"

"I know he will, but having Ben arrested will disturb him more."

"Maybe, but—"

"No buts. I'm not calling the police."

Her mother's blue eyes bore into her. "I've handled these situations before Clare. I know what I'm talking about. And for your information, I'm not always wrong."

"I never said you were wrong."

Her mother studied her a long moment. "You didn't have to. Your expression said it for you." She headed for the door.

"Where are you going?"

Her mother turned back to her, her gaze razor sharp. "To do damage control."

Clare sagged back into the bed and prayed that's all her mother did.

~

THE CEREMONY WAS picture perfect just as Clare had envisioned. It was after the minister told Ethan to kiss his bride that Ben did just as her mother predicted.

"Lay one on her, son," Ben hollered.

Ethan's fingers tightened around her arm.

Clare leaned close and whispered in his ear. "Don't let him ruin our day."

"I'm trying, but he's not making it easy."

She flashed him a big smile. "Start by laying one on me, big guy."

He did just as she requested and kissed her until she was certain stars dropped from the heavens and sprinkled stardust over them.

Applause went up, drowning out her father-in-law's drunken shouts. But as the reception got into full swing, Ben continued to drink and his behavior became more obnoxious.

After they cut the cake, then Clare went to freshen up. When she returned, she scanned the room for her husband and found him with her mother.

Ethan hugged her mother. "Thank you for handling this. I can't tell you how much I appreciate it."

Clare moved to Ethan's side and slid her hand into his. "Appreciate what?"

"Your mother—"

"Nothing for either of you to worry about." Her mother's smile appeared forced. "You two go dance and enjoy the party."

Ethan smiled at her mother, then swept Clare up into his arms. "Dance with me."

Before she could respond, Ethan had her on the dance floor. Clare's gaze tracked her mother as she took a seat next to Ethan's mom. She hadn't seen or heard Ben since he'd made a ruckus when Ethan tossed the garter.

"Where is your Dad?"

Ethan shrugged, his gaze making a quick sweep over the dwindling crowd. "I don't know. He could have left."

"Without saying goodbye or taking your mother? I don't think so. What's going on, Ethan?"

"Nothing is going on."

His blank expression was too blank. It was as if he wiped it clean so as not to expose his thoughts to her.

She looked over at her mother, then up at Ethan. "What were you and my mother really discussing?"

The song ended. Ethan guided her off the dance floor and away from the milling friends and relatives. He took her hands in his.

"I understand that you want to protect me from your family, but I'm a big boy, Clare. I can handle them—their distrust and even their outright dislike if I have to."

Clare started to comment, but Ethan held up his hand to stop her.

"No, they have not said anything rude or disparaging. They have been kind and gracious throughout their stay here, including and most especially, your mother. She was determined to shield me from my father, so that he wouldn't ruin my day. And she did a fine job of it, I might add."

"How so?"

"She very graciously suggested that your father wanted to walk along the lake, and asked Dad if he would be his guide. To spare me any further embarrassment your father left his only daughter's wedding early for me. That was an awfully nice thing to do, don't you think?"

It was, and a definite improvement over her mother's earlier suggestion that they call the police. Perhaps if she'd discussed the situation with her mother rather than immediately dismissing her suggestions, she might have gained two things. First, they could have prevented Ben's behavior and saved Ethan some embarrassment. Second she might have a gained a greater appreciation of her mother.

"Yes, it was."

Much as she didn't want to admit it, her parents had swooped in and saved the day.

Ethan gave her that smile that warmed her clear to her toes, then he kissed her. His warm breath tickled her cheek as he leaned down to whisper, "So, what do you say we blow this party and start our own?"

Her insides melted and her knees suddenly turned rubbery. "Oh Ethan, you say the nicest things."

PRESENT DAY...

The warmth of the memory of her wedding day faded away into the dark sky. Hope had been an endless commodity back then. The world had been theirs for the taking. Young, naïve and head-over-heels in love, it never occurred to her it might not always be that way. Would she and Ethan make it to another wedding anniversary?

The long, keening howl of a wolf sent Clare jackknifing to an upright position, and pain cutting through her from the sudden movement.

A growl rumbled low in Bailey's chest as another howl echoed over their shelter.

Clare eased out of the sleeping bag and added more wood to the fire that had reduced to a pile of orange glowing coals while she'd been daydreaming. As soon as she had it blazing again, she crawled back inside and secured the zipper.

The howling stopped, but Bailey's hackles remained straight up as she stared through their nylon enclosure. Another low rumble in the canine's chest set Clare's nerves on edge. Even Ballistic, whose sleep was rarely disturbed, was awake, ears perked, tail twitching and on full alert.

An ear-piercing yowl echoed over the tent. Clare froze, her blood ceasing to pump as she realized wolves were the least of her worries.

9
____

Ethan pulled up in front of his house and stared at the sky, so black not even a sliver of the moon showed through the clouds. His earlier memory of Clare remained so vivid in his mind he could feel her presence as if she sat next to him. But she wasn't here. She was lost, alone and possibly hurt, or God forbid, dead.

No! He would know if she were dead. Everyone said that when a loved one went missing, but would he actually sense her passing? More likely, he was kidding himself, blocking out the pain of the inevitable he couldn't, or wouldn't, face.

Could he go on if something happened to her?

He climbed out of the truck, and went in to check on the kids before he met back up with Noah and Rudy. Both boys were asleep so he made some coffee, then took a quick shower to revive himself.

Stepping into the steaming water, he was surrounded by Clare. He unscrewed the top of her herbal shampoo and sniffed. Her signature scent filled the shower. He snapped it closed and stuck his head under the spray of water to wash away the scent that only reminded him of her absence.

He pounded his fist against the tile. He missed her, missed them. Their marriage had become an empty shell—barren, fragile.

It seemed the best parts of their life together died with Grace. The little intimacies between them. Gone. The warm body tucked in bed beside him. Gone. The hand gently pressed to his chest. Gone. The softly whispered words of love. Gone. And without that closeness, he wasn't certain he'd ever be whole again.

So why hadn't he just given up and called it quits?

Because life without Clare was unthinkable, that's why.

"Dammit to hell." He shouted out his frustration, his fear, hoping he'd feel better, but he didn't. He never did. Anger wasn't an emotion he could control, and not being in control scared him almost as much as losing Clare. Control equaled stability and security.

He turned off the water, dressed, and went downstairs. Rain pounded the window pane while he sipped his coffee and worried about Clare. He tried not to think about the day Grace died, but with the second anniversary of her death just past, he couldn't seem to avoid it.

A deafening blast of thunder rattled the windows and the foundation.

Ethan flinched when a jagged slash of lightning struck the lake. The blinding white light lit up the sky and for an instant he saw a face reflected in the window.

Sculpted cheekbones, pert nose, wide eyes. "Grace."

No sooner had her name slipped from his lips than the image vanished.

He shook his head to clear the grogginess and the insanity that had made him think he'd just seen his daughter's reflection in the window. He needed to stay focused on Clare, the one female in his life he might be able to save.

He took out his cell phone and dialed his voicemail, then snapped it closed when there were no messages.

Jack's voice startled him. "No word from Mom?"

Ethan turned from the window to face his eldest son. "No."

"You sound surprised. Were you really expecting a message?"

Ethan looked back outside as the wind whipped the lake into a wild froth similar to the tempest brewing within him. "Yes, I guess I was. Wishful thinking I know, but I can't seem to help myself."

"She's okay, Dad. Mom knows how to handle herself out there."

"I thought it was my job to reassure you kids?"

Inside that six-foot-two frame lurked a man, but to Ethan he would always be his little boy. Funny, as a parent he never considered how it would feel to see his son grow into a man.

"You grew up when I wasn't looking, before I was ready." Ethan took another sip from his mug and swallowed the coffee and the pain of time marching on. "I'm sorry about yelling at you earlier. I was upset, but what were you thinking, drinking and driving?"

Jack rolled his shoulders and averted his eyes. "I dunno."

"I think you do."

The thunder rumbled in the intervening silence.

"Talk to me. I want to understand, I want to help."

Jack's eyes suddenly locked with his. "I was just trying to numb the pain."

Ethan closed his eyes as understanding dawned. How many times had he considered the same escape? Every minute of every day since Grace died, but knowing he could become his father had kept him sober.

"I know it's hard, but there are other, safer ways, to deal with your pain. You could have killed yourself or someone else."

He wrapped his arms around Jack and hugged him. "Promise you'll come to me or someone else when you need help dealing with Grace's death."

Jack twisted away. Anger burned deep in his eyes. "This wasn't about Grace."

Ethan pulled back and shook his head. "Then what?"

"You and Mom. You two are going to split up, aren't you?"

Ethan clutched the mug tighter as his world took a nosedive. "You think your mother and I are splitting up?"

"Don't you?"

Ethan slumped back against the window sill. Apparently he and

Clare weren't as good at hiding their animosity as he'd thought. "I didn't realize you'd noticed."

"It's hard not to with the way you and Mom tiptoe around each other."

"Your mom and I have no plans of separating." That was the honest truth. That wasn't to say they weren't teetering on the brink of it.

"I love your mom. I can't imagine life without her." And God willing, he'd find her alive, and well, and get another chance to make it right between them.

"I need to get back out there. Noah and Rudy are waiting for me."

Jack's fingers clutched Ethan's sleeve. "Don't leave me here, Dad, please. I need to do something other than sit and think. I want to help look for Mom."

Ethan studied his son's earnest expression. "I treated you unfairly yesterday."

"You were trying to protect me."

"I was, but I was wrong."

Jack's smile was wry. "You were being my dad."

"I was. Today I'm still your dad, but a dad who's a little more understanding and a little less angry."

"Does that mean I can help search for Mom?"

"Yes."

Ben stepped into the room. "I'm going, too."

The quiet intensity in his youngest son's eyes so reminded Ethan of Clare. Would he ever see that cross between stubborn insistence and fearlessness on her face again? God, he hoped so because it prodded him out of bed in the morning and made the day bearable.

"Who will man the phone?"

"Sarah. She'll be here as soon as we tell her to come," Jack said.

Noah's calm, unflappable wife Sarah, a perfect choice to man the phones. "Call her and tell her we're leaving in ten minutes."

Ethan started for the stairs to grab a clean shirt from his room.

"Dad," Jack called after him.

He turned and faced him. "Yeah."

"Did you remember Grandma and Grandpa were flying in tomorrow?"

Damn, he'd completely forgotten. That was a phone call he'd love to pawn off on someone else. Somewhere deep inside he'd known this day would come. Known he'd have to call Clare's father and confess he hadn't protected his only daughter. Ethan had done everything he could think of to shield her from harm, but trouble stalked women like Clare. Women who took the world by storm. Fearless women. You might be able to postpone trouble, but you never fully evaded it.

"No, I'd forgotten. Thanks for reminding me."

"No problem."

Ethan went to Clare's office and sat down. Her office chair squawked when he slumped into it. He inhaled a fortifying breath, then dialed his father-in-law. The phone rang four times before the maid answered in a sleep garbled voice.

"Benton residence."

"I'd like to speak with William, please."

A moment later Clare's father came on the line. "Ethan, what's wrong?"

"I'm sorry to call so late, but Clare is missing." It surprised him to realize he regretted breaking the news to him this way. They'd barely been civil to one another since Grace's death, but he and William Benton had one thing in common. They both loved Clare.

"What do you mean 'missing'?" His voice was calm, but underneath that polished exterior Ethan sensed his father-in-law held it together with a wing and a prayer. Just as he was doing.

"She went out on a photo shoot this morning and didn't come home."

"What about her cell phone?"

"She's not answering."

"Because she doesn't have service or because she can't?"

"I don't know, but I do know this, if anyone can survive out there, it's Clare."

He might not have been able to keep her out of harm's way, but he'd made sure she could take care of herself if anything happened.

"Why did you encourage her to do this?"

Ethan waited for remorse to settle on his shoulders, but it didn't. He carried his fair share of blame with Clare, but not for this.

"You can fault me for not finding out where she went today, but I won't shoulder guilt over supporting her career choice—a career she loves. She's an extremely gifted photographer, and she would have been miserable doing anything else. I did everything I could think of to protect her, short of asking her to stop doing what she loves."

"What's being done to find her?"

Ethan despised that arrogant tone of entitlement. "Search and rescue is looking for her. We will have helicopters in the air as soon as the weather lets up, and I'm heading back out now to join the search."

"What can we do to help?"

The offer surprised him considering how unavailable they'd been when Grace died. "Are you still flying out tomorrow?"

"Actually, Alexandria phoned Clare this morning and told her we'd decided to come on Thursday, but we could—"

"What time did they talk?"

"I'm not sure—" William stopped short. "When did Clare go missing?"

"I left the house at eight this morning, and that's the last time I saw her."

"Hold on."

Ethan heard the murmur of voices while William conferred with Clare's mother. He came back on the line a moment later.

"Alexandria talked to Clare on her cell phone at nine-thirty your time."

"Did she say where she was going?"

"No. All she said was she'd be losing service soon because she was headed into the forest."

Ethan swore. He'd hoped that Clare had given her mother some indication of her destination. Still, they might be able to pinpoint her location when she answered the call and then they'd have a clue where to search.

"You'll keep us posted about Clare."

A command, not a request, and it left a bitter taste in Ethan's mouth. How must Clare have felt when she asked them for money after Grace died when he'd been unable to work and the bills were mounting? He'd never considered that. He'd only been concerned with his own shortcomings. His own ineptitude.

Ethan leaned forward in the chair determined to find the same courage Clare had and ask her parents for help.

"I need someone by the phone. I've got a friend coming in right now, but she can't stay indefinitely."

"We'll catch the next flight out. What about Ben and Jack?"

"They're joining the search."

"Do you think that's wise?"

Why did he resent the question when he'd wondered the same thing himself? "They've both had search and rescue training, and they'll be with me or another experienced team member the entire time."

"You're their father. I know you'll do what's best for them." That perfectly cultured voice held a hint of derision.

The hair bristled on the back of Ethan's neck. "I've got to go."

"Ethan."

"Yes."

"Promise me you'll bring my little girl home safe and sound."

"I'll do everything in my power to find her." Ethan disconnected the call and prayed he'd be able to keep his promise.

He stared out the window, his gut churning like the waters of Lake Serenity. Under the glow of the porch light Ben lugged his gear to the truck, and Ethan wondered, not for the first time, if having children had been a wise decision.

Seventeen years of parenting and he asked himself that now. He loved kids, but teaching someone else's children was far different than raising your own.

Why hadn't he told Clare he didn't want children? Because only a heartless bastard could refuse her. And he might be a lot of things, but a heartless bastard he wasn't. So, he'd made the decision that he would be a father in more than just name only. He would be the best damn father he could be.

A smile inched up his lips when he remembered that night all those years ago she'd taken out what looked like a mile-long scroll, rather than the two page list from her pocket.

Eighteen years ago...

A draft blew under their front door as the north wind rattled the windows and sent more snow into the single-pane glass. Ethan grabbed the metal poker and squatted to stir the fire.

"Reason number one: I like kids and so do you," Clare said.

A hard point to argue with since he was a teacher and did indeed like kids.

"Reason number two: We're not getting any younger."

Ethan turned from the mantle and staggered, grabbing his shirt above his chest and twisted the fabric into his fist as if in pain. "I think it's the big one, Clare."

"Ha, ha, very funny. And for your information, you do a poor Red Foxx imitation." She sipped her wine. "I wasn't implying you were old, only that I don't want to wait forever to start our family."

Ethan tossed another piece of wood on the fire then glanced over at her. "Two years is hardly an eternity."

"I never said it was."

He brushed the dirt from his hands, then plopped down beside her on the battered tweed sofa and dropped his head onto her lap. "Okay, what's number three?"

She set her wine glass back on the end table, and massaged his scalp as she read the next item on the list. "Nothing smells as good as a baby's breath when they're sleeping."

Ethan cupped her breast through the soft pink sweater. "Yup, there's just nothing like the smell of puked-up formula."

She countered his response. "Number four: Breastfed babies don't emit an offensive odor."

"Says you."

"Says me." She gave him one of those smiles that always turned his brain to mush followed by that stern, stop-interrupting-me look, before she moved on to number five.

"Reason number five: Being the most tired you've ever been in your entire life and the most happy."

"Now there's the best reason you've given so far."

His cynicism didn't diminish her enthusiasm. It was clear she wasn't giving up until she convinced him.

Finally, she reached the end of her list, her eyes bright and eager. "We get to have lots and lots and lots of sex."

He capitulated even though he knew the lots of sex would change after the baby arrived. That selfish, immature side of him wished things could stay as they were and that he'd never have to share her. Deep down in his heart of hearts, he feared he'd turn out to be as big a disappointment as his father at parenting. He pushed his fears aside.

Being a pragmatic man, and a man who knew a lost cause when he saw it, he slid his hand under her sweater and released the clasp on the front of her bra.

Clare gasped. "What do you think you're doing?"

"Getting started." He lifted her sweater and took her nipple into his mouth.

Clare moaned. "I love you, Ethan."

He released her nipple and shifted so that she was beneath him, then made love to the only woman he'd ever loved.

ETHAN FILLED the kitchen sink with hot, sudsy water and began washing the breakfast dishes. He paused and rubbed at the acrid burn in his belly, a constant companion for the last four months since Clare announced her pregnancy. Clearly karma, or a quirk of fate had been at work to make sure Clare got pregnant their first try.

Soapy water splashed his face as he vigorously scrubbed the casserole dish and chastised himself. What had he been thinking when he'd agreed to start a family? He wasn't father material, and God knew his father certainly hadn't been a positive role model.

Benjamin Burke was everybody's pal, but nobody's father. While he played the life of the party with skill and never failed to offer a shoulder and a beer when life went sour, his friends and his booze always came before his family.

Fear haunted Ethan, constantly nipped at his heels. What if he turned out just like his father in the parenting department? He didn't even have his mother to fall back on as an example of good parenting. While she didn't drink to excess, she had enabling down to an art form. Never once had she put her son's best interest first. The slightest inkling of controversy sent her scurrying for cover.

In public, his father was Mr. Congeniality, but in private, he was Mr. Indifference. He'd never laid a hand on Ethan physically. Apathy had been the weapon of choice.

Ethan studied the modest house he and Clare had moved into two years ago. It was a palace in comparison to the series of shacks he'd grown up in. Whenever the landlord got fed up with his father's empty promises of payment, an eviction notice arrived. It was a cycle Ethan knew intimately, and one he was determined not to repeat.

He and Clare didn't live in squalor by any means, but neither did they live like royalty. Not that he'd ever be able to buy her a mansion, but he at least wanted their names on a mortgage rather than a month-to-month lease. He wanted, craved, a home of their own, a place that belonged to them, a place where no one could force them to leave. He wanted stability, something he'd never experienced, and if he had to take a second job to achieve that goal, he would.

"Ethan, ohmygod come quick."

The plate slipped from his fingers and splashed a geyser of soapy water over the counter when he turned and raced to the bedroom. "What's wrong?"

She smiled and waved him over to the bed. Her hand pressed low on her belly.

Most women would have been despondent when their street clothes became too snug in the first trimester, but not Clare. She'd been ecstatic and immediately swapped her tee-shirts and jeans for smock tops and elastic waist pants that would take another three months to actually fit. Anyone but Clare would have looked ridiculous. She glowed.

He crossed over and sat down beside her.

She grabbed his hand and pressed it to her stomach just below her bellybutton.

"Can you feel it?"

Her stomach gurgled. "You had me race in here to tell me you're hungry?"

She shook her head, her thick blonde hair gracefully swirling from side to side. "No silly. I called you in here so you could feel your baby move. Ohhhh, there it is again. Did you feel it?"

No, he hadn't because he'd been too absorbed watching Clare's eyes widen in wonder.

"There it is again."

This time he felt the faint flurry deep in her womb, and while he appreciated the fact their baby made his or her presence known, clearly he didn't have the same sense of awe for the event Clare did. Wisely, though, he withheld that bit of information, the same as he had all the other times Clare's enthusiasm outshone his.

He forced a smile. "Yeah."

Clare playfully punched his arm. "You did not. You only said that to placate me."

"What if I did?" Ethan teased.

She tugged his arm so that he laid beside her and kissed him. "I think it's incredibly sweet that you would do that to make me happy. Actually, I suspect a lot of what you do is more for my happiness than your own."

She propped her head on her hand. "You know what else I think?"

"No, what?"

Her eyes sparkled with barely suppressed merriment as if she knew far more than he did, which wouldn't surprise him in the least.

"I think you are going to be a wonderful father."

A band of pressure tightened his chest. Her unwavering faith in him shimmered in her eyes. His breathing hitched when panic slowly crept over him. Could he live up to her expectations? Or even more terrifying, could he stand seeing her faith in him diminish if he disappointed her?

"Ethan?" She gently brushed the hair from his forehead. "No one says you have to be a perfect dad, just the best one you can. That's all any of us can do."

He wanted to believe her, wanted to believe it was that simple. That he could do his best and everything would work out happily ever after.

"Ethan." She squeezed his hand. "Talk to me."

He pushed his demons aside. "But what if my best isn't good enough? What if I end up like—" He couldn't voice the fear that had been locked inside him since the moment he'd learned Clare was pregnant.

"You're not your father, Ethan." Her fingers feathered through his hair and she stared deep into his eyes. "You're not your father," she repeated, her voice laced with steel this time.

Her words penetrated the tightness in his chest. Maybe he could do this. Maybe history wouldn't repeat itself. Maybe he could beat the odds and be the parent his father hadn't been.

He linked his fingers with hers. "I love you."

"I love you, too."

Their baby moved against his hand in apparent approval, and for the first time, he believed he wouldn't become his father. Clare was his salvation, and he would do anything, *anything*, to maintain her faith in him. And achieving that meant being the parent his father hadn't been.

THE MONTHS FLEW by in a blur of doctor visits, childbirth classes, and turning the tiny spare bedroom into a brightly-colored nursery. Clare embraced it all while Ethan clung to her coattails and her belief in him. The terror he'd felt early in the pregnancy abated, but he still didn't share his wife's enthusiasm.

That changed, however, the instant his son curled his tiny hand around his finger. From that moment on, he'd been transformed from the tin man without a heart, to a man utterly, completely, and hopelessly in love with his firstborn son.

PRESENT DAY...

The front door banged shut and Ben trudged into the kitchen, snapping Ethan from the past. He wondered, not for the first time, how Ben and Jack had gone from babies to miniature adults overnight.

Did Clare feel the same aching loss over the passing of time that he did? He wished he knew. He wished they could talk like they used to, that they could hold each other and share their burdens, rather than hug separate sides of the bed.

He went upstairs to get a fresh shirt, and paused in the stairwell to study the portraits Clare had done of the kids.

He stared at Grace's photo. What had he been thinking when he'd suggested he and Clare have a second baby? Had it been a mistake or the best decision of his life? If they hadn't gotten pregnant, there would have been no Grace and no losing Grace. But the thought of never knowing his daughter, never holding her, never loving her was almost as unbearable as losing her. And losing her had turned his soul inside out.

He shifted his gaze to Ben's photo. The baby neither of them planned on, but both cherished. Their golden child. The baby who smiled, and cooed, and never cried. His sunny disposition provided a constant joy and their greatest blessing. He'd been named after

Ethan's father—certainly not his idea, but the right one, and he was glad Clare had insisted.

He loved his children and he would die for them, would have died for Grace if he'd had the chance. Ethan didn't regret becoming a parent. They might have endured some rough spots, but the very idea of being without Clare and the kids left a vast emptiness within him that was too terrifying to consider. Life might not be perfect, but the alternative, life without his family, was unthinkable.

10

———————

Another blood-curdling yowl echoed through Clare's nylon tent.

The hair on Bailey's hackles rose.

The logs shifted. A spray of sparks shot into the dark sky.

Golden eyes glittered in the firelight.

A growl rumbled deep in Bailey's chest.

Clare restrained her. If she gave the command, Bailey would rip through their shelter to protect her.

The mountain lion howled again. The shadow of its sleek, muscular body cast over the tent.

Clare tightened her hold on the collar. "Stay."

Another spray of sparks shot up into the sky.

The cat leapt back. Its tail twitched. A moment later it spun around, leaped over a downed tree and disappeared into the night.

A faint cry from the mountain lion sounded from much farther away. Clare's grip eased on Bailey's collar and her shoulders slumped forward.

A minute later she crawled out of the tent and added more wood to the fire. Shivering violently, she wiggled into the sleeping bag.

Ballistic shoved his way inside the bag, bumping her hand with his head. She began petting him, and he purred.

Clare reared back and looked down at him. "What's with you? You never purr."

Ballistic gave her a haughty glare through narrowly slit lids, then snuggled deeper against her side. The tension flowed out of her as he continued to purr.

A contented sigh slipped past Clare's lips, and a smile curved her mouth as she stared into the flickering firelight and remembered a happier time, a time when she'd thought her marriage would last forever.

~

TEN YEARS AGO…

"Eight years. Can it really be that we've been married that long? It seems like yesterday I first saw you hanging upside down from that tree." Ethan's tender smile took her back to that day.

Clare twirled her wine glass, watching the clear liquid sparkle in the candlelight. "And you were so darn cute in those Levis and polo shirt. I kept thinking I never had a science teacher who filled out a pair of jeans the way you did."

Ethan's smile widened. "I guess it's a good thing I snatched you up before one of my colleagues did."

"Hah, your memory fails you. I was the one who had to finagle a date from you that first time."

"It wasn't like I could hit on you with twenty eighth graders looking on. And for your information, it was a pretty lame date at that. I mean, promising to bring the photos back for the class to see was an excuse one of my students would have concocted." His dark eyes danced with mirth.

"It was not lame, and it just goes to show what you know. Every one of those kids knew you were interested in me."

"No way."

"Way."

"How?"

"It wasn't a difficult leap. Your face had a giant neon sign that flashed, 'I want to jump your bones.' The same as it does now, I might add."

Ethan pretended outrage. "I have more discretion than that."

Clare shook her head in exasperated amusement. "Why do all men think they are being subtle, when in fact, their intentions are so blatantly obvious?"

Ethan's fingers glided up the inside of her leg. "Maybe because we'd never get any if we weren't."

Laughter bubbled out of Clare. "Oh you poor sex-deprived man."

Ethan's eyes twinkled. "I am. Will you take pity on me tonight and transform me from deprived to fulfilled?"

"I think there's a strong possibility—"

Clare's phone rang just then. She glanced at the screen and saw it was the babysitter. "Jennifer, is something wrong?"

The romantic evening that they'd planned for weeks dissolved when ten minutes later she and Ethan raced home to deal with two sick children.

Their intimate evening became a distant memory as well as the surprise Clare had intended to share.

Clare's stomach grumbled several hours later, reminding her she hadn't eaten dinner. In-between rocking Grace and Jack while Ethan took the sitter home and picked up Tylenol, she managed to scarf down a peanut butter sandwich. It had been enough to tide her over until Ethan returned and she could make something more substantial.

But something more substantial never materialized between cuddling and soothing one fever-ravaged body while Ethan comforted the other. The clock struck midnight when Clare finally collapsed on the sofa.

Ethan joined her a minute later with a plate of saltines, cheese, and two glasses of milk.

He leaned his head back against the sofa and closed his eyes. "How long do you suppose they'll sleep?"

"If we're lucky, thirty minutes, but more likely ten."

Clare sipped the milk Ethan handed her, then nibbled on a saltine. She closed her eyes and sighed as the crackers and milk settled her queasy stomach. Music drifted from the stereo, soothing her frazzled nerves and exhausted body.

She turned her head toward Ethan and opened her mouth to tell him her surprise.

Before she could, he asked a question of his own. "How long were you going to wait to tell me?"

Her eyes widened in surprise. "Tell you what?"

"About the baby."

Ethan's dark gaze studied her.

She'd never perfected the art of deception, and with Ethan, she was a complete and utter failure.

"How did you know? I only just figured it out a couple of days ago."

"You weren't drinking your wine."

"Ah."

"So when were you going to tell me?"

"Actually, I'd planned on telling you tonight, but things kind of went haywire."

His gentle smile warmed her through and through. "I'll say."

Starting a family hadn't been a priority for Ethan. Clare knew if the decision had been left to him, they would have remained a couple.

And if she were totally honest with herself, there were days she wondered if she'd made a mistake pressing him to start a family. She loved Jack and Grace, but two children were a responsibility and a burden at times that felt overwhelming. And now they were adding an unexpected third to the mix.

"I know it's not something we'd planned."

"No, it certainly isn't, but we'll muddle through."

"Muddling through" wasn't exactly the glowing endorsement she'd hoped for. She'd wanted one of them to be thrilled at the prospect, or at least happy about the unexpected surprise. Muddling through filled neither of those requirements. But it was more than the words he uttered that troubled her, it was the tone of his voice that left her uneasy. Then again, she hadn't exactly done cartwheels when she'd seen the positive mark on the pregnancy stick. Truth be told, she'd been downright disconsolate when she'd been forced to face a reality she hadn't planned on or wanted. She'd been looking forward to more time for herself. More time with Ethan.

Van Morrison's voice flowed out of the speakers.

Ethan held out his hand to her. "Dance with me." His warm breath whispered over her cheek.

His dark eyes were bloodshot, his hair mussed and the tee-shirt he'd swapped for his dress shirt sported a glowing pink Tylenol stain on it. Even so, he was still the most handsome man who'd ever asked her to dance.

She slid her fingers into his outstretched hand, and he gently eased her to her feet. They swayed to the music as the pop and hiss of the fire played accompaniment.

Suddenly every logical, sensible reason not to have another baby dissolved like smoke up the chimney and joy bubbled within her. Ethan was right. They would muddle through. It wouldn't be easy, but they had each other, and that was enough.

The song ended and so did the temporary reprieve when Grace's sharp cry echoed from the bedroom.

Ethan lifted his face from her hair. "I was having this fantasy about the two of us alone and naked—"

Clare pressed her fingers to his lips. "I can't deal with fantasy when reality is screaming her lungs out."

He smiled and kissed each of her fingertips, then released her. "I promise fantasy will become reality one of these days soon."

Their eyes held for long moments until Grace's piercing demand was joined by Jack's.

~

Present day...

Embers glowed when Clare returned from her stroll down memory lane. She'd been so incredibly overwhelmed with a third baby. No time for work, no time for herself, and yet she'd loved every minute of it. She and Ethan had been a unit, they'd had each other to lean on. She wanted those days back.

Clare eased out of the sleeping bag. Bailey cracked open an eye, but didn't move when Clare ordered her to stay. By the time she'd finished adding more wood to the fire, her teeth chattered again. She slipped back into the sleeping bag. She needed sleep, but her mind remained fixated on the past, and one question continued to haunt her.

Would everything she and Ethan shared be enough to salvage their marriage?

11

E than climbed into the truck and started the engine, Ben and Jack wedged in beside him. They'd been searching since midnight, and the steady rain had switched to icy, needle-edged sleet.

The faint light of dawn lightened the sky as Ethan turned onto the main road and headed back to the base camp. He needed to check in and get coffee to warm his body and drive away the icy fear in his heart. Not that anything could do that short of finding Clare.

The radio channel faded out and Jack put in a rock CD. Nickleback blasted out of the speakers wailing about not being able to see the signs of a failed relationship.

Why had it taken Ethan so long to see his relationship with Clare was in trouble? It was like the group was privy to the day-to-day workings of his marriage.

And hadn't his marriage become a Hollywood horror like the song described? Why had he turned away from the one person who understood him? He wished he knew.

Finding Clare was only half the battle. Winning back her trust and her heart was another matter all together.

The song ended as he pulled into the base camp. He shifted into park and one question haunted him. Would he get a chance to make it right with Clare?

Ethan shut off the engine, and his fear as he climbed out of the truck. After checking in, he left the boys with the group of search-and-rescue people and went to sit under a cover set up a few feet away.

Ethan took a drink, the coffee scalding his throat. A deputy sheriff, still wet-behind-the-ears, swaggered over to him.

His tough-guy-fresh-from-the-academy attitude would have amused Ethan any other time. All it did now was irritate him.

"Mr. Burke?"

"Yes."

"I'm Officer Harris. I need to talk with you about your wife."

Ethan found the man even more offensive when he compared him to the other deputy sheriffs he'd worked with on search and rescue. Bill Jenkins and Rich Tompkins were experienced patrolmen Ethan had partnered with on a dozen different search-and-rescue operations, and he'd always admired how they maintained authority and respect without being overbearing. This kid needed to spend some time with those two and watch and learn from seasoned veterans.

"Fire away," Ethan said.

"When was the last time you saw your wife?"

"A little before eight yesterday morning."

"And you haven't seen or talked to her since?"

"No. I left a message on her cell phone about an hour later, but she didn't return my call."

"Is that unusual?"

Ethan shrugged, eyeing Harris while he sipped his coffee. "Just depends on where she is and if she checks her messages before she loses service. Sometimes she can get out with her cell phone, sometimes she can't."

"And she hasn't tried to call you?"

Ethan bristled. The sleepless night and worry over Clare had left him irritable and edgy. "Like I told you a minute ago, no."

"Did you two have an argument that turned physical?" His tone oozed sarcasm.

"This is beginning to sound like an interrogation. Do I need an attorney?"

"It's procedure, sir."

"It doesn't sound like procedure for a woman lost in the mountains. It sounds like procedure for foul play."

"Was there foul play involved in your wife's disappearance, Mr. Burke?"

The urge to rearrange his pretty-boy face and give it some character with a well-placed punch was tempting. Instead, he stilled his temper and his fists and answered his question. "My wife is lost, or she's been in an accident, both things that are out of my control."

"You haven't answered my question, Mr. Burke. Did you and your wife argue yesterday morning?"

"No."

"But something happened, didn't it?"

Ethan blew out a weary breath. "I snapped at the kids." He wasn't about to tell him that what happened couldn't really be classified as an argument. Indifferent shrugs and glaring stares weren't healthy vents of anger. He and Clare needed to air their grievances, but Ethan feared if he ever released the anger festering inside him, he'd do irreparable damage to his marriage.

Most of his hostility was directed at himself, at letting Grace die, but he resented Clare, too. Why didn't she tell him about their financial problems instead of running to her parents? Why did she have to prove his father right?

Maintaining a civil relationship with his in-laws when he knew they expected Clare to come to her senses and leave him, was hard enough. But now he owed them money, a lot of money. Thirty thousand dollars to be precise because the initial ten thousand hadn't been enough to tide them over until Ethan recovered from the accident. And even with the monthly payments they made, it would be another eighteen years before they paid them off.

But pay them off he would if it was the last thing he did, even if he had to take three jobs to do it once Jack started college.

Ethan rose and stared down at the kid. "Why do you suspect I had something to do with my wife's disappearance?"

"We checked your cell phone and there's a message on it dated yesterday morning at nine-thirty. Why didn't you tell us about the message?"

"Because I didn't know about any damn message, that's why. And for your information I have at least fifty witness to my whereabouts yesterday." Ethan pulled out his cell phone and called for his messages. Sure enough there was an apology from Clare, but no hint of where she was headed.

After Ethan put his phone away, Harris prodded him some more. "Your wife sounded upset."

"I don't know what you heard, but we had a disagreement. That's all. Could you trace the call?"

"We checked your phone records, and she was north of the city limits."

"That's all you got?"

"Yes. We can't pinpoint her exact location."

"But she was north of town."

"Yes."

"That's something." Ethan had hoped for more, but at least they could narrow their search to the north.

He looked at Harris. "Are you charging me with something?"

Harris' eyes turned icy as he stared back at him. "No."

Ethan headed over to speak with Pete McKlosky, the search-and-rescue coordinator. His cell phone vibrated against his hip before he reached Pete to update him. Hope surged, then fizzled and died when his father-in-law's voice came over the line instead of Clare's.

"Ethan, I just wanted to let you know our flight was ahead of schedule and we're at the house now. We'll handle everything on this end."

"Thank you."

"Has there been any sign of Clare?"

"No, but I just got a message she left on my cell phone yesterday morning."

William's tone was sharp and clipped. "I assume she didn't say where she was headed."

Ethan's hand clenched the phone. "No, she didn't." He blew out a breath, and the knot of tension in his stomach eased. "It did tell us she was alive after she talked to Alexandria."

Ethan swore under his breath. "I'm sorry, I didn't mean to imply—"

"Of course. As you so astutely pointed out, we know she was alive and well at that time, so we will focus on that. If there are any resources you need, all you have to do is ask," William said.

Ethan stared up at the dark sky and watched the snowflakes come down. "Not unless you can do something to move this cold front out so we can get helicopters into the sky to search for her."

"The one thing my money can't do." William cleared his throat as if it were clogged with emotion.

"I'm going to find her, William."

A dry chuckle crackled over the line. "You know, if anyone can do it, I believe you can."

"I won't stop until I find her. I believe Clare is alive, and well, and just waiting for me to figure out where she is."

"I know that. When you can, we'd appreciate updates."

"I will."

Ethan jammed the phone back in his pocket. How different this conversation had been compared to the one they'd had the Christmas after Ben's birth.

Ten years ago...

Clare hung up the phone and returned to the sofa. Her features were stiff, and her eyes glistened with unshed tears.

Ethan looked up from the papers he'd been grading. "I take it your mother turned down your invitation for Christmas."

"Yes. They're having their annual Christmas extravaganza and can't cancel."

Ethan silently absorbed the information while carefully weighing his response. He pushed the science reports he'd been grading aside and gave Clare his full attention. "I know you want your parents to spend more time with the kids, so why don't we go out there for Christmas?"

"We don't have the money to fly us all out there."

"We could drive."

"With Jack, Grace and a six-week-old baby? That's insanity, besides my mother made it abundantly clear they don't have time for bonding with their grandchildren. That's what a nanny does. Their time is too valuable for something that trivial."

"Surely they'd make time if we went out there."

"They won't."

The hurt in her voice gnawed at Ethan. Clare had had the financial stability he'd craved as a child, but she'd still come away from her childhood feeling unloved and unwanted.

"Why don't I try talking to her?"

"It won't do any good. It has to be her way or nothing."

A trait mother and daughter shared, and an insight Ethan wisely kept to himself. Ethan slipped off his reading glasses and rubbed the bridge of his nose. "What can it hurt for me to try?"

Clare's eyes snapped with barely suppressed fury. "Just leave it alone, okay? Seeing their grandchildren isn't a priority."

Ethan started to respond when Ben's wail from the nursery stopped him.

Long after Clare disappeared down the hallway, Ethan stared out the window into the blackness that had settled over the landscape.

What could it hurt to call them? Maybe they would listen to him.

Ethan went into the kitchen and dialed his in-laws. The maid picked up on the second ring, and he asked for his father-in-law.

"Hello, Ethan. How have you been?"

"Fine."

"And my new grandson?

"Growing and changing every day."

Ethan inhaled. He'd stalled long enough. Time to get to the reason for his call. "I needed to discuss Christmas with you. We'd really hoped you and Alexandria would be able to come out and join us, but we understand you have other commitments. Clare and I were talking, and we'd like to bring the children to your place for the holidays."

Silence.

Finally, William said, "We won't have much time with the party we're hosting, and we'll have guests over most of the season."

"Surely you'll have time to see your daughter and grandchildren?"

No response.

"What is it you're not saying?"

William cleared his throat. "There will be a lot of politicians and celebrities here that would bore you."

Resentment simmered, but Ethan ignored it. "Maybe it would be better if just Clare and the kids came out."

"I believe Alexandria made that suggestion to Clare earlier, but she didn't want to be separated from you."

Warmth replaced resentment. Clare had been protecting him.

"Maybe you could persuade Clare to change her mind?"

Ethan was ready to agree, then stopped. He would not allow his in-laws to put a wedge between him and Clare.

"No, I think Clare is right. We shouldn't separate the family during the holidays. Of course if your plans should change, you're always welcome here." He paused a moment, then said, "Clare would really love to see you both."

When William didn't respond, Ethan said goodbye and hung up the phone.

He stared out at the moonlit landscape. A falling star soared through the sky as the discussion with his father-in-law replayed in his head. Clare had been protecting him by lying about her conversation with her mother.

Shutting off the lights, he followed the glow of the nightlight to the nursery and the woman who loved him enough to protect his feelings. Leaning against the doorjamb, he watched Clare nurse their son.

Ben's deep blue eyes shifted to focus on him as he continued to suckle at his mother's breast. His eyes sparkled as a smile gradually loosened his suction.

Clare's gaze followed Ben's. "He was almost asleep until you walked in."

"Sorry," he said, but he wasn't. It warmed him in places that had been left cold and empty during his childhood that his presence alone had the ability to make his son smile. He cherished that unconditional love. It was a feeling he never grew tired of and kept him returning for more.

"You are not." Annoyance tinged Clare's voice, but her eyes sparkled with merriment.

"I'm sorry about earlier. I shouldn't have pushed you. I just knew how much you wanted your parents to see the kids. We'll spend the holidays here and have a wonderful Christmas, I promise."

Her soft blue eyes glistened in the dim light. "Thank you."

Ben's very loud and very satisfied burp interrupted the moment.

Clare smiled up at him. "Clearly your son has finished eating, so I'll let you change him and rock him to sleep while I go soak in the bathtub."

He crossed over and accepted the cooing baby from her. She readjusted her shirt, then vacated the rocker. As she started past him, he reached out and brushed his fingers over her cheek.

She stopped and stared up at him.

"I really love your pink nightgown."

Her nipples drew tight under her shirt, and Ethan's heart pumped double time.

"I might know the one you mean."

"Then perhaps when you finish your bath you could slip it on and dance with me."

"That's a definite possibility." Her sultry voice sent the blood straight to his groin. "I wouldn't turn down a little wine either."

"I'll have it waiting."

As Clare sashayed off, he wondered how he'd been so fortunate to win her heart.

Ben's chubby palm slapped his cheek. He looked down at his son who cooed and smiled up at him.

Thirty minutes later, Ethan managed to get Ben changed and to sleep. He raced into the kitchen for the wine and their fancy wine glasses and took everything to the bedroom. He had just put in a CD when the bathroom door swung open and Clare stepped into the dimly lit room. She smelled of warm, sweet woman, and it was all Ethan could do to keep from throwing her on the bed, skipping the romance and foreplay and just pump his brains out.

Fortunately, he managed to tame his libido and hand her a glass of wine.

She smiled, and Ethan's gut twisted as lust consumed him again. He took a healthy swallow of his drink, set his glass down and swept Clare into his arms.

Her soft laughter was far sweeter than the music coming from the stereo. He pressed her close so he could feel those hard, pointy nipples jab into his chest.

Clare tilted her head so they were eye to eye and batted her eyelashes. "Why, Mr. Burke, I do declare you are holding me a tad too tightly. What will my mama think?" She used a really poor imitation of a southern drawl that was music to his ears.

Ethan toyed with the lacy strap of her nightgown, a smile parting his lips. "Frankly, Mrs. Burke, I don't give a damn what your mama thinks."

Clare's smile widened, and her eyes shone with wicked delight. "Is that so?"

"It is."

"What exactly are your intentions, Mr. Burke?"

The song ended and he took her glass and set it on the dresser. Slowly, he lowered the strap from her shoulder. "I intend." He moved his lips to the tender juncture between her neck and shoulder, inhaled her musky scent, then kissed her.

He raised his head. "To kiss every inch of —"

He paused again as he moved his lips up the smooth, white column of her throat, halting at the enticing nub of pink earlobe that winked out from under her silky blonde hair. He nipped rather than kissed, and her gasp sent another surge of blood to his groin.

His tongue ringed the pink shell of her ear. "—your body."

She shivered. "I believe you're trying to seduce me, Mr. Burke."

Ethan's other hand slipped to the breast he'd partially revealed. "No doubt about it. Are you objecting?"

He flicked her nipple and she moaned. "Oh my, no."

They swayed to the music while Ethan continued his exploration. His lips moved to the arch of her chest. He slid off the other strap and pink fluff pooled at her waist. Her full breasts glowed in the soft light, and Ethan hungered to sample them, but he resisted.

Instead, he pulled off his shirt and looped his arms around her so her breasts pressed against his bare chest as they swayed to the slow, sensual beat of the music.

Clare's soft murmur sent him to the edge, but the rake of her nails from his chest to navel was nearly his undoing.

"You're overdressed, Mr. Burke." That sexy southern drawl was far more potent than any aphrodisiac.

He swallowed with difficulty. "What do you suggest?"

Her warm breath tickled his ear. "Strip."

Wicked, wicked woman. "Your wish is my command."

The music shifted to a faster beat as Ethan slid his jeans over his hips. He watched Clare's breathing hitch. So did his.

He wanted to rush, wanted desperately to find his release inside of her, but he kept himself tightly restrained so he could linger, savor each moment with her.

When he finally stood naked before her, she stared at him with the same dark intensity she studied her photos. It was as if she'd touched him, but she hadn't. As impossible as it seemed, his erection grew as her gaze continued to sweep over him.

"Well, do I meet with your approval, Mrs. Burke?"

Passion burned deep in her eyes. "Y-Y-Yes, most certainly. Do carry on, sir."

And Ethan did just that. Carried on, carried under, carried over until they were sweaty, gasping for breath and sated.

PRESENT DAY...

The memory faded and the tight fist that had been squeezing Ethan's heart increased. He ached to revive the closeness he'd had with his wife. The easy banter, soft laughter and the intimacy. He stared up at the breaking dawn over the vast wilderness and prayed Clare was hunkered down waiting for help to arrive.

12

———

The world had never felt so enormous, and Clare had never felt so alone when she stared out at the dark sky and watched the rain continue to pour.

A flash of light drew her attention. A helicopter. Hope surged then died in the space of a breath when she realized the light was too high in the sky for a helicopter. It actually looked like a falling star, but that would be impossible to see through the thick cloud cover.

She shifted her position and groaned. Every inch of her body ached from her encounter with the airbag the previous day. What she wouldn't give for a good long soak in the bathtub to ease her aching muscles. Instead, she crawled out of the tent and added wood to the few remaining coals.

The sharp bite of the wind had her scurrying back inside and snuggling into her sleeping bag. Ballistic huddled up next to her and she was grateful the mangy feline provided her with the comfort of his purr and the warmth of his body.

When her shivering subsided, she relaxed and felt much less alone. As she drifted between wakefulness and sleep, her mind drifted back to the first Christmas with Ben when life had its disappointments, but she and Ethan still supported each other.

Ten years ago...

A high-pitched childish giggle alerted Clare that Jack and Grace were awake and headed downstairs to see what Santa had brought them.

She cracked open an eye to witness dawn breaking.

A burp drowned out Ethan's snore and drew Clare's attention to Ben who had just finished his pre-dawn snack. Rosebud lips curled into a blissful smile as his mouth slipped off her breast. His sweet baby breath filled her nostrils and contentment settled over her. She traced a finger over his cheek and marveled at the silky softness of it. Tears pricked her eyes as it occurred to her just how blessed she was to have found Ethan and carved out this life.

How could her parents not see what a wonderful man she'd chosen? How could they care more about appearances than seeing their grandchildren?

Their loss.

If that was so, then why did the ache in her chest refuse to subside? Why did she desperately wish for a Christmas miracle that would have them downstairs waiting to surprise her?

Pipe dreams, Clare. Appreciate what you have.

A tear slid down her cheek before she could pull back her emotions. It rolled off her chin and landed on the top of Ben's head. Another followed and she sucked in a deep breath as she struggled for control.

A calloused finger caught the next tear before it dripped off of her chin.

Startled, Clare looked up. Ethan's dark gaze scrutinized her.

"Crying is a heck of a way to start Christmas." His finger caught another tear. He carefully slipped his arm under her shoulder so as not to disturb the baby.

Clare offered him a shaky smile. "Postpartum blues."

Ethan pressed her head to his chest. "It's okay to be sad that they're not here, Clare."

Another wave of unhappiness swept over her. "Oh Ethan. Why don't they want to see their grandchildren?"

"I don't know. I'm sorry they aren't here for you."

"It's not your fault."

"It is. We both know I embarrass them, that they think I'm just a backwoods Idaho mountain man."

Clare swiped at her damp cheeks. "If you know so much, smart guy, then you also know there's no one I'd rather spend my holidays with."

His smile lifted her spirits. "Is that so, Mrs. Burke?"

"It is."

A giggle echoed up the stairwell followed by the rattling of a package.

"I hear a couple of little urchins downstairs," Ethan said.

"Old news. They went past while you were sleeping."

A gurgle of amusement followed by an unsteady finger that reached up to brush Ethan's stubble-roughened chin announced the newest member of the family was awake.

"Looks like someone else is ready to see what Santa brought." Ben waved a chubby hand at Ethan.

Clare's heart warmed when Ben smiled up at them. He might not have been planned, but sometimes the best gifts arrived unannounced and unexpected.

Ethan squeezed her shoulder. "I promise you we will make this a memorable Christmas."

Clare offered him a watery smile. "You've never let me down, so I know you'll succeed this time, too."

Ethan slid his arm out from under her and cupped her face with both hands before he kissed her. "I love you."

The baby began to fuss and Ethan scooped him up, holding him above his head.

"I wouldn't do that," Clare warned a second before Ben threw up all over him.

She pursed her lips. Three children and the man still hadn't learned not to lift a well-fed baby over his head.

Clare fought hard to keep a straight face. "I guess you were right."

Ethan cocked a jaundiced eye at her. "How so?"

"This is definitely going to be a memorable Christmas."

ETHAN'S PARENTS arrived mid-morning with more presents for the kids. Jack and Grace had barely finished opening their presents when Ethan's dad fixed a glass of eggnog laced with a double shot of rum. He downed a second glass before they sat down to eat the turkey dinner Ethan had prepared.

The meal went surprisingly smoothly, but underneath Ethan's genial expression, Clare sensed tension. The smile that didn't quite reach his eyes and the fork clenched so tightly his knuckles whitened indicated how much his father's drinking disturbed him.

After all Ethan had done to make this a special holiday for her, Clare desperately wanted to do the same for him. She turned to her father-in-law. "Ben, would you mind helping me clear the table?"

Ben grabbed his glass and a platter and disappeared into the kitchen without a word of complaint.

Clare saw the protest building in Ethan's eyes and squelched it. "Ethan, didn't you promise Jack a ride on his new sled?"

"I want to go, too," Grace cried, when Jack jumped out of his chair.

The kids raced out of the room, Dot trailing after them.

Clare reached for Ethan's plate, and his fingers twined around her wrist. "I know what you're up to."

She arched a brow at him. "I don't know what you're talking about."

He smiled and this time it reached all the way to his eyes. "The hell you don't, and thanks."

She lightly kissed his lips. "We're a team, remember?"

She started to pull back when his hand slipped behind her head and held her lips to his as he deepened the kiss.

Clare resisted the urge to fan her face when he released her. "Oh my." The words escaped on a halting breath.

Ethan pressed her hand to his chest. "How much longer until we can find some time alone?"

If the house hadn't been filled with children and his parents she'd have told him immediately, but since they weren't alone, she tempered her response. "Sometime between next week and eternity."

"I'll be sure to mark my calendar." A twinkle sparkled in his eyes. "Don't strain yourself with the cleanup. I don't want you to overdo."

Clare watched him walk away, and she couldn't help but notice a very definite skip to his step.

Focusing on clearing the table she headed into the kitchen. Her father-in-law joined her a moment later.

He poured straight whiskey into his glass and swirled the amber liquid while he watched her. "So, are you playing intermediary between me and my son?"

Clare smiled at him as she set the dishes on the counter. "I just thought you two could use a break, that's all."

"Just because you convinced him to name the baby after me doesn't mean I have to like you." He took a healthy swallow of his drink.

"Doesn't mean you don't either, Ben."

He eyed her over the rim of the glass. "You've got more spunk than I gave you credit for."

"You have always underestimated me. Do you still think I'm going to break his heart?"

His eyebrows shot up in surprise. "Ethan told you what I said?"

"No, I guessed."

Ben stared down into his drink. "I'm sorry." He emptied the glass in a single swallow.

Clare shrugged. "You spoke your mind. I don't fault you for that. You have a right to your opinion. I don't happen to agree with it, but that's okay, too." She smiled. "Bet you thought I'd be long gone by now, didn't you?"

He set the glass down and looked her square in the eye. "Yeah."

"I'm glad I proved you wrong."

He studied her a long moment. "Me too. I just wish Ethan was as forgiving as you."

Clare patted his hand. "You and Ethan have a lot more history than you and I do." She turned on the water and added soap to the sink. "Trust me, it's a whole lot easier to deal with you than my parents."

"They're fools for not coming."

Tears filled Clare's eyes. Ben was far from the ideal father-in-law, but at least he cared enough to spend time with his grandchildren. Probably because he was part child himself. Regardless, he was here, and her parents weren't. What did that say about them? Nothing good for sure, Clare thought as she plunged her hands into the warm, soapy water.

~

SEVERAL DRINKS later Ben started a tipsy game of roughhouse with Grace and Jack.

Clare winced when they banged into the coffee table and upset her teacup.

Ethan shot a warning glare at his father as he hurried off for a towel.

"Jack, Grace, why don't you two run upstairs and bring down some of the new games you got for Christmas?" Clare suggested.

Grace ignored her mother and scrambled onto Ben's back. She cried in delight when he trotted around the room like her own personal pony.

Not about to be left out of the fun, Jack tackled his grandfather and sent an already unsteady Ben tumbling to the floor. Grace rolled off his back and crashed into the Christmas tree.

The tree tilted sideways then righted itself. The ornament Clare had bought for their first Christmas fell, and the fragile glass shattered against the hardwood floor.

Ethan returned with the towel to mop up Clare's tea as silence descended over the room. Grace's lip trembled just before she burst into tears.

"I'd like to have a word with you outside, Dad," Ethan said.

"It's cold out there. Let's talk in here." Ben rolled onto his side and rested his head on his arm as if nothing had happened.

"Naptime." Clare handed the baby to Ethan and gathered Grace into her arms.

Jack stifled a yawn. "I'm not tired."

"If you're not asleep in fifteen minutes, then you can get up." Clare ushered the children upstairs.

When Clare returned, Dot had just finished sweeping up the broken glass, and said, "It was an accident."

"Yes, it was an accident, but a preventable one if Dad hadn't been drinking and hadn't allowed the horseplay to get out of hand," Ethan said.

Clare took the baby from Ethan.

"I don't know what you're so upset about, son. It was just an ornament. I'll buy you another one."

Clare inhaled a steadying breath. "It wasn't just an ornament, Ben. I bought that for our first Christmas. It was one of a kind."

Ben swiped a hand through the air, his voice slurred. "Just a bunch of sentimental nonsense."

The baby began to fuss. Clare swayed to settle him.

Dot leaned the broom against the wall and sifted through the broken glass. "I think I know where I can find one of these."

Clare shook her head. "I don't think so. We bought it in Spokane, and the store has gone out of business."

That ornament had cost far more than their meager budget allowed, even being on sale. It had been a symbol, something to mark the beginning of their life together.

Dot patted her arm before she headed to the kitchen with the dustpan. "I'm sure I can find something close."

"There now, everything's all taken care of. Time for a drink." Ben got to his feet and swayed before he took a step toward the kitchen.

Ethan's hands balled into fists. "I think you've had enough to drink."

His father leaned against the wall and glared at him. "Who the hell do you think you are telling me when I've had enough to drink?"

"I'm your son, and this is my house, and I won't have you destroying our property then walking away without being accountable."

"Your mother said she'd find another one."

"It's not Mom's responsibility to make this right. It's yours."

His mother returned from the kitchen. "I don't mind, Ethan."

"I do. I mind that you always make it easy for him to be irresponsible. I mind that you are always scurrying around trying to make things right. I mind when you always stand beside him even when he's wrong. I mind that you enable him to continue drinking."

Dot's eyes went wide, then glassy with tears. "I think it's time to go, Ben." She went to the closet to get their coats.

"This is why he continues to drink, Mom. You would rather take him home than admit he's an alcoholic. I love you, but if you continue to be his enabler, it will put a rift between us that won't be easily repaired."

His mother's gaze moved from him to Clare, begging Clare to intervene.

Clare stood firm and squeezed Ethan's hand.

His mother's voice turned shrill. "You would cause a family fight over an ornament?"

Ethan shook his head. "This isn't about the ornament. This is about my father being an alcoholic. This is about me having to be the parent when neither of you could. I was the one who worked to keep a roof over our heads. I was the one who worked so we had food. And what did you do?"

Dot's face went scarlet, but she didn't respond.

"You gave him the money I earned to buy alcohol. How could you do that?"

His mother's voice shook. "How can you do this? How can you ruin Christmas?"

"You just don't get it, Mom. It's not me. Just once I wish you'd side with me."

Clare held Ethan's hand tighter as he shook with anger. He didn't buckle under his mother's obvious pain, and Clare had never been prouder of him.

Dot faced her. "Talk to him, Clare. Make him see the truth."

"Ethan has already seen the truth. Ben needs help, and so do you. You need counseling Dot, so you can help him. Please do it before something more happens than a broken ornament."

A tear slid down Dot's wrinkled cheek. She turned away, pulled on her coat and walked out the door. Ben stumbled after her.

The baby fussed and Clare sat down in the wood rocker to feed him. When Ben fell asleep, Clare laid him in his bassinet, then went to find Ethan.

She found him in the kitchen washing the dessert plates. She came up behind him and slid her arms around his waist.

"I'm sorry about your ornament." His voice was so quiet she barely heard the words.

"I am too, but you were right. This wasn't about the ornament. This was about your father's alcoholism." Clare placed her body between the sink and Ethan and looped her arms around his neck. "I know you wish this hadn't happened today, but you did the right thing."

"Then why do I feel so rotten?"

"Because in order to do the right thing you had to tell your mother some painful truths no child, even an adult child, should have to say. I'm so proud of you." She brushed her fingers over his cheek, then kissed him.

Soapy fingers pressed into her blouse, and Clare shivered when Ethan pulled her snug against him. He broke away and trailed kisses down her neck. "Is it eternity yet?"

Clare stared at him in confusion. "What are you talking about?"

"You said it would probably be eternity before we'd be alone to make love again."

Warmth spread through her. "Will twenty minutes be enough time?"

Ethan's smile was the best Christmas gift she'd ever received. "Long enough to get to heaven and back. What do you say?"

Clare curled her finger at him and winked. "Take me away."

PRESENT DAY...

Clare's lips curled into a smile as the memory faded. Why couldn't their passion take her away from reality anymore? Why couldn't Ethan's presence alone still do that? There had to be a way they could heal and start again.

She stared at the flickering fire and Grace appeared, smiling. The wind whistled through the tent, and she swore it carried Grace's voice humming their favorite song.

Clare's voice wobbled when she sang the words. "Take me home where the green grass grows. Let the wind blow through me, take me home where the sky is blue and the air is fresh."

Grace's image wavered with the firelight.

"Home where my heart belongs. Home where I'll wait for you always." As Clare sang the last refrain the wind caught the words and carried them and Grace away.

Clare continued to hum the melody long after her daughter's image and voice faded from her mind.

Hope replaced despair. She wouldn't give up. She would get home to Ethan and the boys, and she would find a way to reach Ethan and save their marriage.

Losing Grace had robbed her of Ethan's tender looks across a crowded room, the gentle sweep of his fingers across her back, and the whispered words of love before dropping off to sleep. She wanted it back. She wanted a real marriage, and when she made it out of here alive, she wouldn't settle for anything less.

13

————

Jack walked alongside Noah, periodically calling out his mom's name. They climbed a ridge and Noah paused.

"Noah?"

He didn't respond.

"Earth to Noah."

Noah blinked and focused on Jack. "Yeah."

"Do you miss Matty? Do you miss all the stuff we used to do, the games and trips we all went on?"

Noah blew out a long breath. "Every single day."

Finally, someone who understood what no one else could.

"Let's take a break." Noah dropped his backpack and sat on a downed tree.

Jack joined him. He missed Matt almost as much as he missed Grace. They called each other frequently and texted all the time, but it wasn't the same as hanging out.

At first Matt came home every weekend, but then the visits came less often as Matt's parents fought more and more. They still planned to room together when Jack went to college next fall, and that couldn't come soon enough.

Noah tugged off his gloves and twisted the top off of his water. He took a long drink, then swiped the back of his hand across his mouth.

"It-it went so fast, all the fishing trips with you guys. I loved it all."

Jack missed going fishing with Noah and Matt, but most of all with his dad. It wasn't like they hadn't tried after Grace died. They'd hiked into one of their favorite fishing spots after his dad recovered, and they pretended to enjoy the day. In truth, they'd been miserable without Grace. It was just too painful to be there without her.

He'd told no one about the trip except Matt, the one person he could talk to about anything, including Grace. And Matt had an instinctive way of knowing when to nod, when to stay quiet and when to talk.

Noah stared at Jack, and it was as if Noah had read his mind. "It was never the same after Grace died," Noah said.

"It wasn't."

"I-I wish I knew how to make it better, make it like it used to be."

Jack picked up a stick and jabbed it into the snow. "We can't."

"That doesn't mean we should have stopped trying. We should have given it more time."

"Do you really think that?" Jack winced at the wistful tone that said far more than he'd intended.

"I do. And after we find your mom, me, you, and your dad are going to drive down and pick up Matty and have a guy's fishing weekend. Matty's always talking about this great place he and his pals go steelhead fishing, so I think we should give it a try."

Noah slung an arm around his neck and rubbed his knuckles on Jack's scalp just like he'd done for as long as Jack could remember.

Jack laughed and ducked his head, his heart lighter than it had been in months. Some things never changed, and suddenly Jack had hope they would find his mom and life would get back to normal. Well, as normal as life got anymore. And a weekend away from Paradise Falls, and seeing Matty, would be the perfect therapy.

ETHAN STOPPED when he came upon Noah and Jack sitting and talking. A sudden, completely irrational rush of jealousy struck him, and he had to still the urge to yank his son and Noah apart.

Goddammit, he wanted to be the one to give Jack a noogie, but Grace's death had changed the relaxed camaraderie between them.

Ethan kicked a snowdrift.

What was wrong with him? He didn't behave this way. Noah wasn't competition for his son's affection. The real problem wasn't Noah. The real problem was, Jack was slipping away, and Ethan was clueless about how to repair their relationship. But, it hadn't always been that way. There had been a time his son thought he walked on water.

~

SIX YEARS AGO...

"Dad, look at that."

Ethan skipped a rock across Lake Serenity, then came up alongside Jack. He followed the direction Jack pointed and saw a house nearly overgrown with trees and dense underbrush.

"Can we go over there?"

"Sure. Let's go."

Jack took off at a run, forcing Ethan to pick up his pace to keep up with the ten-year-old. Twenty minutes later they'd circled around to the house. It clearly hadn't seen human habitation in some time.

"Let's go inside."

Ethan snagged the back of Jack's shirt and kept him from climbing onto the rickety porch. His oldest had inherited the daredevil gene from his mother. Not altogether a bad thing, but there were times Ethan wanted to rein him in without curbing his zest for life.

"Not a smart idea." Ethan pressed a foot to the bottom step and it snapped. "How about we check it out from the outside."

They circled the house. When they returned to the front porch, Ethan pushed aside the knot of bushes that blocked the lake.

Transfixed, Ethan stared at the Canadian Rockies that stood sentinel at the mouth of the lake. The snow-tipped peaks glistened in the afternoon sun and reflected in the calm glacial-blue waters of Lake Serenity. Screw the house. He wanted that view every morning when he rolled out of bed and the last thing he saw at night before he went to sleep.

He made another tour of the house this time taking a closer inspection of the foundation and walls. He stepped back to look at the roof. The place needed a lot of work, but that didn't scare him. In fact, just the opposite. It challenged him. He wanted this house. Wanted to turn it into a home for his family.

"Dad, wouldn't this be a cool place to live?"

Ethan looked down at his son and ruffled his hair. "You know I was thinking the very same thing. We just have to figure out how to convince your mother."

"That's easy. We cut back these bushes and trees so she can take pictures of the lake and the mountains from the porch."

"You know your mom pretty well."

Jack's stance turned cocky. "Sure. She's my mom."

"What about me? Do you know me, too?"

Jack gave him an exaggerated eye roll. "Dumb question Dad. Course I do. You're my dad."

"So, how would you convince me to buy this place?"

"I already did. I brought you here."

"You didn't know the house would be here."

"No, but I thought we could build one here. But this is better. There's already a house here."

"And you think that's all it will take to get me interested?"

Jack's forehead puckered while he studied him. "You're ready to go get Mom and bring her here. That means you want it, doesn't it?"

Ethan determined his son knew him better than he knew himself. "Yes, I want it."

Jack pumped an arm in the air.

"Hold on. Just because I want it doesn't mean your mom will, or that it's for sale, or that we can afford it."

"You gotta believe, Dad."

Ethan had spent his childhood banking on miracles, secretly hoping something or someone would whisk him away to a better life. A childhood. He'd finally given up that fantasy when his father drank away the rent money Ethan had earned cleaning stalls after school for Mr. Casey. He'd faced the cold, hard facts. Believing got you squat. Believing wasn't what created change. Only back-breaking work did that.

Fortunately his son lived a different life. One based on faith, and miracles, and Ethan sure as hell wasn't going to tell Jack the truth. Besides, a tiny part of him still wanted to believe.

~

"KEEP YOUR EYES CLOSED."

"They're closed, but don't you think it's time you told me where we're going?"

"Patience."

"I've had my eyes closed for ten minutes. I'd say I've been pretty tolerant."

Ethan turned onto the dirt road that led to Lake Serenity. "We're almost there."

He pulled up behind the house and parked the car then helped Clare out. He led her to the front where he and Jack had trimmed the bushes, then positioned her so she faced the lake.

He removed the blindfold. "Okay. Open your eyes."

Her eyelids fluttered open. Her gasp was the reaction he'd anticipated. "It's spectacular." Her gaze circled the lake, then stopped when she came to him. "Where are we?"

"Lake Serenity."

"It's beautiful. Why are we here?"

"Actually, it was Jack's idea."

Clare's brow furrowed. "Why?"

"He has this idea we should live here."

"Here, on the shore?"

Ethan gestured behind her. "Here, in this house. After we rebuild it of course."

Clare turned and gasped a second time. "Tell me you didn't encourage him."

"Sorry."

"Ethan, this-this place isn't habitable."

"No, it's not. But it could be." He tried and failed to keep the wistful note from his voice.

Clare pressed her foot on the middle step of the porch. It broke with no exertion on her part just as the bottom one had for him. She arched a brow. "Are you going to show me the inside?"

Ethan shrugged. "Okay, so it's in need of some repair."

"It's in need of a bulldozer."

"Maybe, maybe not. I think the structure is sound, other than the porch of course and the roof will need to be replaced at some point."

She pointed to the front door. "Animals are living in there."

"How do you know? You haven't been inside."

She leveled a stare on him that brought instant silence to the children when they'd pushed her just a little too far. "I don't need to go inside to know that."

"So we gut the inside and rebuild."

"Are you serious? You really want to leave our home?"

"It's tiny."

"It's cozy."

"We're wedged into it. Here we could have all this space." Ethan's arm encircled the house and property.

"You really want to undertake this?"

"I do. I know it will be a lot of work, but look." He turned her so she faced the lake again. "Every day we could have this view from our house, from our bedroom, if that's what you want."

A tiny whimper of pleasure sufficed as a response, and Ethan knew he'd pushed the right button. The photographer inside her didn't care about the living accommodations, she cared about the picture.

She continued to soak in the view, her voice faraway when she spoke. "You really think we can do this?"

"I do."

"You do remember we have three children."

"Yes."

He pointed to the lake. "Think about the view."

She sighed. The sound fell somewhere between a moan and ecstasy.

Ethan linked his fingers with hers. "What do you say we inaugurate this place and make it ours?"

"Here in the dirt?"

"I was thinking more on the shore with some wine and the blanket from the trunk."

Clare's eyes turned electric blue. "Now you're talking."

PRESENT DAY...

Ethan blinked away a snowflake that landed on his eyelash. He missed those days with Clare when they'd worked hard and played harder. They'd been a team.

He peered through the wild swirl of wind and snow to watch his best friend and his son.

Why couldn't that be him? What had caused the strain between him and Jack?

He'd worked hard to be a good provider, a loving, caring father, so what happened? The accident happened. It poisoned everything and everyone around him. If only he could turn off memories of the accident the same way he switched off the alarm clock every morning, but he couldn't.

If he didn't get his act together one day soon Clare would leave him, and some other man would be the person his sons confided in.

14

Shivering, Clare climbed out of the tent to rebuild the fire. She stared up at the dark sky and saw only the vaguest shape of a fat, snow-laden cloud. The sky felt as vast and deserted as her campsite.

No stranger to solitude with her job, somehow this was different. A seclusion she had no control over.

It was day two and the animals filled part of the void, but not all. She needed human contact, human interaction. Rescue.

She shook off the melancholy and put a log on the fire, then reached for another one from the dwindling pile. She'd be lucky if she managed to keep the fire going much longer.

She sorted through the remaining pieces and sharply drew back her hand. She swore and leaned closer to the fire to examine the splinter in her index finger.

How many slivers had she picked from her hands while she and Ethan built the house? Too many to count. Even with as much work as rebuilding it had been, she'd loved working with him. Loved what they had accomplished with hard work, blood, sweat—and a multitude of slivers.

∾

Six years ago…

Late spring sunshine warmed Clare's face as she pried up another board from the rotted porch. She and Ethan had been working every weekend and a lot of evenings since the weather warmed and their house on Lake Serenity cleared escrow.

Clare sat back on her haunches. Well, calling it a house might be a stretch. While it turned out the structure itself was sound, the rest of the house had been gutted.

A deep sense of satisfaction warmed her when she reflected back over the last several weeks. She and Ethan had made steady progress, and an image of the home they envisioned slowly began to take shape.

It was particularly satisfying to create something from their own sweat and blood––a new experience for Clare. Housekeepers and staff had been delegated to handle what her mother deemed mundane chores—never her daughter. And while Clare could certainly appreciate that most chores become tedious at some point, they also empowered her. They gave her a sense of confidence that she was capable of doing things she'd never imagined.

Laughter echoed from the back of the house. Curiosity drew Clare in search of the source and a much needed break.

"On your mark. Get set." Ethan clicked the stopwatch in his hand and threw down his arm. "Go."

The ring of five hammers pounding nails into two by fours along with laughter and shouts of encouragement from Noah and Ethan filled the air.

Noah had arrived with his two kids, thirteen-year-old Matt, and eleven-year-old Jessica, while Clare had been working on the porch. As usual he and Ethan had found a way to both work and entertain the kids.

Grace threw up her hands. "Done."

Jack and Matt finished a second later followed by Ben. At four-and-a-half he worshipped the older kids and mimicked them. Jessica continued to lightly tap her nail. From birth she'd been the girly-girl of the group as Noah fondly referred to her.

Grace wrapped her hand around Jessie's. "You gotta hit it hard, Jessie, or it'll never go in." Together they gave the nail a good thwack.

It still amazed Clare how well the Tomboy and the Glamour Girl got along.

Jessie handed the hammer to Grace. "You finish it."

Grace neatly sent the nail home with a single swing.

"Everybody ready for round two?" Noah's voice boomed across the lake.

Clare watched while Noah and Ethan set the nails for round two, then headed back to finish the porch.

She picked up the pry bar and jammed it underneath the rotting two by four, pulled it up and tossed it into the growing pile of lumber.

A hiss drew a screech out of her—an excellent imitation of Jessie's.

She jumped back. A pair of glowing green eyes stared at her from the dark depths beneath the porch.

"Ethan!"

Another hiss.

She scampered back several feet and plowed into Ethan as he charged around the side of the house.

He grabbed her around the waist and steadied her. "What's wrong?"

Clare pointed a shaky finger at the porch. "Something is under there."

"Could you tell what it was?"

"It has green eyes, and it hisses."

"A snake."

Clare shuddered. "No!" Reptiles were at the top of her don't-want-to-be-within-a-hundred-miles-of list.

"So, it's not a reptile?"

Was that amusement twinkling in his eyes? "It was too dark to see what it was, but there's probably a lot of spiders under there."

Trepidation replaced amusement. The man might slay dragons, but not spiders.

Sufficiently chastised, his expression turned somber. "My guess would be probably a raccoon, but it could be a fox or a skunk."

Clare took several quick steps back. "A-a-a skunk. Get that thing away from our house."

Ethan smiled. "Why don't I see what it is first?"

Clare gestured for him to proceed.

He got a flashlight and went over to the porch. "Mama raccoon and babies," he called out a minute later.

Clare exhaled heavily. Breaking fingernails and sweating like a heat wave in the dead of summer in Oklahoma was one thing, but there were limits. No wild animals in her home or under her porch.

She moved in close enough to see the mother and babies. "Oh, they're so cute."

"Until they grow up and become a nuisance."

Clare had seen first hand the extensive damage these creatures could do. "So, how do we relocate them?"

"I'm not sure. I'm going to call Kevin and see what he suggests."

Kevin and Ethan went to high school together, and Kevin was a biologist for Fish and Game now.

Ethan finished the call a couple minutes later.

"What did he say?"

"He's bringing over a trap, but he said the key is to close off the area and anything else that might attract them. That will encourage them to look for somewhere else to live. We'll probably have to keep trapping and removing them until we get this closed in."

Clare picked at the sliver in her finger. "What do I do in the meantime?"

"If it were me I'd keep pulling up boards." His eyebrow arched in challenge. He didn't think she would keep at it with the raccoons. Silly man. He should know by now she was a woman who stared down her fears and came out the victor.

"Got any gloves?"

Her chest expanded when he smiled and handed her a pair of

leather gloves from his back pocket. He believed in her and her ability, or was it merely his way of keeping her working?

Whatever the reason, he got her busy again, and in the end, that was all that mattered.

By sunset they'd captured the mama raccoon and her babies. Noah took his crew home, and Kevin and Ethan relocated the raccoons. Clare and the kids began picking up the tools.

Grace gathered up a screwdriver and hammer. "Why can't we camp here?"

Clare loved it here, too, but after a long day of working she wanted a warm shower and a comfortable bed. "We're spending most of our days here."

"Yeah, but I want to sleep under the stars."

Clare smiled. If she could, Grace would spend every waking minute outdoors summer and winter.

"How about this. Once we move out here you can have some friends over for a campout in the backyard."

Grace's eyes sparkled. "Really?"

"Really."

"Oh Mom." She danced circles around Clare. "This is going to be so much fun."

She continued to chatter as they cleaned up, and Clare would have given anything for just a smidgeon of that energy to see her through until bedtime.

She left the kids to finish picking up the tools and went to close up the house as best she could. She'd just sat down on an old tree stump to watch the kids toss rocks into the lake when Ethan pulled up. He came up behind and massaged her shoulders.

"Long day."

"Mmmm humm." Clare's body went lax as he continued to knead her sore muscles. "And we've still got dinner to make and laundry to wash."

"Don't worry about dinner. I've got it covered."

"Bless you." She groaned when he worked his magic on the underside of her right shoulder blade.

His warm breath tickled her ear. "If you keep making noises like that I'll be thinking it's more than my massage at work."

Clare leaned her head back to see his face. "Do you seriously have the energy to do anything more than massage my shoulders?"

Dimples formed in the corners of his mouth. "Try me."

"I wish, but I'm not sure *I* have the energy."

"Maybe a long soak in the tub will transform you."

The soak sounded heavenly, but she suspected she'd be lucky to stay awake for it.

Ben's howl of fury drew Clare from the daydream to their four-year-old in a tug-o-war with his older brother.

"I think it's time we got these kids home, don't you?"

Ethan sighed and nodded.

Several hours later Clare made her way to the bedroom to shower, then drop into bed. She'd bid Ethan goodnight and left him watching the baseball scores on television. She pushed open the bathroom door and the room hung heavy with the scent of midsummer rain. Candles flickered around the tub filled with her favorite bubble bath and so did Clare's heart as it swelled with love.

She'd married the sweetest man on the planet. She stripped off her clothes and stepped into the toasty water that slid over her body like velvet. Her aches and pains magically dissolved with the bubbles. The candles sent her into a trance that she didn't come out of until the water turned tepid.

She released the plug and climbed out of the tub, her skin rosy and her body relaxed and rejuvenated. She slipped on her robe then went in search of her husband since the bed was still neatly made. She could hear the murmur of the sports channel and followed the sound. Ethan's gentle snores emanated from the recliner. Clare smiled, grabbed a blanket and drew it over him. She pressed a kiss to his forehead, then turned off the television and went to bed.

～

Present day…

The campfire flickered the same as the candles that had ringed the bathtub. Clare missed Ethan. She'd forgotten what a sweet, considerate man she'd married. How she wished he were by her side right now. Sure they had their problems, but there were many, many good times she cherished. Memories that sustained her now when hope of rescue faltered.

Clare added another log to the fire, then crawled back into her tent. The distant yip of coyotes sent a shiver over her. She'd never spent a night alone in the wilderness. Hiking through the mountains by herself in daylight was one thing, but alone at night was something entirely different. She didn't like it, didn't like it at all.

15

"Clare."

Ethan's voice had eroded to little more than a whisper after calling Clare's name for hours. It was a nearly useless endeavor as the wind gobbled up his voice and carried it along the narrow mountain ridge. Regardless, he continued to shout out her name.

It beat doing nothing at all.

He trudged through the forest, Noah and Rudy spread out on either side of him, the boys walking alongside Noah.

Ethan ducked his head when heavy rain slapped his face.

How he wished Bailey were here. She would find Clare. No, better she was with Clare, protecting her, doing her job. It was the reason they'd gotten her. When the kids were young they'd combined family outings with Clare's work, but as time went on too many other activities and social obligations had consumed them and ended those trips. As a result, Clare had started doing photo shoots alone after Ben started school.

Ethan had been fine with it until the day she crossed paths with a mountain lion. That day the reality of the dangers she faced came home to haunt him.

She'd been lucky and a little too cavalier to suit him. But once his eyes were opened to the risks her job entailed, there was no going back. That moment he'd decided she needed protection.

A branch snapped to his right and he froze. A pair of golden eyes stared at him through the swirl of wind and rain and snow.

A mountain lion poised and ready to strike blocked his path.

All those nights he'd lain awake worrying about Clare being attacked. Instead, he was the one in harm's way with nothing but his wits to protect him.

FIVE YEARS AGO...

"Clare."

Ethan awoke with a start. His skin was clammy, and his heart pounded against his chest like Tommy Aldridge drumming for Whitesnake. His sigh of relief echoed in the dark bedroom when he turned over and found Clare sleeping peacefully beside him.

A shudder went through him as he gathered her into his arms and held her close.

She stirred, her voice groggy with sleep. "Ethan."

"Hummm."

"Is something wrong?"

"No, why?"

"Your heart is pounding. Did you have a bad dream?"

Bad dream didn't come close to describing the nightmare he'd experienced. Hell was a more appropriate description. That's what life would be if he ever lost the woman curled into his arms as he'd done in his dream.

"You could say that."

She yawned. "Do you want to talk about it?"

He didn't want to burden her with his fears now. He kissed her forehead. "Later. Go back to sleep."

"You sure?" She stifled another yawn.

"Positive."

Clare's body relaxed and she quickly fell back asleep. Ethan held her close, the scent of fresh mountain breeze wafting from her hair eventually soothed him back to sleep, too.

DAWN FILTERED through the blinds when Ethan awoke several hours later. Clare continued to slumber peacefully at his side. Rather than toss and turn and disturb her, he slipped out of bed and went downstairs to start the coffee.

After it finished brewing, he poured a cup, put on his coat and went out on the deck. He leaned against the railing and watched the sun inch up over the jagged purple peaks of the Canadian Rockies.

The crisp March wind nipped at his ears and nose. He wrapped his hands around the coffee mug and let the warmth seep into him.

A pair of arms slipped around his waist and soft breasts pressed into his back.

He set his mug on the railing and pulled her in front of him. "You're up early."

"I was lonely all by myself in that big bed."

Ethan's hands clasped over her stomach, and he rested his chin on the top of her head.

Clare picked up his mug and took a sip of his coffee, then offered him some.

"You finish it."

She took another sip. "So, are you going to tell me what upset you last night?"

The sun burst over the mountain, and its warmth spread over Ethan, but it did nothing to chase the fear from his heart. He'd married a woman who hung upside down from trees, who thought nothing of leaning over cliffs or backpacking into the wilderness alone.

He wrestled his demons into compliance, then said, "You."

Clare tilted her head so she looked him in the eye. "What do you mean, me?"

"It bothers me that you go into the mountains alone."

"It's my job, Ethan. I don't have much choice but to go alone, especially now that the kids have so many activities. There just isn't time on the weekends."

"I know, but it still worries me."

"What's the alternative?" Clare asked.

"We could get a dog."

"A dog?"

Clare loved the mountains, but all Ethan saw was danger lurking up every tree and behind every bush. He'd been considering this for quite some time and felt it was a reasonable solution. "We could train it to protect you and to carry your gear."

Clare shook her head even before he'd finished speaking. "A dog is a lot of work to take care of and to train. I don't want to take on that responsibility."

Ethan remained calm, determined to win this one.

"I'm not asking you to do it on your own. I'll be here to help. The kids can pitch in, too."

"I don't know."

Ethan turned her so she faced him fully and clasped her hands tightly between his. "Please, Clare I need some peace of mind. I can't constantly wonder if this will be the day you don't come home. The day I lose you forever. Don't make me go through that every time you go out."

Clare's eyes softened and her shoulders relaxed. "I-I never considered how this affected you. I only thought about my feelings. I seem to do that far too often lately. I'm sorry."

She gently pressed her lips to his.

Ethan threaded his fingers into her sleep-mussed hair and deepened the kiss. They were both breathing heavily when he pulled back to stare down into her eyes. "Promise me you'll at least think about getting a dog."

She looped her arms around his neck and kissed him again. "I promise."

Ethan slid his hands under the waistband of her flannel pajamas and cupped her bottom. "What do you say we go back to bed and warm each other up?"

Clare smiled and her eyes warmed with desire. "A quickie. Wonderful idea."

Ethan leaned closer, a grin tilting his lips before he kissed her long, and deep, and thoroughly.

He lifted her into his arms. "I don't do quickies." He carried her upstairs and proved beyond a doubt that speed had no place when it came to making love.

PRESENT DAY…

Ethan had been terrified something would happen to Clare out in the mountains alone—in particular he'd worried about mountain lions stalking her. Ironic he was the one face-to-face with one.

Another yowl lifted the hair on Ethan's scalp. He raised his arms high to appear larger.

The cat remained tense. Ready to pounce.

"Ethan," Rudy called out. "I heard a mountain lion."

"Yeah. I see it."

"Holy shit. I'm coming."

Seconds passed. Ethan stood stock still, kept his arms wide, waiting for help to arrive or the cat to attack.

As suddenly as it appeared, the animal spun around and disappeared into the thick knot of trees and brush.

Ethan's shoulders sagged, and his head dropped to his chest. "Clare, where are you?"

He stared into the brush where the cat vanished moments before. "I'll find you, I swear it."

"Ethan." Rudy's yell cut through the howl of the wind.

Ethan expelled a haggard breath. "Over here."

"Where is it?"

"Fortunately, something scared it off. We should warn the others.

And make sure Noah and the kids know. I lost sight of them awhile ago."

Rudy contacted base and sent out the warning, much to Ethan's relief. He was still shaky, and he wasn't sure he would have been able to keep his voice steady.

He sent up a silent prayer to keep Clare safe until he got to her. She had Bailey, and she was smart, tough and resourceful. She would survive until they found her. He couldn't lose her. They'd been through too much. Shared too much. And when he found her, he would fix what had broken between them.

16

———

Hunger pains woke Clare from a fitful sleep. She fed the animals, then peeled the wrapper on another nutrition bar and took a bite.

It wasn't much of a breakfast, but it was certainly better than nothing. She chewed slowly. A chill swept over her that was partly from the cold, and partly fear and loneliness. Had she spent the last of her nine lives just like Ballistic curled up next to her?

She studied the persnickety cat. Perhaps his friendliness amounted to pity rather than a softening toward her. It seemed the more likely scenario given their turbulent relationship up to this point.

As if on cue, his eyes cracked open. He stared at her through narrow slits. Then again, maybe not. Ballistic didn't possess an ounce of compassion.

Clare turned away when another chill swept over her that set her teeth to chattering. Wrapping her arms around her waist she attempted to control the quaking, but the tremors increased rather than decreased. They had nothing to do with the cold and everything to do with fear cutting a hole in her stomach.

A low whine drew Clare's attention to Bailey. The dog stared at her with big sad eyes that asked what she could do to help.

Clare patted the space next to her. "Come here, girl."

Bailey released another pitiful whine before complying. She dropped her head on Clare's shoulder and laid a paw over her heart.

Slowly Clare's shaking subsided, and as she calmed down, she snaked an arm around Bailey and snuggled into her.

"I'm so glad you're here with me." Clare stared at the gray, dreary landscape and realized she wasn't far from the place she'd found Bailey and brought her home.

FIVE YEARS AGO...

"Clare, I can't concentrate at work because I'm worried about you. I need some peace of mind even if you don't. I want a dog for you to take into the mountains."

Ethan's concerns echoed in Clare's head as she drove up to McKenzie's Meadow. She collected her camera bags from the SUV and started to hike in. The weight of her gear slowed her down.

While Ethan had made some valid points about the benefits of adopting a dog, Clare continued to balk at the idea. Training would take a phenomenal amount of time that she couldn't spare, plus there was a part of her that resented his constant worry that had progressively increased over the years.

Of course, getting a dog wouldn't just be protection, it would also be companionship. And truth be told, she was lonely. She missed the times Ethan and the kids joined her, but it had been a tradeoff. She'd never really felt free to work without Ethan's constant worry hanging over her. She'd known when she accepted his proposal he'd want to rein her in. She'd thought at the time his concern solicitous, charming and thoughtful, but more and more it felt constraining. Didn't he trust her judgment? She knew how to take care of herself.

But a dog. Clare just couldn't wrap her mind around it.

A whimper caught on the breeze.

Clare froze.

A flock of geese passed overhead, their honking echoed long after they'd disappeared into the clouds.

Deciding the whine had been her imagination, she began walking again. She hadn't taken two steps when a sharp, high-pitched yip stopped her.

She followed the sound to the edge of a steep embankment. At the bottom a puppy had its foot trapped under a boulder. When it saw her, its tail thumped the ground and sent up a cloud of dust.

The puppy barked nonstop while Clare dropped her gear, scrambled down the embankment, and soothed the frantic animal.

Clare lifted a fallen tree branch and wedged it under the boulder. After several failed attempts to lift the boulder, she paused to swipe the sweat from her forehead. Trying again, she managed to raise the rock high enough to free the puppy.

Clare scooped the half-starved mongrel into her arms and climbed back to her gear. She took the water bottle from her pack and poured some into her hands. The puppy immediately lapped it up. She continued to pour until she emptied the bottle, then grabbed her sandwich and fed chunks of it to her.

Clare checked the injured leg. The puppy yipped when she rotated her foot.

Clare grabbed her gear and was about to set off when the puppy's fluffy hair rose up on her back, and a ferocious snarl erupted.

Clare's gaze tracked the puppy's to where a wolf stared back at them, its hackles raised and teeth bared.

The pup sprang forward. Clare grabbed it by the scruff of the neck and slowly backed away.

The wolf snarled in response to the puppy's growl. Clare backed down the trail to the SUV and didn't relax until she and the puppy made it safely inside the car. Shoving the key in the ignition, she looked out the windshield.

The wolf stood directly in front of the car, teeth bared.

With shaking hands, she put the SUV in gear and drove off.

The puppy circled the passenger seat next to Clare three times then flopped down. Clare smiled when a beleaguered sigh slipped past the pup's lips a second before she closed her eyes and went to sleep.

Ethan was right. She needed protection.

The puppy squirmed and turned onto her back. Clare reached over and scratched the exposed belly. Somehow the fates had known she needed a little nudge in the protection department because rather than find that protection on her own, *it* had found her.

A WEEK LATER, Clare folded laundry and smiled down at the puppy, named Bailey after a family vote, asleep at her feet. Bailey had settled into the Burke household as if she'd been there from the beginning.

Clare gathered up Grace's laundry and headed upstairs, the puppy racing ahead and nosing open the door.

Grace's laughter carried into the hallway. "Bailey, where have you been?"

Clare tapped on the partially open door, and when she got no response, she entered.

Grace held Bailey in her arms. "Mom! What are you doing in here?"

Neatly folded clothes slipped from her arms and scattered over the floor. "What is that?"

Grace set the puppy on the bed and yanked on her shirt, covering her belly button. "Nothing."

"That wasn't nothing. That was a ring in your navel. A ring I specifically told you you couldn't have. Where did you have that done?"

Grace pursed her lips and plopped down beside Bailey.

"Don't tell me you did it yourself."

She hugged Bailey close. "What if I did?"

"Then I'm taking you to see the doctor. It could be infected. Let me see it."

Grace scooted back against the headboard, clutching Bailey

against her chest with one hand and using the other to hold her shirt down. "Stay away from me." Her screech could be heard across the lake.

Clare inhaled and brought her temper under control. A battle of wills would get her nowhere. "Grace, calm down and talk to me."

She shot her a mutinous glare.

Clare leaned an elbow on the dresser and drew in a deep breath. "Why did you disobey me?"

Grace averted her eyes. "I didn't."

"Funny, but the piercing in your belly button says you did. And just so we're clear, I specifically said no piercings."

"I didn't get a piercing."

The mulish thrust of her jaw gave Clare pause. Her daughter might be stubborn and headstrong, but so far as Clare knew, she didn't make a habit of lying to her.

"Okay, if it's not a piercing, what is it?"

Grace buried her face in the puppy's fur. "It's a clip on."

Relief raced through Clare. "Why didn't you say so?"

Grace's jaw jutted out. "Why did you come barging into my room? No one respects my privacy."

A twinge of remorse skittered over Clare. A teenager deserved some privacy.

"The door was open, but I should have waited. I'm sorry." She sat down on the bed and stroked Bailey's silky fur. "I forget you're growing up."

"Try harder."

"I will." She lifted Grace's chin so they were eye to eye. "That doesn't mean you are allowed to disobey me when I slip up."

Grace peered at her through a swag of purple-streaked hair. A hesitant smile played on her lips. "Okay."

Clare pressed a kiss to the top of her head. Her stubborn, determined daughter was growing up too fast, and too much like her. She wanted her to stay a little girl, but at the same time she saw hints of the talented, intelligent woman she would become. She was stretching her wings, wanting to be independent and Clare remembered those feelings. But it was much easier to experience them than it was to watch her daughter go through them.

Bailey squirmed between them. Clare sat back, and the puppy flopped onto its back, its tail thumping in rapid succession against the quilt.

She and Grace laughed and the tension between them eased. Bailey turned out to be more than protection. She became the shaky bridge between Clare and her daughter.

Present day...

Bailey's cold nose pressed into Clare's cheek. She hugged the dog, grateful once again that fate, karma, or whatever supernatural force that had been at work that day had brought them together.

She was equally grateful that Ethan had had the foresight and the persistence to insist they get a dog. Even if Bailey hadn't found her, Ethan wouldn't have given up until they'd gotten a dog.

And that made Clare just as certain he would be equally unrelenting in his search for her. He wouldn't stop until he found her.

17

───────

"Dad, are you and Mom getting a divorce?"

Ethan dropped the tailgate with a heavy thud. Had the strain between him and Clare become so obvious that Jack and even Ben noticed?

"Why would you think that?" He took out the thermos of hot chocolate and poured two cups, then propped a foot on the corner of the bumper.

Ben shrugged and settled himself on the tailgate. "Because you never laugh any more. You never go on Mom's photo shoots, or look at her pictures, or sit and talk to her like you did before —"

Ben ducked his head and stared down at his chocolate.

Ethan sat down beside him and slung an arm over his shoulder. "It's been hard on all of us since Grace died, but I still love your mom very much, and I have no intention of getting a divorce."

He prayed Clare felt the same way, but after the way he'd behaved since the accident, he couldn't be certain.

"It's my fault you and Mom aren't happy, isn't it?" Ben's earnest expression ripped a crater-sized hole in Ethan's heart.

Ethan hugged him tight. "Your mother and I are just going through a rough stretch."

"But you wouldn't be going through it if I hadn't wanted to go fishing. Grace would have been at home, you wouldn't have gotten hurt, and you and Mom would be happy."

"No! Ben, listen to me. This was *not* your fault."

Ben traced his finger around the edge of his paper cup before looking up at him. "But you blame yourself, and if you're blaming yourself, then I was wrong, too."

His words caught Ethan by surprise. It never occurred to him anyone knew about the guilt he carried. Would always carry. "That's different."

"How?"

"I'm your dad, the adult. It's my job to protect you, and Grace, and Jack."

Confusion filled Ben's eyes. "But there was nothing you could do."

"I should have paid closer attention to the weather. I knew a storm was brewing. I should have made sure the boat would start. I should have saved both of you." His hand squeezed the cup so tightly hot chocolate spilled over. "It was my job to save you both."

Ben eased off the tailgate. "If that's how it works being a dad, then I don't think I ever want to be one."

Ethan watched Ben open the passenger door and an ache filled his chest that matched the ache in his soul he carried from losing Grace.

Tossing his hot chocolate into the snow, he slammed the tailgate closed, venting the anger and frustration vying for dominance. His world crashed that day two years ago and every day since he'd worked to pick up the pieces and carry on. His life was unraveling again and he was just as powerless to stop this train wreck as he'd been to save Grace.

Pushing his turmoil aside, he climbed into the truck and headed back to base. The trip was silent and awkward. As soon as they arrived, Ben went to find Jack while Ethan checked in.

He changed direction when Randy Tompkins pulled up in his patrol vehicle.

His carefully schooled expression sent Ethan's imagination into overdrive. "Have you got news?"

Randy climbed out of the mud-caked four-by-four Blazer. "A logging truck went over the canyon off Forest Service Road A-Thirty-two sometime yesterday."

"Was there another car involved?"

"I don't know."

"What does the driver say?"

"Nothing. He's dead. I'm headed up there now, and I thought you might want to tag along." Randy glanced over at Ben and Jack. "Don't bring the kids, Ethan. If Clare was involved—"

His words trailed off, but Ethan understood precisely what he hadn't said. If Clare was involved, the odds of her surviving were remote.

"Let me talk to Noah."

Randy nodded. "I'll get some coffee while you get them taken care of."

"Thanks."

Ethan continued on to the command center. He found Noah conversing with Pete. "Can we talk in private?" he said to both men.

They followed Ethan over to a stand of trees out of earshot, and he quickly filled them in on what Randy had just told him. "This is an area Clare goes to frequently, so it's logical she could have been there and involved in the accident. I don't want the kids there. Noah, could you take them somewhere else to search until we know something?"

"Yeah. I was just about to head out to Moosehead Ridge. I'll take them with me. Do you want to say goodbye?"

Ethan shook his head. "If they see my face, they'll know something's up."

Noah studied him a long minute, then nodded his agreement. "Contact me as soon as you know something."

Ethan turned to Pete. "I'll follow Randy over, then radio you with an update."

"If there's any indication Clare was involved, we'll focus our search from that point," Pete said. "How about I get you a cup of coffee and food while Noah gets the kids off."

Ethan's stomach rumbled in response to the suggestion of food. Even though the idea of eating was unappealing, he needed to keep his strength up. "Yeah, I'd better eat. Thanks."

He watched Pete walk off, then blew out the breath he'd been holding since Randy told him about the accident. He tried to block out the vision of Clare's twisted and mangled body, but couldn't, so he prayed for a miracle instead.

AN AMBULANCE PULLED AWAY as Ethan and Randy arrived at the scene of the accident. Snow had been falling for several hours and the road was already ankle deep in it. The forest service truck that had found the big rig was parked behind another patrol car. It belonged to none other than wet-behind-the-ears Officer Harris.

"What have you found?" Randy asked.

Harris cast a distrustful look at Ethan. "What's he doing here?"

Randy gave the junior officer a hard stare. "Hoping like hell his wife's car wasn't involved in the accident."

"He's a person of interest."

"In what?"

Harris' suspicions were as plain as Ethan's footprints in the fresh-packed snow. "His wife's disappearance."

"Says who?"

"Me. I contacted his cell phone provider and there was a message from his wife yesterday morning that he never told us about."

Randy turned to Ethan. "What was the message?"

"She said she loved me and would see me tonight."

Randy cocked a brow at his subordinate. "How exactly does that make him a suspect?"

"He didn't tell us she'd called him."

"Why didn't you tell us about the message?" Randy asked.

"Because it didn't come through until he asked me about it. I'm guessing that Clare must have been out of the area when she called. In the past, that has delayed messages we leave for each other."

"Now that we've got that misunderstanding cleared up, what happened here?" Randy studied the accident scene.

Harris scowled at Ethan a final time, then focused on his superior. "We suspect the driver had a heart attack and died, then went off the road."

"Any signs of another vehicle being involved?"

"We just finished removing the victim from the truck and getting him into the ambulance. I haven't had time to check."

The forest ranger who'd discovered the accident walked up to Randy. "Do you need me for anything else?" He glanced up at the sky where the snow continued to come down. "I'd really like to get down the mountain while I still can."

Randy shook his hand. "No, go ahead. Thanks for your help."

"No problem."

Randy started walking. "Let's start here and work our way up the road. If there was another car involved and it went over, there will be signs. Broken trees, bushes, car parts."

They didn't go two hundred yards before Ethan spotted a group of trees with broken limbs. The tip of a muffler jutted out of the snow bank.

Ethan ran forward. "Randy, here."

He dug it out and pulled it up, then looked down the canyon. He couldn't see anything between the thick cropping of trees and heavy underbrush.

Ethan headed back to his truck to get his gear. "I'm going down."

"That's suicide in this weather." Harris' comment was an observation not a criticism, and Ethan appreciated the difference, but it didn't change his mind.

Randy grabbed his arm. "Ethan, I've got to agree with the kid. This is too big a risk. I can't let you do it. We need to wait for the rest of search and rescue to get here."

Clare was down there. Ethan felt it, sensed it, could swear a voice inside him led him to her.

"Somebody went over, and my gut is telling me it's Clare. I'm not waiting for everyone else to get here. I'm going down to find out, now. Tell me you wouldn't do the same thing if it was your wife."

Randy said nothing, then finally nodded and released his hold on him. "We'll cover you from up here."

Ethan got his gear and minutes later dropped over the cliff. As he scaled down the snow-covered rock, it struck him how much he missed going on outings with Clare. Missed being a part of her work.

He'd shut Clare out the moment he'd learned about Grace. He'd laid helpless in that hospital bed, the beep of the monitors keeping time with the mantra in his head.

Failure, failure, failure.

He'd saved one child and killed another.

Everything had gone wrong after the accident. His family was falling apart and it was all his fault.

$\sim$

Two years ago...

Ethan worked the third wind knot out of Ben's line. He wondered fleetingly if roofing might not have been the enjoyable alternative to fishing. He looked over at Grace sullenly thumbing through a magazine, her feet dangling over the side of the boat. He'd gotten nothing but single-word responses from her since he'd vetoed her staying home alone.

"I got one, Dad." The broad grin on Ben's face dissolved his annoyance.

It wasn't a huge fish, but Ben didn't care. The fun was in the catching.

An hour later, clouds rolled in over the river.

"I'm cold. Can we go home now?"

The first actual sentence his daughter had directed at him all afternoon and it was a complaint.

Ethan studied the sky to contain his irritation, then nodded. "We'd better head in."

"Do we hafta? I want to fish some more."

Grace rolled her eyes. "Some of us don't want to be struck by lightning."

"Some of us just have a stick up their butt."

"Dad! Did you hear what he said to me?"

He had and Ethan remained silent to keep from agreeing with Ben. Instead, he put away their rods and went to start the engine. To his annoyance it refused to turn over.

The gentle breeze that had kept them cool all afternoon began gusting over them. The fluffy white clouds turned dark and threatening.

"Grace, get out the lifejackets." He moved to the back of the boat and took off the engine cover.

"Do this, Grace. Do that, Grace. I'm not your slave, you know."

Ethan's temper jumped a notch, but he focused on the engine and didn't rise to Grace's bait.

White caps broke over the side of the boat as thunder rumbled. Ethan pumped the ball pushing gas into the motor to prime the engine. He turned the ignition.

Nothing.

Why did the damn thing have to choose now to refuse to start?

A wave broke over the bow of the boat sending water onto the floor.

He cranked the engine again.

Still nothing. Not even a damned spark.

The boat rocked hard to the left as another wave slammed into them. Lightning arced across the sky. A boom of thunder blotted out the roar of the raging wind.

"I don't see why we can't get a good boat instead of this piece of junk."

Ethan's temper snapped. "Grace, shut up. Stay close to Ben."

Grace pursed her lips and she folded her arms over her chest.

Ethan turned back to the motor. He swayed from side to side and nearly lost his footing when another wave struck the side of the boat.

"Dad." Ben pointed to a tree that had toppled into the water. They were headed directly for it unless he got the boat started now.

"Hang on to Ben."

Grace clutched her brother to her side. Fear replaced belligerence.

He pumped the ball again, then turned over the engine. It hesitated, then fired to life. He spun the steering wheel hard and pushed the shifter down. The boat shot forward.

They missed the tree by inches. Another wave broke over the bow, soaking the floor a second time.

The occasional sprinkle turned to a pounding rain as Ethan headed for the boat launch. Lightning flashed and lit up dark sky. The boat launch came into view, and Ethan pointed the boat toward it.

Another flash of lightning angled out of the sky. It struck a tree hanging over the riverbank and cleanly severed it down the center. The tree crashed onto the boat, flipped it over, and tossed them into the icy water.

Ethan surfaced to find nothing but water, wind and black swirling water.

Consciousness returned in slow building waves of pain. An insistent beep grated on Ethan's nerves until finally he cracked open an eye. The only light in the room came from the neon-green glow of the monitor. Clare's head rested on the bed nestled against his stomach.

What was he doing here?

He wiggled his toes and all ten moved, but the action sent pain rocketing up his left leg. He sucked back a groan and lifted his head to see it was in a cast.

Clare stirred and sat up. "Ethan." Her voice sounded clogged with sleep.

"What happened?"

"You were in a boating accident."

Ethan had to force the words out. "How bad am I hurt?"

Clare sat on the bed next to him. "You have a broken femur on your left leg and what the doctor called an incomplete spinal injury."

Ethan absorbed the information like blows to his body. He moved his right leg, then wiggled the toes on his left foot and winced. "My legs move."

"And that's a good sign. The doctor says we'll know more as the swelling subsides."

"But I'll be able to walk."

"After some intensive physical therapy."

"How long?"

"Six to seven months. Right now the important thing is to rest and allow your body to recover."

He sagged back into the pillows, fatigue zapping his strength. He studied Clare closely. She held back something more.

Fragments of the accident filtered into his foggy brain. The tree crashing into the boat. Surfacing. Grabbing Ben. Swimming back for Grace.

Where were Ben and Grace?

He clutched her hand. "Where are the kids? Are they okay?"

She squeezed his fingers. "Ben's fine." She laid her other hand on top of their interlocked fingers. "You would be so proud of him. The instant you left him on shore he ran for help and they rescued you."

She looked away, but not before her eyes turned hollow.

The infernal beep of the monitor kept time with the pounding of his heart. "What about Grace? How is she?"

Clare started to speak, then stopped and cleared her throat. "They searched for hours and hours, but couldn't find her. Finally, they found her body downriver. She-she drowned."

Ethan stared at the monitor beeping his vitals, but he didn't see it. All he saw was his daughter begging him to save her.

His last words to Grace spun round and round in his head. "I'll get you out of here. I promise."

His sweet baby girl. Dead.

"Ethan?"

He didn't respond. Couldn't respond. Couldn't get the words out of his throat. Couldn't get anything out. Emptiness filled him.

Clare's arms went around him. She whispered words of comfort he couldn't comprehend. One thing remained crystal clear. His daughter was dead and he was to blame.

ETHAN SURVIVED the days and weeks following Grace's death on painkillers and sleep.

He desperately wanted to give up, be with Grace, but he couldn't. He had a family that needed him. And he had to recover.

Anxiety became a companion Ethan shared breathing space with on a full-time basis. His recovery dragged, and the medical bills mounted daily. On top of that, Clare had had to hire a roofer to finish the job he'd started, which also added to their debt.

To keep his mind off Grace, he pushed himself and his physical therapist to the brink of exhaustion, but it did nothing to relieve the fear gnawing a crater-sized hole in his belly that he had become as irresponsible as his father.

Guilt over Grace's death took the form of anger, and it simmered within him day and night. Grace's death—his fault. Not getting the roof done—his fault. The mounting bills—his fault. Clare having to deal with everything on her own—his fault. And his worst fault — using Clare as his scapegoat. She deserved better than to have him harp at her day and night, but he couldn't stop himself. Clare carried his responsibilities and hers, and yet he lashed out at her for his inadequacies. Blaming her was easier than facing his own short-comings.

He stared out the window as Clare took the mail from the mail-box. Another of the many mundane chores he couldn't do. Two months after the accident, he barely got out of bed on his own.

He heard the kitchen door open and close. The tromp of Clare's feet against the mat as she kicked off the snow and removed her shoes. The quiet swoosh of her stockinged footsteps echoed down the wood floor to the makeshift bedroom she'd made for him in her office.

She stopped in the doorway. Her eyes were like lasers piercing his back.

Fury pumped through his veins. He didn't want to be checked on. Didn't want to be helpless.

He kept his back to the door hoping she'd leave him alone.

She didn't.

"What do you want, Clare?" He kept his tone calm, but the irritation was unmistakable.

"I thought maybe you'd like to get out of bed."

In truth, he'd rather stay right where he was, but that wasn't an option. He slowly turned and faced his wife. The effort left him breathless and angry.

"Bet you never planned on being married to a helpless waste of a human being."

Clare crossed over to the bed and sat down beside him. "I have never once thought that."

"Liar. Women like you want a strong man."

Clare arched a brow. "Women like me?"

"Yeah. Why else would you have married a nobody like me?"

"I married the man I loved. The man of my choosing."

"Who just happened to be the exact opposite of the kind of man your father would have chosen for you."

Her nostrils flared and her eyes flashed with fire before she controlled her anger. "Ethan, I married you for the reasons I just stated. Not to antagonize my father." She smiled, a devilish twinkle lighting her eyes. "Antagonizing my father was just a nice side benefit."

Her snappy comeback put Ethan in his place far quicker than any angry response. Still, he kept waiting for her to call him on his behavior. To cry uncle, especially when he was so clearly in the wrong.

Ethan landed on the rock ledge with a jarring thump back to reality. The disintegration of their marriage started with a snipe here, a cold shoulder there. Before he knew it, a wall of silence had been erected bit by bit, hour by hour, until the effort to communicate became too much of a struggle.

He began sifting through the snow for evidence that a vehicle had been here. He found a side mirror. A rear bumper hung over the ledge. He pulled it up, and his blood froze as solid as the ice forming on the rock ledge where he stood.

KV13T0.

Randy's voice crackled over the radio. "Ethan, have you found anything?"

"A license plate."

"Give me the number, and I'll run it."

Ethan gripped the snow-crusted plate. Coldness seeped into him. "Don't bother. It's Clare's."

Silence.

"Any sign of the car?"

Ethan studied the broken tree trunk that showed the path Clare's car had taken. He took his binoculars from his jacket pocket and peered through the heavy snowfall, but couldn't see the bottom of the canyon.

"Ethan, are you there?"

Ethan closed his eyes and fought off the panic. She wasn't dead. He refused to believe she was gone. Still, the odds of anyone surviving a fall like that were astronomical.

"Yeah, I'm still here, and there's no sign of her SUV. I don't know if it landed here, and then fell the rest of the way, or if it just lost parts as it tumbled down."

"Any sign of Clare?"

"No, she's not here."

Another lengthy silence. "Get back up here so we can drive down and find her."

He didn't say it like a recovery effort, he said it like a search and rescue.

Grace's voice whispered in his head, "She's alive."

Until they found a body, there was hope, and Ethan would cling to it with every fiber of his being.

18

Clare crawled out of the tent to add more wood to the few remaining coals of the fire. The sharp bite of the wind had her jamming her hands inside her pockets. Blinking the raindrops from her eyelashes, she studied the steady rain that became more and more interspersed with snow.

Clare stomped her feet and rubbed her arms to disperse the chill, and estimated the temperatures had dipped several degrees. If it continued to fall, she would be in serious trouble, and she'd need better shelter than a nylon tent.

She stared up at the sky, hoping for a break in the cloud cover or the wind, but saw no sign of either, which meant the helicopters wouldn't be flying and the search for her would remain on the ground. And that would be impeded by the weather, too.

Ethan had told her time and again that chances for a successful rescue doubled and tripled if the person managed to get to a road. She focused on that, rather than all the odds that were stacked against her, and reviewed her options.

First choice, the road, but getting there might be impossible. It would take hours of hiking—a risky endeavor since the snowfall could increase and she'd be stranded in the elements.

Clare studied the landscape. She estimated where her SUV went over the canyon and another option took hold. If she followed the river, she might be only a couple of miles from the cabin where she and Ethan had been snowed in all those years ago. If she could get there, it would provide shelter for several days, possibly longer if need be, and significantly increase her chances of survival. And Ethan would have that on his list of sites to check.

Her decision made, Clare loaded her backpack with as much gear as possible, then left a note on the steering wheel explaining her destination. After putting out the fire, she and the animals set off, Ballistic riding in his usual spot on top of Bailey's back.

They climbed over snow-slicked boulders and fallen trees and made surprisingly good time until they reached Topeka Falls. A good/bad scenario. Good, because Clare knew she was only about a mile from the cabin. Bad, because the trail had disappeared under thick, dense brush. She would have to hike away from the river until the brush thinned again, which would consume valuable time she couldn't afford.

Clare checked her watch. She'd been hiking for two hours. She unhitched Bailey's pack to let the dog rest before they continued on.

Bailey loped over to the river and splashed in chest deep, taking long slurping drinks before lying down in the water. Ballistic, in sharp contrast to his canine pal, tip-toed along the riverbank, then leapt onto a rock and leaned down to gingerly lap at the water. Two polar opposites, yet best of friends. Clare guessed the old saying about opposites attracting was true. It had certainly been the case with her and Ethan. The question was, did it make for a strong, lasting relationship or only lead to friction and eventual collapse?

Separation, *divorce*?

She'd never envisioned life without Ethan, or perhaps in truth, she hadn't allowed the idea to settle and take root.

Clare brushed the snow from a nearby boulder and sat down to rest. Bailey circled several times in the snow then laid down. Ballistic promptly curled into her side, then immediately fell asleep.

Clare envied their ability to find sleep so effortlessly. It seemed she rarely slept anymore. Since the accident, she'd been in a constant state of anxiety. She'd lost her daughter, and a day hadn't gone by since that she didn't forget how fragile life was, or how easily someone you loved could be taken away.

TWO YEARS AGO...

Clare watched Ethan sleep from her office doorway. Her eyes tracked the rise and fall of his chest. She often stopped and watched him to reassure herself he was alive and well. The deep purple rings beneath her eyes she saw in the mirror every day attested to the nightmares that routinely disturbed her sleep. Nightmares of death, of morgue tables, of hospital beds.

She'd come within a heartbeat of losing Ethan. Every time she went to the hospital she watched the monitors, fear skittering through her at the slightest fluctuation. She continually begged God not to take Ethan. And even as Ethan became stronger and the doctors assured her he would survive, she continued to watch the monitors. And once he came home, his breathing.

"What are you staring at?"

Clare blinked and focused on the curt man who stared back at her. The husband she'd begged God to save, the husband she'd needed so desperately to confide in, lean on to get her through the loss of their daughter, had transformed into a surly stranger.

The man that survived wasn't the one she needed. "Just checking to see if you needed anything."

"You can't give me what I need."

She ignored the snarled response the same as she had in the two weeks since he'd returned home from the hospital. She knew he was in pain mentally and physically, but her patience was wearing thin. Between minimal sleep and a sulky patient, she teetered on the breaking point.

She swallowed the sharp retort and kept her voice light. "Try me."

Ethan's frown deepened before he turned his back on her.

Her voice wavered when she spoke. "I know you're hurting, and I want to help you through this."

He rolled back to face her and winced. "You can't help me. No one can help me. I should have died. I should be the one dead and buried."

The naked pain on his face cut through Clare and pushed aside her fatigue and resentment. She rushed to his bed and kneeled, clasping his hand. "No! Don't say that. Don't think that. I need you. Jack and Ben need you."

A film of moisture glazed over Ethan's eyes. "You'd be better off without me."

"Never." She squeezed his hand. "I love you. I need you. I can't get through this without you."

His eyes probed hers. "That's a lie. You don't need me. You never have. You're strong. You're a survivor." He pulled his hand from hers. "I'm tired. I want to sleep." He closed his eyes and faced the wall again.

The doorbell rang as Clare reached out to touch him. Her heart heavy, she left the room. The emptiness in his eyes haunted her. It might very well be the medication talking, but she suspected it was more than that.

She opened the front door and found Dot standing on the porch.

Dot stepped inside and closed the door. "What's wrong?"

Clare's tenuous hold on her emotions slipped. Her tears flowed in great gushing sobs that shook her entire body. She tried to speak, but the words wouldn't come.

Dot hugged her tight until the worst of it passed, then guided Claire to the kitchen and pressed her down into a chair. "Has something happened to Ethan?"

Clare shook her head. While she slowly gained control of her emotions, Dot brewed a fresh pot of coffee. When it was done she poured them each a cup and sat across the table from her.

"When was the last time you left the house?" she asked.

Clare shrugged. "I'm not sure."

"Then it's time you did."

"I can't leave Ethan alone."

"Who said anything about leaving him alone? I'm here and perfectly capable of watching after him for a few hours."

"What would I do?"

"You will call your friend Sarah, have lunch and forget about everything for a couple of hours."

Dot's take-no-excuses tone shocked Clare speechless. Her mother-in-law wasn't a take-charge kind of woman.

She handed Clare the phone. "Call Sarah and then you go upstairs and take a nice long soak, put on something pretty and go out and have some fun. And don't come back here until dinnertime. Understood?"

Clare took the phone and called Sarah, who immediately agreed to meet her for lunch. She hung up, then tried to put her cup in the dishwasher, but Dot took it from her and shooed her upstairs.

"Go on. I'll manage everything here."

Clare filled the tub with warm water and extra bubbles and let the water envelop her. Tears flowed again along with the water, and she cried until she felt cleansed inside and out.

CLARE MET Sarah at the trendy North Shore Bistro that had opened the previous spring. They took a corner table, away from prying eyes and listening ears.

After they ordered, Sarah sat back and studied Clare. "You look like hell."

Her comment brought a burst of laughter from her. "Thanks a lot."

"You aren't taking care of yourself."

"I've got a lot of responsibilities."

"And you will do no one any good if you fall apart. Thank God Dot made you get out. So, how's Ethan?"

Clare avoided Sarah's probing gaze. "Fine."

"In other words, still being a prick."

She could never put anything past her friend. "I never said that."

"Didn't have to. He's a man, he's injured, and he can't fend for himself. They all become pricks at that point."

Clare laughed. Sarah rarely used coarse language, but today it felt fitting. Sarah always knew what to say to make her feel better.

Their wine arrived and Clare sipped her drink.

"So, tell me how you're doing, and don't give me any of that que-sera-sera Doris Day nonsense. I want the unvarnished truth."

Emotion welled in Clare's chest, and it felt as if it would burst right out of her. But it didn't. It came out in a whimper. "Horrible. I can't sleep. I can't eat. Tell me this is going to get better. Tell me I won't always have this empty space inside of me where Grace used to be."

A sheen of moisture filled Sarah's eyes. She wrapped her arms around Clare and held her close. "It will get better. I promise you it will, but maybe you'll need help."

Clare pulled back to look at her friend. "What do you mean?"

"I mean a good counselor could help."

"Do you have someone in mind?"

"Actually I do." Sarah reached into her purse and handed her a card.

Clare clung to the card and Sarah's words for the lifeline they were. Over the next days and weeks the counselor, and Sarah's words, were the only thing that kept her sane in the midst of insanity.

PRESENT DAY...

Loneliness enveloped Clare as she stared out over the river. She missed Sarah. She'd kept her sane during the worst moments of her life. Without her and the therapist, she'd never have gotten through Grace's death and Ethan's convalescence.

Clare's gaze swept over the landscape. Normally the vastness of the wilderness filled her with wonder, but today it was her against the elements. She stared at the pool of water and blinked when Grace's reflection stared back at her. Perfectly clear, every inch of Grace visible from her purple-streaked hair to her slightly tilted nose and aquamarine eyes. The blue of her eyes was even bluer than the water. Bluer than she remembered.

Clare looked up and Grace's shimmering image hovered over a boulder at the edge of the water. She was so close Clare could touch her, but she didn't reach out for fear she would vanish.

Grace smiled and Clare's loneliness disappeared.

Long after the vision evaporated, Clare felt her daughter's presence. While she was still alone, she wasn't forlorn any longer. Actually, she wasn't alone. She had the animals, she had a plan and she would make it out alive.

19

———

Ethan tucked Clare's license plate in his backpack and climbed up to the road. The burn in muscles unused to climbing was preferable to the fear gnawing his gut.

Maybe Clare's father was right. Maybe he should have convinced her to do something safe.

Something she would have hated.

He reached the top, and Harris and Randy helped him over the edge. The snowfall had increased, reducing visibility.

Headlights broke through the sea of white, and Ethan recognized the approaching vehicle as belonging to one of the search-and-rescue members. More headlights followed and soon they had a group ready to head out. They were about to set off when Noah pulled up.

Ethan looked at Noah's truck, anxiety rippling through him. He didn't want the boys here. "Where are Jack and Ben?"

"I left them with Rudy."

Ethan released the breath he hadn't realized he'd been holding. Noah was true blue. "Thanks."

"For what?"

"For not bringing the boys and for coming." Ethan hadn't realized until now just how much he needed his friend's support. He pulled

Noah in and gave him a quick hug. His throat raw, he choked out, "Thanks."

Noah squeezed his shoulder. "We're going to find her and bring her home."

Ethan stepped back suddenly overcome with emotion. "We'd better get going."

They got into their pickups and started down the narrow dirt road to recover Clare's body.

"Mom's alive."

Grace's voice filled him with resolve. Until he saw Clare's body, until he confirmed her death with his own eyes, she could be alive. And he would cling to that hope until the last ember flickered and died.

They followed the road until it became impassible with snow and unloaded the snowmobiles. An hour later, they still hadn't reached the SUV, but Ethan refused to give up just as he refused to give up after the accident even though he'd wanted to. He might be a lot of things, but he wasn't a quitter.

Two years ago...

"Let's go again."

Ivan Preston, Ethan's physical therapist pushed the wheel chair up behind him. "You've done enough today."

Ethan's hands clenched the parallel bar. "I haven't done nearly enough." Enough would be when he walked unassisted. Anything short of that was unacceptable.

"Ethan, I know how badly you want to be fully recovered, but pushing yourself too hard won't make it happen either."

Ethan blew off the warning. He could live with strained muscles. What he couldn't live with was being dependent. He wanted his life back. He needed his life back. Pushing himself kept him from thinking about Grace and how he hadn't saved her. And that was more than enough reason to keep at it.

He took a step forward. Sweat beaded his forehead and dripped into his eyes. His arms shook with the effort of holding himself upright. A baby had more strength than he did.

Ivan shook his head. "This session is over."

"You can end the session, but you can't stop me from continuing to work these muscles." Ethan grabbed his crutches and maneuvered himself onto the rowing machine.

When he stopped rowing, Ivan squatted in front of him. "You are not the first patient to ignore my advice. You managed to push yourself beyond your limit this time, but there is a price. The body is only capable of so much, Ethan."

"I think you don't have enough faith in my body. You're treating me like an invalid. I'm not. I can go longer, and I'm going to."

"I'm pushing you exactly as hard as you need to be pushed for the injuries you've sustained."

"You are coddling me." Ethan grabbed his crutches and struggled to his feet.

Ivan threw up his hands. "Why is it I have two types of patients. Those who won't do anything to assist in their recovery, and those who don't know when to quit."

Ethan hobbled out of the session determined to push his recovery to the limit.

❧

As SOON AS he and Clare got home Ethan went inside and fell asleep. He woke up an hour later sore, but not so sore that it stopped him from continuing his workout.

He made his way to the garage where Jack had set up the equipment Ethan needed to work out at home.

First, he rode the exercise bicycle. When he finished, he went to the rowing machine. His arms were weak and shaky by the time he finished.

"What are you doing?"

His head jerked up, and he caught sight of Clare in the doorway. "What does it look like I'm doing?"

"Ignoring Ivan's advice."

Why didn't anyone trust him, most of all his wife? "I know what I'm doing."

The skeptical expression on her face angered him further. "So, you know more than a trained physical therapist?"

"In this case I do." He jammed the crutches under his armpits and headed to the parallel bars.

Clare rolled up her sleeves. "At least let me help you."

Ethan held up a hand. "I'd rather you didn't."

"Ethan, I can see you're tired. Let me at least stay in case you need help."

"I don't need your help, Clare. I need your support."

Her eyes widened. "You've always had it."

He positioned himself in front of the bars. "Really? It sure doesn't feel like it when you second guess my every move."

Her brow arched. "So, my opinion doesn't count?"

He set the crutches aside and clasped the bars. "In this instance, no."

The flash of hurt that crossed her features gave him momentary regret.

"Fine. Call me if you need anything."

She was gone before he could respond. Before he could apologize. Not for continuing with the workout. For shutting her out.

He just wished she could see he did what he did for them. He had to return to work before they lost everything. It would be a hell of a lot easier if everyone, including Clare, stopped telling him what to do.

He took a step. His arms trembled, but his leg stayed steady. He took another step and another. He reached the end of the bars, sweat drenching his tee shirt. His ears rang and his arms turned rubbery. Even so, he pushed on.

He started back and made it halfway to the other end when a sudden spasm in his left leg sent him tumbling to the floor. He heard the crack of bone before blackness absorbed the pain.

PRESENT DAY...

Ethan gripped the handlebars of the snowmobile tighter. His determination not to give up on Clare was as strong as it had been during his physical therapy.

He pushed hard, always had. It was the only way he knew how to get ahead in the world. If you didn't stand up for yourself someone took it from you. A lesson he'd learned from his father, and one he'd carried with him into adulthood. And he would use that determination to bring his wife home safe and sound.

—————

20

Clare paused to catch her breath and get her bearings.

Bailey whined.

Clare removed her pack to let her get some water and rest for a few minutes.

The dog trotted down and drank from the river then came back and flopped at Clare's feet.

Clare reached into her backpack and gave the animals a treat, then sat down to rest a moment.

The chill wind penetrated her jacket and told her the temperatures had dipped. Getting to the cabin, building a fire, and putting on warm clothes motivated her to keep moving. Or it had until she sat down and fatigue set in. All she wanted was to curl up and go to sleep.

She shook off the lethargy and pushed to her feet. Keep moving. Keep Ethan and the boys in your line of vision.

They needed her. At least the boys did. Her husband, she wasn't as confident about. Their marriage teetered on ground as slippery as the ice underneath her feet. Ethan might still love her, but he no longer confided in her. There had been a day when he'd told her everything, and she needed that intimacy back because without it she was like a plant deprived of water—slowly withering away.

Could they recapture what they'd lost? Could they go back to the way it had been?

No.

Going back wasn't an option. Best case scenario would be to piece together a new and better future. And that was exactly what she intended to do when she got home.

No matter how resistant Ethan was to the idea, she wouldn't back off. She was through pretending; tired of being alone and married.

She'd been the one who'd broken the trust between them. She'd done the unthinkable when she'd asked her father for money without consulting Ethan. Of all the things she regretted this was the one thing that had sent her marriage into a downward spiral from which it hadn't recovered.

TWO YEARS AGO...

Clare punched in the numbers she'd known by heart since childhood, then immediately hung up the telephone.

She couldn't do it, wouldn't do it. She had her pride, her dignity to consider, damn it. She wouldn't grovel. She wouldn't ask her parents for money.

For over twenty years she'd maintained her financial independence. While it had been rough at times, she'd treasured the skills she'd acquired, from making home-cooked meals to learning to sew their clothes. She even cherished the extras they'd done without. They were badges of honor, and she wore them with pride.

Clare looked at the pile of bills. They mocked her, reminded her that her dignity didn't equal cold, hard cash. And with Ethan's sick leave running out next week, she didn't know where she'd get the money to cover those expenses.

Pride wasn't a luxury she could afford any longer.

She'd had no time for photo shoots between caring for Ethan and the kids, especially when Ethan's rehab took a series of unexpected setbacks. What if someone new and fresh snatched her markets away from her? That would mean starting from scratch, and rebuilding her base, which could take months, or years.

Resentment simmered, groundless and unjustified, but it formed a knot in her belly that wouldn't ease. Her gaze shifted to the window, to the icy winter wonderland she longed to photograph. She missed the bite of cold on her cheeks and nose. Oh to be out there working instead of trapped inside with a man who resented her very presence.

She stared at the telephone as if by osmosis she could make their financial problems magically disappear. Unfortunately life was never that simple. It required sacrifice, and for Clare, that meant groveling. It meant forfeiting her pride for her family's well-being.

She punched redial and waited as the phone rang once, twice, three times before her parents' housekeeper picked up. She asked for her father and moments later he came on the line.

"Clare, it's good to hear from you. It's been awhile."

She winced at the subtle note of censure, or perhaps it was just her own guilt. No question any guilt she felt was justified since she didn't contact them as frequently as she should.

"It has been awhile."

"How's Ethan?"

"Better since the last surgery after breaking his leg and back on track with his rehab."

"What is his prognosis these days?"

"We're hoping he'll be walking unaided soon."

Clare's unsteady breathing filled the gap in conversation.

"So I gather there's a purpose to your call since you haven't asked after your mother and me."

Clare exhaled a long breath strewn with regret. "I'm sorry, Dad. I've got a lot on my mind and manners seem to be out of reach these days."

Rather than accept her apology, she was greeted with stony silence.

She exhaled again and sought the courage to do what she'd sworn never to do.

"You can release all the tortured breaths you want, Clare, but it still won't tell me what you need."

Suddenly she was sixteen again, and bitterness swept over her the same way it had all those years ago when he'd manipulated her with money. She didn't want to be under his rule again. She didn't want his money, money that gave him the ability to make her feel obligated, to bend her to his will.

"How much do you need, Clare?"

"I-I didn't ask you for money."

"No, you didn't, but it is why you called, isn't it?"

She longed to deny his assertion, but she couldn't. She'd applied for a loan from the bank, but with Ethan unable to work and her reduced income, they'd turned her down. She'd even considered taking an advance on their credit card, but the most they could qualify for was a few thousand dollars, not nearly enough to get them through.

"I need a loan."

A resigned sigh met her ears. "How much?"

She twisted the telephone cord around her fingers until they turned blue. She hated that tone, like he'd known from the day she walked away from her inheritance that she would come crawling back. Oh how she wanted to tell him she didn't need his money, didn't need him, but the stack of bills beside her didn't permit her that indulgence.

She swallowed her pride. "Thirty thousand."

"I'll wire you the money today."

"Don't you want to know why I need the money?"

"I know why, but even if I didn't, I'd send it to you."

"No questions asked?"

"None."

"Why?"

This time her father released a haggard breath. "We really have grown apart, haven't we?"

"Were we ever really close?" Clare's tone came out soft and wistful when she'd intended hard and cynical.

"Actually, we were, but I doubt you remember when you used to come rushing into my arms after I'd been gone."

Those were memories she'd blocked because they were too painful to recall, especially with all the hurtful disappointments since.

She focused on the present rather than the past. "We'll pay the money back, but we'll need a twenty-year note."

"There's nothing to pay back. The money is from your trust fund."

"I don't want it."

"The money is yours whether you want it or not."

Another edgy silence, and Clare swore she could hear molecules splitting in the interim.

"Why is it you can never accept anything from me?" Her father's voice broke with what sounded like tears.

Ridiculous. He never became emotional. Never.

"Because, Dad, that money is tainted and there are always strings attached to your gifts."

Even though she spoke the truth, she wished she'd kept that bit of insight locked inside, spared them both the additional loss of intimacy. But the words were out, and she couldn't take them back.

He cleared his throat. "You'll have the money today, and if you need more, I'll arrange it so you can contact the bank directly rather than call me."

Before she could respond, a dial tone sounded in her ear. Tears blurred her eyes as she stared out her office window at the iced-over creek as frozen as her heart. Why couldn't things be different with her parents? Why could they only exchange polite but deadly barbs at one another? Why couldn't they—why couldn't *she* put aside the past and build an adult relationship with them?

A tear trickled down her cheek. In one fell swoop, she'd thrown away her pride and severed whatever flimsy relationship she had with her father.

Clare wiped away the tears and rose to finish cleaning up the breakfast dishes. She halted when she saw Ethan blocked the doorway. She hadn't heard his approach, hadn't heard his crutches thump against the hardwood floor. Stealth was something he'd perfected since his accident, and from his harsh expression he'd overheard her conversation with her father.

They stared at one another, neither speaking, but both saying volumes with their silence. Finally, Ethan turned away.

"Wait."

He faced her. "For what, Clare? For you to castrate me?" He slapped his forehead. "Oh, wait, you've already done that. Tell you what, next time give me some notice and I'll make an appointment with a doctor. At least that way I'll be anesthetized, so I won't feel the knife."

Clare swallowed around the expanding lump in her throat. "I'm sorry, but what should I have done?"

His vacant stare lacked the spark of fire his anger generated moments ago. "Consult me. I am your husband, aren't I, or have you taken care of that, too?"

This time the heavy thump of his crutches slapped against the hardwood floor.

Long after the sound faded away she stared at the doorway. She replayed their argument in her head and suddenly, it hit her. She hadn't just sacrificed her pride today, but Ethan's. And chances were, he had far less to spare than she did.

PRESENT DAY...

Clare swiped at the tears frozen to her cheeks. Regret weighed heavily on her. If only she could go back. If only she could have a do-over.

She shook off the notion. Regrets took time and energy she didn't have. She needed to push forward.

Whistling to Bailey, she strapped on their gear, and set off as the snowfall thickened.

They reached the top of the waterfall an hour later and stopped to rest again. Clare's breath fanned out in white puffs as she studied the fog-shrouded mountains.

She blinked when a snowflake landed on her eyelashes. Several inches of snow had fallen since she and the animals had taken their last break. Exhaustion nipped at her and urged her to curl up and go to sleep.

Bailey leaned into her thigh and stared up at her with dark trusting eyes.

Quitting wasn't an option.

Clare blew out a breath, then straightened her spine. Bailey and Ballistic depended on her, her children needed her, and she hoped Ethan did, too.

She and Ethan might have their problems, and many of them her doing, but she wasn't ready to give up, or give up on the two of them.

She would get to the cabin. All she had to do was put one foot in front of the other. As long as she kept moving, she would make it out of here and get back to Ethan and the boys and salvage her marriage.

21

———

Ethan stared at the mangled, twisted remains of Clare's SUV. During the long ride down the canyon he'd clung to the faint hope Clare had somehow survived the crash, but no one survived a fall like this. No one.

Ethan barely felt Randy's hand on his shoulder. "Ethan, did you hear me?"

He blinked and focused on his friend. "What?"

"I said, stay here with Noah, while we search the SUV."

Ethan nodded, shut his eyes and prayed for a miracle. But with each prayer he uttered, he became more and more convinced the miracle he'd been banking on had slipped through his fingers.

The words "she's alive" rang in Ethan's head, and warmth filled him even though he knew the odds she survived the crash were nonexistent.

The typical laughter and off-color jokes were replaced with a sharp, stilted silence. It was so quiet in fact, every footstep echoed as the men crossed over to the wreckage. Metal groaned when they pried open the car door, then suddenly, amazingly, Ethan heard Randy's jubilant shout, "It's empty, and she's left a note."

Ethan's eyes snapped opened. Hope replaced despair. He raced over to Randy and the others with Noah on his heels. "What does it say?"

Randy looked up from the note. "She's gone to a cabin upriver. Do you know where?"

"Yes, it's a cabin we stayed in years ago, maybe three miles upriver."

"Is there a faster way there rather than following the river?"

"On snowmobile."

"Then you, Noah, and Paul go to the cabin on snowmobile. The rest of us will start upriver on foot. If she's at the cabin you can contact us, and if not, you can start downriver from there until we find her."

As Ethan set off with Noah and Paul, he hoped this could be his second chance with Clare. Because of him their daughter was dead, and Clare had had to ask her parents for money—something she'd have never done otherwise. It ate at him that he was the one who'd forced her to do that. She'd been so proud of their independence, of the fact they'd made it on their own, and he'd taken that away from her. He had to move beyond the guilt and blame, but he was mired in it. He'd tried therapy hoping it would help and stop Clare from nagging him, but nothing changed.

SEVEN MONTHS AGO...

"Here's crazy for you. I have this recurring fantasy Grace is alive. That she's hiding from me. Waiting for me to find her."

The silence that followed Ethan's statement was as awkward as when he'd asked Tricia Stanford to the seventh grade spring dance.

The counselor's face didn't show a hint of surprise, doubt, or sympathy. Just a steady, unflappable, thoroughly annoying calm. It was as if he'd known, expected even, that Ethan was going to say that. So why, after confessing his deepest fear, didn't he feel unburdened?

Ethan stared down at his shoes. "So what now?"

"You keep talking. To me. To Clare. When you go it alone it gets ugly," Bruce said.

An easy concept in theory, but in practice the hardest thing he'd ever done. Talk to Clare. Tell her that not only had he let their daughter die, but now he was crazy, too.

"And if I do this, it will help?"

"Not overnight."

"How long?"

Bruce lifted a shoulder. "This isn't an exact science, Ethan. A lot will depend on you and Clare. How willing you both are to work on your relationship."

Non-fucking committal as usual.

Bruce studied him a moment. "Grief is like going to war. You have to do battle with real grief until you conquer it, or it will eat you alive."

Ethan gave a slow thoughtful nod. Yeah, he did feel like he'd been at war.

"Tell me about Grace."

A smile momentarily relieved his tension. "Clare was the one who pushed to have Jack, but a second child was my idea. I still remember the first time I held Grace in my arms. She was perfect, an exact replica of Clare. I loved Jack, but Grace and I, we just clicked from the beginning. The moment she started walking, she became my shadow. She loved all our trips into the mountains for Clare's work. I taught her to fly fish while Clare worked. If I had my tool belt on, she insisted on having one, too. She was easy to be with, easy to parent."

"But that changed."

Ethan gave a single sharp nod, the tension threading back through him. "The instant she became a teenager, she stopped being my little girl. Everything changed. Her hair, her clothes, her attitude. She challenged everything I said and did."

"She spread her wings."

He'd never considered it from that perspective. In truth, he'd felt abandoned and floundering. His little girl was leaving him behind.

"Tell me about the accident."

Discuss memories he'd worked nearly two years to bury? He considered walking out, looked longingly at the door, but in the end remained. Silence hadn't lessened his pain, so what did he have to lose by talking about it?

"I took Grace and Ben fishing."

Correction—he'd coerced Grace into going. What had happened to the little girl who'd begged to tag along with him and Jack?

"What happened?"

Ethan stared out the second-story window at Lake Pend Oreille. Fluffy white clouds reflected off the still water, and boats dotted water. A scene eerily similar to the one on the Serenity river the day Grace died.

"I spent the afternoon teaching Ben to fly fish, tying on flies, and taking wind knots out of his fishing line." He hadn't really minded, in fact, it had been a pleasant reminder of past trips with a younger, less-militant Grace.

"So, it was a pleasant outing?"

"Yes."

"What about Grace?"

"She wasn't thrilled to be there."

"Why not?"

"She wanted to stay home, but we were afraid of what she'd do if we left her alone."

"Like what?"

"Like get a piercing or a tattoo."

"Did you have reason to think she'd do that?"

"Clare found her using a clip-on in her navel, and she'd done some henna tattoos with her friends."

Bruce studied him a long moment. "Would it have been the worst thing in the world if she'd have done either of those?"

"You think we overreacted."

"I've heard a lot worse things that fourteen-year-olds do."

Bruce's comment was probably on target since it had been a point of contention with Grace. Grace had reminded them they'd allowed

Jack to stay on his own at that age, but Jack was different. He hadn't wanted belly rings or tattoos.

"How did she react to going?"

"She whined and pouted and demanded to know why she was being forced to come." It wasn't the fishing she objected to, it was being with him. Anything he did, she did the reverse.

"But you stayed."

"Yes. Ben was having fun, despite Grace's complaints, and I didn't think it was fair to cut his trip short just because she didn't want to be there."

"Life isn't fair."

"No." A fact Ethan knew with certainty.

"So you stayed."

"Until the storm started to roll in. I told Grace to get the lifejackets. She kept baiting me until I—I told her to shut up."

Ethan looked away as shame washed over him yet again. What kind of father spoke that way to his daughter?

"What happened next?"

"I headed for shore. We were almost there when lightning struck, hitting a tree and capsized the boat. One minute we were upright, the next we were in the water."

Ethan's bones ached as he remembered the icy water, so cold his arms and legs moved like strings on a marionette.

"I broke the surface and called out to the kids. Grace and Ben were tangled up in the tree, and the current was pulling them under.

"Grace's foot was wedged between two branches. I pulled on the branch and Ben popped free. I swam him to shore, then went back for Grace. I dove under to free her foot. It wouldn't budge. I tried to break the limb, bend it. It started to give, then the tree shifted."

"Daddy, help me." Grace's cry was the last thing he remembered before the tree slammed into him and knocked him out.

"So you did everything you could to save her."

Ethan blinked and silenced Grace's voice. "Yes."

Bruce's steady gaze held his. "Do you believe that, Ethan?"

"What?

"That you did everything within your power to save her."

"Yes."

Was that a flash of skepticism he'd seen in Bruce's eyes?

"What do you remember about those days right after Grace died?"

"Not much. I was barely conscious, and when I was, they pumped me full of painkillers."

Not that he'd cared. He'd have done anything to numb the pain. He'd desperately wanted to give up, to join Grace, beg her forgiveness, but he couldn't. He had a family that needed him.

"And you didn't attend the funeral?"

"No."

"Did you see Grace's body?"

"No." And thank God. He wanted to remember the tow-headed little girl who'd believed in Santa Claus and thought her daddy was Superman.

"Is it possible that's why you fantasize that she's alive?"

Was it? "What difference would it make?"

"Seeing her body would have given you closure, made her death absolute."

"You think I don't know she's dead?"

"You dream she's alive."

He did more than dream it, he fantasized about it.

Ethan shrugged. "I can't change the past."

"That's true."

Something in Bruce's tone gave him pause, made him wonder if he'd seen more than Ethan had wanted him to.

"Tell me about your recovery."

"It was slow, slower than I'd anticipated. The medical bills nearly bankrupted us. Clare had to hire a roofer to finish the job I'd started, putting us deeper in debt."

"So you pushed yourself."

"Hell yes."

"Why?"

To keep from thinking, from having to deal with the fear gnawing a crater-sized hole in his belly that he'd become his father. Not an alcoholic, but a man who couldn't support his family.

"So I didn't have to think about Grace." Ethan's jaw clenched, and tension coiled inside of him. Anger consumed him. It had become a permanent fixture within him.

"You're angry."

"Hell yes."

"At yourself."

"Yes."

"At Clare."

His fingers dug into the smooth leather arm of the chair. Anger suffocated him. Clare was his scapegoat.

"Yes. She deserved better than me harping at her day and night when she took care of me after the accident."

"So you took out your frustration on her."

"She carried my responsibilities and hers."

"Give me an example."

It shamed him to admit how he'd treated her, but maybe his penance was to acknowledge his shortcomings. "Clare was shoveling the drive one morning. I was pissed I couldn't do it, so I yelled at her."

"How did she react?"

"She didn't. It was as if I hadn't said anything."

"She refused to engage."

"Yes. Why did she keep taking my shit? Why didn't she fight back? Why did she have to be so damned pleasant and make me feel like the jackass I was?"

"Maybe she made allowances because you were injured and still recovering."

Ethan shrugged. "Maybe."

"What did she do when you couldn't draw her into an argument?"

"She started shoveling again."

"And that pissed you off."

"Yes. I told her Jack should be doing it, and to leave it for him to do when he got home."

"Did she?"

"No. She said a storm was due in, and she didn't want to wait."

"Perfectly logical." Bruce leaned back in his chair, looked at his notes, then at Ethan. "So how did you respond?"

"I told her she shouldn't coddle him."

"Did that get the rise out of her you wanted?"

"No. She said he did more than his fair share, and since he was at school, she was helping him out. That's what being part of a family meant."

"Was that all she said?"

Ethan blew out a breath. "She said maybe I was the one she was coddling and shouldn't."

"How did you respond to that?"

"I didn't. What could I say? She was right. I behaved like a spoiled brat."

Or rather he'd been behaving like Grace before she died. "I—I kept waiting for her to give up on me, to cry uncle, but she never did. Not even when I was so clearly in the wrong."

"Do you think it was wrong to express your anger?"

"I didn't have a right to treat her the way I did."

"No, you didn't, but you have a right to your anger. You have a right to be angry your daughter is dead, that life at that moment sucked. Do you think if you had told Clare that she would have understood?"

His question stopped Ethan cold. Would she? Or more importantly did he deserve her compassion? "I didn't deserve her sympathy."

"Why?"

"I was the best husband and father I could be." The man his father hadn't been.

Bruce gave him a thoughtful nod. "In order to be a good husband and father, is there room for error?"

"None."

Bruce made a note on his pad of paper, then looked Ethan square in the eye. "Have you considered the burden that puts on your family?"

Ethan snapped his head up. "How can being a good parent be a bad thing?"

"It isn't, but striving for perfection is a pressure cooker waiting to blow." Bruce studied him a long moment. "Is it possible your guilt stems from the fact that your last words to Grace were in anger?

ETHAN STEPPED out into the warm spring sunshine and crossed to his truck, his insides churning like a shaken soda can.

He climbed into the cab and slammed his fist against the dash. Wasn't counseling supposed to make him feel better?

He stared into the rearview mirror, and the man in the reflection was suddenly a stranger. The man who stared back at him had felt his daughter slipping away long before death claimed her. And in his heart of hearts, he *was* just a little relieved their battles had stopped. That way he could pretend he'd still been the perfect dad and Grace's idol.

IT WAS LATE when Ethan got home from his session with Bruce. He grabbed a beer and went outside. He eased down into the lawn chair on the small patio set back from to the house hidden in a cluster of trees beside the hot tub. He stretched out his legs and stared up at the stars winking across the velvet canopy overhead. Sipping his beer, he wondered if one of those shining stars was Grace.

Had it really been a year and a half since she'd died?

Silence enveloped him along with the sharp stab of loneliness. Why couldn't things be different between him and Clare? He wanted to hold her, bury himself in her and wash away all the painful memories. But Clare wasn't interested in a physical relationship with him any longer. She claimed her diminished sex drive wasn't because of him, but he knew better.

She'd withdrawn from him, and could he blame her? No. Who wanted to be with someone full of anger and guilt?

As if she'd been privy to his thoughts, Clare materialized out of the darkness and approached the hot tub.

He took another sip of his beer and watched as she opened the lid. Steam billowed out, glowing against the black sky.

She shrugged out of her robe, and he could make out the silhouette of that lush body he so desperately missed.

"Kind of late for a soak, isn't it?"

Clare gasped and swung around to face him. She pressed a hand to her chest. "You scared me to death."

"Sorry," he said, but he wasn't. He'd wanted to drive some honest emotion from her, and for once, he'd succeeded.

She stared at him. He couldn't read her expression, but her discomfort was obvious from the way she grabbed her robe and clutched it to her chest.

They'd gone from relaxed and comfortable with each other to veritable strangers. That realization ripped at his heart almost as much as Bruce's suggestion he was relieved Grace was dead.

Grace. The reason they were both out here tonight. The reason for the distance between them.

He tipped his beer toward the hot tub. "Don't let me interrupt your soak."

Her hesitation spoke volumes. She'd wanted to be alone—no, she'd wanted to avoid him. And any other night, any other day, he'd give her her space, but tonight he needed her. He wouldn't walk away even though that's what he knew she wanted.

Rather than climb into the hot tub, she slipped her robe back on and started past him. He reached out a hand and halted her retreat. Twining his fingers through hers, he eased her onto his lap.

"I've missed you, I've missed touching you." He pressed his nose into her hair and inhaled. He loved the smell of her hair, a breath of fresh morning air.

"Ethan, I—"

He pressed a finger to her lips. "Please, Clare, I need you. Don't turn me away."

When she said nothing more, he trailed his finger from her lips down to the base of her throat, then dipped lower until he cupped her breast. Her nipple pebbled, and she leaned into his touch.

"Ethan, it's been so long." Her whispered words soothed the ache inside of him.

"Too long."

He shifted so that she straddled him. The action caused her robe to gape open, and the sight of all that creamy flesh made his pulse skitter.

The cool spring breeze swept her hair into her face. She pushed it aside, leaned forward and kissed him. A kiss that set fire burning deep within him. A fire that wouldn't be extinguished until he buried himself deep inside her.

"I've missed this too." Her breath warmed his skin as her kisses moved to his chest, his belly, then lower.

Ethan's breath hitched when she lowered his zipper and the back of her knuckles brushed his skin. She fingered the source of his heat. Her touch drove the demons from his soul, the guilt from his heart, and for this space in time, life became what it had been before the accident.

His fingers pressed into the soft flesh of her backside as he maneuvered her over him. A moment later he slid into her warmth. His arms held her against him, his mouth zeroed in on her nipple.

A soft moan escaped from her throat and filled the still night air. They ground out their ache for each other and drove away their grief. Their passion rose higher and higher until the velvety sky became their sanctuary.

The orgasm ripped through Ethan fast and hard, long before Clare reached hers. He slowly came back to earth and brushed a strand of hair from her cheek. "I'm sorry. It's been so long, I couldn't control it."

Clare eased her robe closed. "It's all right. I understand."

She started to rise, but his hands continued to circle her hips, holding her in place. "Give me a few minutes to recover, and I'll make it up to you."

She shook her head and slid out of his hold. "I'm tired. Maybe another night."

He couldn't see her face, but he heard the quaver in her voice. "What's wrong?"

She turned her back to him, but he didn't miss the back of her hand swiping her cheek.

"Nothing's wrong. I'm going to bed."

He adjusted his clothing and rose to block her exit. "Talk to me, Clare. Tell me the truth. What's really going on here?"

"It's nothing, really."

"You and I have a whole different opinion on what constitutes nothing. I call a wife crying after making love to her husband a hell of a lot more than nothing. It's something—a big something."

He gentled his tone. "I'm sorry it wasn't the greatest sex for you, but I'll make it up to you if you just give me a chance." His fingers trailed over her damp cheeks. "It's not like this hasn't happened a time or two before."

"It isn't the sex, Ethan."

When she didn't elaborate, he pressed her. "Then what is it I've done to upset you?"

"It's not you, it's me. I just don't desire sex. It's as if I've shriveled up inside, as if losing Grace took that from me."

"Are you saying you didn't want to make love to me just now?"

"No. I want to make love to you. The desire isn't there."

"I'm not sure I see the difference."

She looked up at him, cupping his face with her hands. "I love you, Ethan. I want to make love to you, but there's this vacant spot inside of me that never gets filled, that doesn't respond to anything."

Clarification. What she was really meant was, she didn't respond to him.

"If you didn't want to make love with me, why didn't you just say so?"

She dropped her hands as a frustrated sigh escaped. "I knew

you'd misinterpret my words. All the books say it's normal. That a lot of women go through this. It's part of the grieving process."

Ethan resisted rolling his eyes. Couldn't there be a conversation between them that didn't revert back to something she'd read in one of those damned self-help books? The first few she'd asked him to read had been one thing, but she'd read dozens of them over the past year and the fact of the matter was, they were both still grieving and still distant with each other. Said a lot for those books in his opinion.

"Books won't bring Grace back."

She whirled around and faced him. "I never said they would."

"But isn't that what you'd hoped?"

Her silence told him everything she didn't say. "She's dead, Clare, and we can't bring her back." Had he said that to convince her or him? After what he'd revealed to Bruce earlier that day he had to wonder.

"I know that. I'm not a child living in fantasy land."

There were times he wasn't so sure. Maybe living in fantasy land was easier than facing the truth. God knows he wouldn't mind a trip down the yellow brick road now and again.

"The answer isn't in those books, Clare. The answer is speaking the truth."

"What truth?"

She was going to make him say it. Fine. "This has nothing to do with lack of desire from grieving and everything to do with you not wanting me, not wanting to be near me." He paused, then asked the question he wasn't sure he wanted answered. "You dread being alone with me, don't you?"

When she said nothing in response, he asked, "Do we have anything in common anymore other than our grief?"

PRESENT DAY...

Fear gripped Ethan deep in his belly. Finding Clare was only half the battle. If they didn't find common ground, they had nothing left —therapy or no therapy.

A low hanging branch slapped Ethan in the face. He managed to stay on his snowmobile, but Noah wasn't so lucky. The branch caught him square in the face and he tumbled onto the ground.

Ethan stopped and ran over to his friend as he struggled to his feet.

"Noah, are you all right?"

"I think so." Noah grimaced when he tried to push to his feet.

Ethan helped him onto the snowmobile seat. "You don't look so fine."

Paul joined them. "Where does it hurt?"

"My shoulder." Noah winced when he moved it.

Paul made a quick evaluation. "You need to get this looked at. It could be dislocated."

Noah shook his head. "It can wait."

"I don't think so." Paul opened the first aid kit he'd brought from his snowmobile and formed a temporary sling while Ethan called in their situation.

"The search is being called off because of the weather, and it will be resumed tomorrow," the radio operator reported.

"Copy that." Ethan turned to Noah and Paul. "They're calling off the search for the night. You two head back. I'm going to go on to the cabin in case Clare is there."

Noah groaned when Paul lifted his arm. "It's too dangerous for you to go alone. I'll come with you."

Even in obvious pain his best friend would continue searching with him. "You need to go back and get that shoulder looked at."

"I can manage," Noah insisted.

"I know you can, but to be honest you're going to slow me down."

Noah said nothing for a long moment. "I don't like leaving you out here on your own."

"I know what I'm doing. Go back and get that shoulder taken care of. I'll radio in as soon as I get to the cabin."

Noah's eyes narrowed, then he heaved a resigned sigh. "You'd damn well better not get yourself killed, or when I get to the afterlife I'm going to kick your ass."

"I won't do anything stupid."

"You know you could be snowed in there for a few days," Paul said.

"I know. If we are, the cabin will keep us warm, and there's water. I've got food, plus I'll bet there's canned food inside, so we'll be fine. Noah, you'll make sure my kids don't behave like their father?"

"I'll be sure they don't act like a damn lovesick fool if that's what you mean."

"It is, and thanks."

Ethan waited until Paul and Noah set off, then he headed for the cabin. Squinting through the heavy snowfall, the cabin came into view thirty minutes later.

He parked the snowmobile and searched for Clare, but found no sign of her.

He started a fire to warm the cabin, and radioed in that he'd arrived at the cabin.

With only a few hours of daylight left, the smart move would be to start fresh in the morning, but his gut told him he had to keep going or lose Clare forever. And he always listened to his gut.

She'd survived the car crash against incredible odds, and she was still out there fighting her way to safety. No way in hell he'd stay put and wait. He was going after her and bringing her home.

22

———————

Clare pivoted to study the area and realized she'd taken photos here just last May, but she'd been on the other side of the river and a little further upstream in a tiny meadow. There hadn't been snow on the ground either.

She'd pictured an award-winning photograph in her mind's eye that day, but as frequently happened, the pictures she'd visualized didn't live up to her expectations. Some of her best photos had resulted from plain, old luck. They were unplanned, unexpected, and caught her totally unaware.

She'd come that day with a vision of early morning mists and swirling fog, but instead she'd been met with a thunderstorm and wild gusting winds that swirled the snow around the mountain peaks.

Ironically, the pictures she'd envisioned hadn't materialized, but instead she came away with a full rainbow that turned out to be one of her best pictures ever. Nothing had gone as expected that day, and it was also the day she'd nearly lost Bailey.

Six months ago...

Squatting, Clare zipped her camera bag closed and paused to stare at the rainbow, the colors brilliant against the black clouds pressed up against the mountain. Her gaze tracked the rainbow as it arched over the snow-capped peaks until it disappeared into the thick growth of trees. She smiled recalling Grace's infatuation with the story of the leprechauns and the pot of gold at the end of the rainbow. She and Ethan had read her the story so often they'd memorized the words.

She tracked the rainbow the opposite direction and wondered if Grace sat at the end of it on top of the pot of gold with those leprechauns she'd loved. Her spirits lifted. She hoped so. She prayed Grace was happy and all her dreams had come true. It made losing her more bearable.

Bailey's hackles rose and a growl rumbled deep in her chest. Still on her haunches, Clare's gaze circled the tiny clearing. A chill swept over her that had nothing to do with the frosty north wind and everything to do with the wild-eyed cat crouched twenty feet away.

She raised her palm to Bailey. "Stay."

She slowly rose and held her arms high and wide to make herself look larger to the mountain lion.

Another growl rumbled through Bailey.

The cat hissed in response, its hunger-starved stare fixed on Clare.

Normally mountain lions avoided humans, but this cat was stalking prey, and she and Bailey were targeted for its next meal.

Bailey's growl deepened, and she lunged forward the same instant the cat pounced. The two animals rolled onto the ground growling and hissing, mud and grass flying as fast as claws and teeth.

One moment Bailey had the cat by the throat and pinned to the ground, the next, a paw slammed her rear flank and sent her tumbling end over end.

The fight was over as fast as it began. Somehow Bailey managed to send the cat limping off, but not before she sustained serious injuries.

Adrenaline still pumping, Clare got Bailey into the car. She raced to the vet, and called Ethan as soon as she had cell phone service.

Ethan arrived at the clinic almost on Clare's heels.

The moment she saw him, she threw herself into his arms, relieved he was there to lean on, to make things right.

"Are you hurt?" His gaze swept over her blood-stained clothes.

Clare shook her head. "It's Bailey's blood. I'm fine."

Ethan pulled her into his arms and squashed her against his chest. "Thank God." His cheek pressed onto the top of her head, and he repeated the words, his voice raw.

"I thought I'd—" He broke off the sentence, but he didn't need to finish it because Clare knew exactly what had gone through his mind.

"I'm fine, thanks to Bailey. You would have been very proud of her."

"I'm just grateful you had her with you." His finger trembled as he tucked a lock of hair behind her ear.

Clare eased back to see his face. His skin was gray, his mouth a rigid slash, his eyes hollow with fear.

For the first time in a long time she read his thoughts, understood perfectly the fear he'd experienced. She'd have reacted the same way if the situation were reversed.

"Clare, Ethan, would you like some coffee while you wait?" Annabelle Green, the vet assistant broke in.

Turning in Ethan's arms, Clare forced a smile. "That would be nice, thanks."

Annabelle's gaze lingered on Ethan. She wasn't the first woman to show an interest in him, but it was the first time Clare wondered if Ethan returned the interest. Since Grace's death nothing had been right between them, and this was the closest they'd been in a long, long time.

Annabelle returned with their coffee, and Ethan barely acknowledged the other woman, to her obvious disappointment, and Clare's relief. He only had eyes for her, regardless of their current difficulties.

They sat down in the molded plastic chairs, sipped their coffee and waited. Ethan's hand rested on her thigh. She traced the bumps and ridges of his knuckles with her fingertip, relishing the warmth, the strength that flowed into her.

"I should have done something more to protect Bailey. I shouldn't have gone into the mountains today. I should have left her at home."

Ethan's dark eyes turned fierce, and his hand tightened on her knee. "No! You did everything right. I'm sorry Bailey is injured, but what happened today is precisely the reason we got her. She did her job. She protected you. If she hadn't been there you could have been seriously injured or killed. I love Bailey, and I don't want to lose her, but if I have to make a choice between you and her, it's you every time."

Ethan hugged her close. "I love you, Clare, and I can't bear the thought of anything happening to you. Promise me you won't go out alone until Bailey is well enough to go with you."

"I-I have to work." Even as she stammered the words the idea of going alone terrified her.

"I know you do, but we'll find a way so that you're not alone. Promise me you won't go by yourself."

Numbly, she nodded, then laid her head on his shoulder.

He stroked her hair. "You scared ten years off my life today. I'm so glad you weren't hurt. I don't think I could have gone on if I'd lost you, too."

For the first time since his accident, Ethan was taking care of her. It felt good. Damn good. It was a tiring thing to carry the weight of the world on your own, and Clare was more than ready to share that burden with him.

James Dawson, their vet, came out a few minutes later. He sat down beside them. "She's going to be fine. There were a couple of deep cuts, but no organs were damaged. I stitched her up, and she should be back to normal in a couple of weeks."

Ethan's hand squeezed her thigh. A simple touch and yet reassuring when chaos reigned.

"Can we take her home?" Clare asked.

"I don't see why not, but she's going to need some care."

"No worries there. She'll be treated like a queen," Ethan assured him.

James gave them a list of instructions, then Ethan carried a still drowsy Bailey out to Clare's car and carefully laid her in the back compartment.

They reached the house a few minutes later. Ethan opened Clare's door for her and helped her out, then stared deep into her eyes.

"What? I'm a mess aren't I?" She smoothed her hair.

He gave her one of those gentle smiles he reserved for the kids when they were upset and in need of comfort. "Terrible."

Clare laughed and playfully punched his shoulder. "Haven't you learned anything in all the years we've been married? You're supposed to lie."

His teasing expression turned solemn. "You've never looked more beautiful or alive." He pressed a soft kiss to her lips.

His words had come from deep inside and moved Clare more than anything else he could have said.

"Why don't you go shower, and I'll take care of Bailey." He carried the dog up the porch steps.

Clare kept pace with him. "I want to sit with her for a few minutes first and get her settled, but thanks."

Ethan started to respond, but stopped when Jack and Ben raced out the front door. They skidded to a halt when they saw their parents.

"Mom, are you okay?" Jack stared at the blood that covered her shirt and jeans.

"She's fine." Ethan carried Bailey inside, his confidence reassuring.

"What happened? Is Bailey going to be okay?"

Clare didn't miss the quaver in Ben's voice. Wrapping an arm around his shoulders, she tucked him against her side as they followed Ethan into the living room. He laid Bailey on her bed.

Clare made it to the chair beside the bed before her legs gave out completely. She tugged Ben down beside her and held him close. Ethan sat on the floor next to Bailey.

Jack hovered as if uncertain what to do.

Ethan settled the matter by tapping the floor and telling him to sit.

The moment Jack was settled, Ethan said, "Your mom and Bailey were attacked by a mountain lion this afternoon."

"Is Bailey going to be okay?" With wide, frightened eyes, Ben stared at the semi-conscious dog.

Ethan squeezed Ben's knee. "She's going to be fine."

"You're sure?" Ben leaned forward and gave Bailey a pat on the head.

"Positive. She's just going to have to take it easy for awhile," Clare said.

Ben laid his head on Clare's chest and curled into her. She held him close, and felt his body tremble. "I'm glad. I didn't want her in heaven with Grace."

The independent ten-year-old turned into her baby again, and they both needed cuddling after what had happened today.

Ethan leaned forward and touched his forehead to Clare's. The simple gesture comforted her. Whatever had been fractured between them had temporarily healed while they faced this crisis together.

It struck Clare how colorless life had been since she and Ethan had become estranged. Her work had paled, her food was bland, and her heart only functioned at half capacity without him to depend on, lean on, confide in.

Ethan's fingers glided over her hair. "I'm going to get you a glass of wine, then start dinner."

Clare swallowed back the lump in her throat. "Thank you."

Their eyes held long moments, then he squeezed Jack's shoulder and ruffled Ben's hair before he rose.

Clare's gaze tracked Ethan until he disappeared into the kitchen. How she'd been fortunate enough to marry a kind, gentle man like Ethan Burke was beyond her.

∽

"Mom." Jack's yell echoed through the house two days later.

"I'm in my office." Clare took out her camera, checked the battery, and made sure the memory card was in place.

"What are you doing?" Jack came to stand beside her.

"I'm getting my gear ready."

"Why?"

Excitement pulsed through Clare. She had an opportunity to get her career back on track. "I just got an assignment from a national magazine."

Stony silence met her announcement.

Clare looked up at her six-foot-two ultra-responsible high school senior.

"You promised Dad you wouldn't go out alone."

His words sent Clare's adrenaline rush into hibernation, and a guilty flush crept up her neck. She'd been caught up in the moment and forgotten her promise, forgotten her own qualms about going back alone. "This is a big assignment."

Jack's body went rigid. His eyes turned so cold it sent a chill through her.

"You have no right doing that to us. You could have died out there. Don't you care about how we feel, what it would do to us if something happened to you?"

"I can't turn this assignment down, besides the odds are it won't happen again."

"I don't care about odds. I care about you. Do you have a death wish? Is this about Grace?"

"No!" Clare gripped his arms. "I love Grace, I miss her. I wouldn't do anything to intentionally end up dead. I have too much to live for —you, and Ben, and your father."

Jack stared down at her and said nothing for a long minute. "I'm going with you tomorrow, and there's nothing you can say to change my mind."

"There's no skipping school in this house." Ethan's voice rang with quiet authority from the doorway.

Jack faced his father, his face still belligerent and unyielding. "I'm not letting her go up there alone."

Ethan crossed over to his son and put a hand on his shoulder. "She's not going alone. You have my word on that."

Jack's posture slowly relaxed. "You swear?"

"I do."

Jack glanced back at Clare. His expression held more than a touch of resentment before he walked away.

"You promised me you wouldn't go out alone." Ethan's voice was low and controlled.

Clare leaned a hip against the desk and faced him. "I know, and honestly I don't want to go alone, but this is a fabulous opportunity to get my career back on track. I've lost a lot of my regular markets, and I'm basically starting over. I need the work."

While that was all true, work also gave her space from Ethan and their problems, but she feared telling him that would fracture their relationship beyond repair.

Ethan exhaled heavily. "I'm sorry, I didn't realize."

"You were in recovery, and I didn't want to burden you with my work problems."

Ethan studied her intently. "A marriage should be about sharing, about give and take, Clare. You never take anymore."

How could she? It had been all give and no take since Grace died. She'd been meeting everyone's needs. There hadn't been time for her.

Ethan touched her arm. "Wait until Sunday, and we'll all go."

That would mean pulling an all nighter in the office to get the photos screened and labeled to meet the Monday deadline, but she'd rather do that than worry her family and go by herself.

Maybe it wouldn't be so bad if they made a family day of it. Maybe it would be like the old days when they'd spent their weekends in the mountains, and they'd been happy.

Studying Ethan's face, she found no sign of happiness, no joy in spending a Sunday with her, only determination.

"Now that we've got this settled I'll go tell the boys."

Another problem solved. Another item to cross off his to-do list.

Why did doing something with her, with his wife, have to be a job, a chore? Why couldn't he embrace their time together with anticipation, eagerness, passion?

Passion.

When was the last time there had been even a hint of passion between them? No, that wasn't accurate. She was the one who had lost the passion, not Ethan.

She'd felt that spark a few weeks ago at the hot tub, but it had burned out before they'd barely begun making love. Clare wasn't even certain that had been passion she'd experienced. All they did anymore was go through the motions of being a couple.

She heard the murmur of Ethan's voice in the next room. She wanted the tender, passionate man she'd married back. But what if he'd died with their daughter?

The mountain peak came slowly into focus as the past shifted back to the present. Clare resumed walking, and in the absolute silence that surrounded her, she had never felt more alone than she did at this moment.

How she wished Ethan were here with her right now. She didn't care if it was with stilted silence, she just wanted him beside her. She'd take that any day to the utter quiet of being completely and totally alone. No matter how bad their relationship was, it beat the hell out of her current situation. She missed his company, missed all the times he'd come with her, taken care of her.

As she trudged through the snow, it dawned on her she hadn't done all the giving. Ethan had sacrificed plenty for her career over the years. Had she ever expressed her appreciation for all he'd done for her? All the trips, the local events and just time to relax that they'd postponed for her career?

No. She'd always accepted it as her due, as if she were the princess and he her devoted slave.

Shame washed over her. How could she have allowed him to continually give and never tell him how much she appreciated his sacrifices?

She just hoped she had the chance to make it right between them, because a life without Ethan was no life at all.

Bailey cut a path through a patch of thick undergrowth.

A branch snapped back and slapped Clare in the face. She stumbled and skidded on an icy boulder. Arms flailing, she grabbed at a tree branch, but the frosty boughs slipped through her fingers.

She fell through a narrow opening between two boulders and the ground rose up hard and fast. The air whooshed out of her lungs, then everything went fuzzy and faded to black.

23

Ethan abruptly stopped the snowmobile and shut off the engine.

"Clare." The wind swallowed his voice. Ethan remained perfectly still waiting for a response.

Nothing.

He reached over to fire the engine, then froze when he heard a faint bark.

"Bailey."

Another bark, this one louder and moving closer.

Ethan put his fingers between his lips and released a loud, shrill whistle. Seconds before he saw Bailey, he heard her galloping through the snow. A moment later she came barreling toward him, burdened down with Clare's pack and a wild-eyed feline clinging to her back. The dog leapt into the air and landed in his arms sending all three of them flying.

Sputtering snow, Ethan laughed while Bailey slathered his face with kisses. Holding the dog at bay, he staggered to his feet and brushed off the snow. Ballistic did the same, shaking his wet fur with a put-upon glare at his ride.

"Bailey, take me to Clare."

She released a joyous bark, waited for the cat to settle on her back, then set off. Ethan followed close on her heels with the snowmobile. Bailey stopped, and Ethan killed the engine. He raced over to where Bailey and Ballistic sat at the edge of a narrow ravine.

Ethan's heart constricted when he stared down at Clare laying prone at the bottom of a ravine.

"Clare."

No response.

"Clare, answer me."

When there was still no response, he ran back to the snowmobile and grabbed his gear. Securing the rope to a nearby tree, he strapped on his harness and stepped off the ledge.

CLARE GRUNTED and started to turn over, then groaned when her ribs protested the movement. She didn't know if it was from the car or if she'd damaged them further when she fell down the ravine.

She struggled to push the fuzziness from her brain and tried to recall what had happened.

The wind howled over her, and she swore it whispered her name.

"Clare."

She listened intently, but heard nothing more. Just her mind playing tricks on her. Perhaps that happened after so many hours of silence. What was the longest she'd gone without some form of human contact? Hours, never days.

Wait, that hadn't been just another human voice —it had been Ethan's. Carefully she turned so as not to put pressure on her ribs and peered up the steep ravine, hoping against hope the voice wasn't a figment of her imagination.

Crushing disappointment weighed her down when she looked up and saw only Bailey sitting on the top of the ridge staring back at her.

Shoving her disappointment aside, she attempted to push into a sitting position. Pain shot up her shoulder. She dropped back onto the snow, sucked in slow breaths and waited for the throbbing in her arm to ease.

Her gaze traveled up the narrow chasm, and Clare realized she was damn lucky she'd had the snow to cushion her fall. She could have been severely injured or killed otherwise.

Snow also meant she had to get out of here or freeze to death. She studied the straight vertical walls covered in snow and ice.

How in the hell was she going to climb that?

"Clare."

Was she losing her mind? She could swear she heard Ethan calling out to her again.

She peered though the blanket of falling snow and blinked.

Was that a man scaling down the rock toward her?

She swiped the snow from her eyelashes and whatever she'd seen vanished. Only Bailey and Ballistic stared down at her.

She was losing it, that's all there was to it.

"Clare."

That was no hallucination.

"Ohmygod, Ethan!"

She wasn't alone. He'd found her, just as she'd always believed he would. Joy bubbled up inside her, and she barely felt the pain as she struggled to stand.

Before she got fully upright, Ethan swept her into his arms.

His hands brushed over her face, then down her body touching every inch of her. "You're alive. Thank God you're alive. I was so scared. I thought I'd never see you again."

His arms tightened around her, and he kissed her.

Clare relished his touch, savored his body against her own, inhaled his scent of earth and new fallen snow, confirmed it to memory.

She traced his face with her fingertips to assure herself he was real and not a hallucination.

"Ethan, it really is you, isn't it?"

The tenderness of his smile left her weak inside. God, she'd missed that smile. Feared she'd never see it again.

"It's really me." Concern puckered his brow. "How bad are you hurt?"

"I've got a couple of bruised ribs from the airbag, and I'm guessing a black eye. I bruised my shoulder, too."

Ethan carefully lifted her shirt to check her injury. He took out an elastic bandage from the pack strapped to his waist and began wrapping her ribs. His hands trembled against her skin as he worked. "When you didn't come home I-I was terrified." His fingers tightened around her waist before he blew out a breath and relaxed them. "It would have killed me to lose you, Clare. I love you more than life."

"I love you, too."

Ethan's eyes shone with love for her. "You know I would never have stopped searching for you, don't you?"

She inhaled a shaky breath. "Knowing that kept me going."

He brushed his knuckles over her cheek before he fashioned a sling for her arm. When he was finished, he lightly pressed his lips to her bruised eye. "What do you say we get you out of here and go home?"

Clare blinked back tears, his gentleness nearly her undoing. She swallowed against the lump in her throat and nodded.

He lifted her into his arms and cradled her against his chest. 'I'll always be here to protect you."

Clare snuggled into him and for the first time in a long, long time she was safe, secure, and content. Ethan had found her, and she'd been given the second chance she'd prayed for.

THEY ARRIVED home late that evening to find a receiving line of well wishers waiting for them. Jack and Ben were the first to race out of the house to hug their mother. Clare's parents followed, then Ethan's parents and what looked like the whole community of Paradise Falls. Clare had never felt more loved.

As soon as the well wishers dispersed, Dot ushered Clare inside and set a steaming bowl of soup and a cup of tea in front of her.

When she finished eating, Clare excused herself to shower. Thirty minutes later, she stepped into the bedroom, clean and refreshed to find Ethan waiting for her with a glass of wine.

"I thought you might like this to settle your nerves."

He knew her well. She smiled and accepted the glass. "You read my mind." She pressed her lips to his. "Thank you."

Ethan's eyes misted as he tenderly brushed a wet strand of hair from her face.

Clare pressed her cheek to his chest absorbing his warmth. "Thanks for bringing me home."

They stayed that way a moment until Clare pulled back. "I'm worn out. I need to sit down."

Ethan helped her into bed. "I'm going to shower. Call if you need anything." His fingers brushed the back of her hand.

The heady high from their reunion pumped through Clare as she sipped her wine. Life felt almost normal again.

A tap on the bedroom door pulled Clare from her thoughts. "Come in."

Jack pushed open the door, but remained in the doorway.

Clare waved him in.

Jack stared at the steam that curled through the partially open bathroom door where Ethan showered. "Could we talk in private a minute?"

"What about?"

"My truck."

"Has something happened to it?"

Jack shook his head. "Can we please talk out here?"

Clare set her glass on the nightstand, eased out of bed and followed him into the hallway. "What's going on with your truck?"

"Dad took it away and grounded me for–" Jack shrugged. "He said indefinitely. You've got to talk to him."

"He wouldn't do that without a reason."

Jack ducked his head. "He found out about McKenzie Meadow."

Clare silently digested that detail. "I'm not sure I disagree with him."

"Come on, Mom. It was just once."

Clare stared up at her son. Suddenly, she didn't care for his wheedling tone or his attempt to pit her and Ethan against one another. "I will discuss it with him, and we'll come to a decision on the truck and grounding together."

Jack snorted. "You didn't do that when Grace came home drunk."

"Grace wasn't driving."

"So it's okay if I drink as long as I'm not driving?"

"I never said that to Grace, and I'm not saying it to you. What you both did was serious, and there are consequences for your actions."

Hostility enveloped the narrow hallway. "I thought you'd keep Dad from freaking out like he did with Grace. Isn't that why you didn't tell him about her drinking?

Was it? She couldn't deny Ethan's constant battles with Grace had worn on her.

"I thought I could count on you to stand up for me–be in my corner."

Clare tamped down her irritation. She didn't like his blatant manipulation. "I'm always there for you, and I will talk to your dad."

Jack heaved a sigh of relief. "Thanks. At least you listen to reason."

ETHAN STEPPED BACK from the door, his hands clenched into fists after hearing Clare promise Jack she'd intervene for him. After everything they'd been through, he'd thought they were a team again, but now he wasn't so sure.

Clare entered the bedroom a moment later and smiled at him, her eyes warm and inviting. One hand curled around his neck and the other the waistband of his sweatpants. "Any chance you'd be interested in a little reunion sex?"

Ethan stared down into those eyes that he'd always depended on for support, but instead he saw betrayal. "Maybe we should discuss how you're going to make me listen to reason first."

Clare's brow puckered, then Ethan saw realization dawn. "You heard me talking to Jack."

"I heard you tell him you'd talk to me and that he was relieved because you were the reasonable one. What exactly are we discussing?"

"Couldn't we discuss this tomorrow?"

"That depends on if it's about the basketball game tomorrow or McKenzie Meadow."

Clare sighed and rubbed her forehead. "It's been a long day."

"Not so long that a moment ago you wanted to have sex with me, or was that how you were going to manipulate me on Jack's behalf?"

Clare's mouth went slack, then her face turned brilliant red. "You honestly think I would do that?"

"I don't know, but I have to wonder with as little sex as we've had in the last year."

Her breath came out in a rush. "And here we go again. I thought this was a fresh start, but clearly it isn't. For your information, I told Jack I would discuss what happened at McKenzie Meadow with you and together *we* would decide how to handle it."

Ethan's temper dissolved. "Oh...I'm sorry I jumped to conclusions."

Clare said nothing for a long moment. "You know, sorry just doesn't cut it anymore. You need to change your behavior."

He reached a hand toward her and she stepped back. "I'm a little sorer than I realized. I'm going to soak in the hot tub. Goodnight."

The bedroom door closed behind her, and any hope of reconciliation Ethan had been harboring went with it.

CLARE WENT through the motions of being a wife and mother. She managed to make it through Grace's ceremony and pretend her marriage was as solid as the headstone they'd just set.

She and Ethan smiled, they held hands, they were civil in public, but in private, away from the children and prying eyes, a hollow empty silence ate at Clare's spirit and made her want to be anywhere but with Ethan. It was as if their joyous reunion had been a dream rather than reality. While he was beside her physically, emotionally he'd abandoned her and he was as out of reach as Grace.

"Clare."

Her mother's voiced jarred her from the merry-go-round of emotions revolving through her head. She turned away from the window where she'd been staring at the lake in a desperate search for solace.

"Yes."

"Your father and I are leaving this afternoon."

Of course they were. Duty called. "I know. I remember."

She resumed her study of the lake, then looked back when her mother cleared her throat.

Clare watched her twist her wedding ring around and around her finger. Could Alexandria Benton be nervous?

Impossible. Nothing intimidated her mother. She had carried on conservations with heads of state and all manner of dignitaries. It was inconceivable she'd be nervous talking to her own daughter.

"Was there something more, Mom?"

"Could you sit down for a moment and talk?"

Clare took a seat beside her. Her mother sat as if she were having tea with the First Lady, but beneath her regal front, Clare sensed a thread of tension.

"I want to apologize."

Her mother was never wrong. "For what?"

"For not being here when you needed me."

Shocked into silence, Clare could only stare at her.

"I'm good at a lot of things. Ask me to plan a party, entertain, organize, and I'm in my comfort zone. The one-on-one intimate conversation is not an area in which I excel and it's where I've failed you. I know you feel I put your father's work before you when you were a child, and to an extent I did, but not as much as you seem to think. I suspect that's normal."

Her mother inhaled, and her hand trembled. "But where I've

really neglected you is as an adult. I haven't been here for you when you needed me. I wasn't here to help with your wedding, when your babies were born, or when Grace—I'm sorry. I've missed out on the major events of your adulthood, and I'll never get them back."

"Why now, Mom?"

She lifted an elegant shoulder. "I-I almost lost you." She paused, blinked away a sheen of moisture and cleared her throat. "I've lost a granddaughter, and I want my daughter to know what a wonderful, talented woman I've watched her become."

Emotion welled in Clare's chest. "Thank you. It means more than you know."

"I was also wrong about Ethan. I judged him unfairly. He's been a good husband and a good father. He was determined to find you, to rescue you. We could never have chosen anyone that would have made you as happy."

Tension flowed over Clare and her mother noticed.

"Clare, what's wrong?"

"Nothing. It's just been an emotional week, that's all."

"I know I've hurt you, but I'm trying to make amends. Isn't there something I can do?" She clasped Clare's hands.

Clare shook her head. "As a child I didn't see you as having strengths and weaknesses, but as an adult I understand. Thank you." She squeezed her mother's hands and relished the moment with her. "I-I know it couldn't have been easy for you to tell me this. I hope we can be closer now."

Her mother slid an arm around her shoulders. "I can see there's something upsetting you."

"I can't discuss it."

Clare leaned her head against her mother's shoulder and recalled a trip to the movies when she was very small, sharing popcorn and laughing.

"So you still don't trust me." Her mother's shoulders sagged.

"No, it isn't that. It's something I have to deal with on my own."

"You know, if my failing is an inability to form close relationships, you've acquired some of my bad habits."

"I've formed close relationships."

"Yes, I suppose you have, but you still hold yourself back. It's that little bit of me in you."

"Perhaps," Clare allowed. "But it doesn't change the fact it's not something I can talk about."

"Surely you can discuss it with Ethan."

"It's something I have to work out on my own."

Her mother arched a delicate brow high on her forehead. "Marriages tend to fail when you can't share with your partner."

Clare didn't respond.

Her mother started to pull back, then suddenly squeezed Clare tight. "I want to help. If you need me, call."

The sweet warmth of her whispered words stayed with Clare long after she left the room. For the first time in her adult life she and her mother had connected. She should be shedding tears of joy, of celebration, but instead her world was crumbling.

ETHAN LEANED AGAINST THE WALL, listening to Clare's muffled sobs, wanting to comfort her, but afraid to reach out. Every day since their return he'd felt Clare slipping further and further away. There was more distance between them now than before her accident.

If only he could go to her, console her, but he knew she'd turn him away. And he just couldn't bear another rejection. They had to find neutral ground and fast. Maybe after her parents left they would have some time alone to sort things out.

He slipped out the side door and walked down to the lake. The pine-scented air was invigorating, and it calmed him. His despair eased. All was not lost. They still had time to mend their fractured relationship.

His father-in-law came outside carrying luggage when Ethan arrived back at the house.

William set the bags on the deck. "Ethan, I have to apologize. I've thought over what you said about Clare's career, and I've come to realize you were right. In fact, I think I've known it for a long time, but I've been too stubborn to admit I was wrong. Clare would have been miserable doing anything other than what she's been doing. You saw that and I didn't."

William gazed out over the lake, then turned back to him. "Grace's death wasn't your fault, and neither was Clare's disappearance. You've been a good husband. I'm sorry."

His words left Ethan at a loss for words.

"I want to thank you, too."

Ethan found his voice. "For what?"

"For keeping your promise to me."

"What promise was that?"

"To bring Clare home, of course."

Ethan studied the older man, searching for any hint of censure, but all he saw was genuine gratitude. "You're welcome."

The words sounded trite, especially when he considered he may have brought her home, but he clearly made her miserable.

More failure to lug around.

Ethan watched a hawk swoop down over the lake and snag a trout from the pristine water. Gripping the fish in its claws, it disappeared into the forest and reminded him of just how easily Clare could slip away.

Pushing aside his concerns about the future, Ethan grabbed the bags and followed his father-in-law to the car. After they closed the trunk, William turned to him. "There's something else I'd like you and Clare to consider. Alexandria and I would very much like to pay for Jack and Ben's college."

Ethan started to protest, but William held up a hand stopping him. "I understand pride, Ethan. I've had too much of it myself. It's distanced me from my daughter. It's resulted in missing out on time with my grandchildren. I had to lose a granddaughter, and then nearly lose my daughter, to realize work can't always come first. Money is easier for me to hand out than my time, and I've done that far too much. I'm not trying to use it in place of myself this time.

Alexandria and I really want to do this. We know you are more than capable of providing for your family."

William cleared his throat, and his eyes misted. "We need to do this, Ethan, so I hope you and Clare will see your way clear and give us this privilege."

"I'll talk to Clare," Ethan promised, suddenly overcome with emotion himself.

"Well, I'd best see what's keeping Alexandria."

Ethan had never imagined a day where talking to his father-in-law would be easier than to his wife.

24

———————

Ethan sat at the bar nursing the same beer he'd had for the last hour. The fact that he preferred a warm beer at the Jolly Tavern, the local dive, to the company of his wife and children right now pretty much summed up his state of mind.

He'd taken a booth in a dark corner where he'd be free of prying eyes and unwanted conversation. He didn't have a clue how his father found him, but he slid into the seat opposite him.

"Mind some company?" his dad asked, clearly a rhetorical question.

"And if I said yes?"

"I'd tell you too damn bad."

"What are you doing here, Dad?"

"Coming to save you from yourself."

Ethan raised his eyes and glared at his father. "What makes you think I need saving?"

"Because you've got a life, and a wife, and children who need you, and you're tossing it all away the same as I did."

"I'm nothing like you." With his pulse throbbing at his temples, Ethan clutched his mug of beer.

His father calmly leaned back against the cracked vinyl, folding his arms over his chest. "Really. Could have fooled me."

Ethan's jaw clenched. "I'm not an alcoholic."

A chuckle momentarily filled the booth. "Definitely not, but your behavior is of a man who's looking to crucify himself. I know self-destructive behavior when I see it."

"And how is that the same as a man who drank away all his responsibilities?"

His father's gaze hardened. "The way I see it, you're tossing aside your responsibilities so you can wallow in guilt. Explain the difference."

Dumbfounded, Ethan opened his mouth to disagree, then snapped it closed when he couldn't think of a response.

"Have you ever asked yourself why you feel the need to punish yourself this way?" His father's dark eyes held him prisoner. "You've lost a daughter. Burying a child is something no parent should ever do, but don't let that tragedy ruin your life. Why are you throwing away the all the good you still have in your life?"

"I don't know." Ethan took a sip of his beer, then cringed when the warm brew slid down his throat.

"I'll tell you why. You're still angry at me, at the fact I wasn't the father you are. So in turn, you don't feel you deserve the life you've made for yourself. You've been waiting all these years for it to come crashing in on you, and when it did, deep down you weren't surprised. In fact, I think you expected it, that you've been waiting for it, and it arrived right on schedule."

His father's words slammed into him. "How do you know this?"

A sad smile creased his father's weathered lips. "Because I've lived it, waited for the other shoe to drop my whole life. I blurred my fears with alcohol. It took losing my granddaughter for me to pull myself up and take a hard look at how I'd hurt the people I loved. I've done things that are unforgivable, things that I'll never make amends for, relationships that will never be as deep or fulfilling as they would have been if I'd faced my shortcomings long ago. I missed out on being a good father, husband, and grandfather."

"So you're saying if I forgive you, all my problems will magically disappear?"

His father shook his head, expelling a weary sigh. "Nothing is that simple. What I'm saying is, you start by forgiving yourself, then everything else will begin to fall into place."

"I don't know how to do that."

His father shoved the beer aside and clasped Ethan's hand. "Then you need to find someone who can help you do it, just like I did."

"I've had counseling, Dad. It was too hard. Too painful."

"Yeah, it is hard and painful, but you've got to keep going until you feel better. You don't give up."

His father's fingers gripped his. "Give me your word you won't give up." His relentless gaze gave Ethan the strength to promise.

His father immediately released him and rose. "Good. I've got to get home. Your mother's holding dinner for me. I'd suggest you do the same."

Numbly, Ethan slid out of the booth, and followed his father out of the bar. Ironic how this time Ethan hadn't come to fetch his drunken father, but rather his father had come to fetch his delinquent son.

He had his father to thank for that change.

"I want to leave him. I'm not happy." Clare stared out the window watching the sun glint off the fresh layer of new snow. The bright light glaring through the window was as painful to her eyes as the words she'd spoken were to her heart.

Bruce looked up from the yellow legal pad. "Will leaving Ethan make you happy?"

"I don't know, but I've got to do something. All we do is argue."

What if she left and was even more miserable?

"About what?" Bruce asked.

Clare pulled in a deep breath. "I didn't tell him Jack had been drinking and driving."

Bruce's gaze studied her a long moment. "Why didn't you tell him?"

Clare waved an arm in the air. "He was busy, I was busy, then the accident happened–" Excuses. She hadn't told him for the same reason she hadn't told him about Grace or asking her parents for money.

Bruce waited for her to continue as if he knew she held something back.

"Just before Grace died, she got drunk with some friends. She begged me not to tell Ethan, and I let her tears sway me, then later I regretted it. I told her I was going to tell him, and then–"

"And then what?"

Tears blurred her vision, but she blinked them back. "She died."

"And you never told him."

Clare shook her head. "At first, I didn't even think of it between the funeral and Ethan in the hospital. It wasn't until I found out about Jack that I remembered."

"Did you tell him then?"

"No." Guilt tinged her voice. Clare pushed to her feet and moved to stare out the window, suddenly unable to sit still. "I was worn down, tired of the constant fighting between him and Grace. They were both so volatile. All it took was a word or a look to set them off, or so it felt at the time. I-I just wanted some peace.

"Ethan can be so...unbending at times. There's no room for error, and he takes everything to heart as if he alone is to blame when something goes wrong with the kids."

"Avoiding conflict won't resolve it." Bruce paused a moment before continuing. "Is it possible the reason you didn't tell him about Grace or asking your parents for money was to avoid conflict?"

Maybe it was.

～

CLARE WENT HOME after her session with Bruce and changed into her running clothes.

Ethan drove up as she stepped out the back door. They'd tiptoed around each other since they'd returned from the cabin two weeks ago.

His gaze slid over her, gauging, judging, analyzing her, and she realized he was carefully reviewing what he would and would not say to her just as she did with him.

"It's cold out," he said at last.

Clare's breath fanned out in a frosty white cloud. "It is."

She went down the steps and turned to the path that led to the lake.

"How was your session with Bruce?"

Clare slowly swiveled around to face him. "I made some progress."

He looked away from her to study the landscape, his tone measured and reasonable when he spoke. "Did you happen to discuss why you've been lying to me?"

She stared at him, anger and guilt battling for dominance. "I should have told you about Jack. I'm sorry."

"Why didn't you?"

"For the same reason I didn't tell you Grace got drunk."

Shock, then anger registered on his face. "Grace drank?"

"Once, right before she died. She went to a party and experimented like kids will do—like I did when I was her age."

His face turned a vivid red. "I had a right to know."

"You did, and I intended to tell you, but then she died and I forgot about it until I found out about Jack."

Bitterness oozed from him. "And you kept that from me, too."

"I did, and I was wrong to do that."

"Why Clare?"

Something in his voice cut through her, made her want to protect him from the truth, but she couldn't. Not any more. "I was afraid it would result in more arguments like you had with Grace."

"Confrontation is part of life. Do you think it's better to just ignore he was drinking and driving?"

"No, of course not. But I also think your need to be the perfect parent is part of the problem."

"Are you saying this is my fault?"

Anger pulsed through her. "No! And that is my point. You take everything to heart, immediately blame yourself. You overreact."

"What should I do? Behave like it's no big deal?"

Clare chewed her lower lip. "I didn't say we shouldn't do something, shouldn't be concerned, but constant conflict with the kids doesn't get to the heart of the problem."

Ethan's stance became unyielding. "That's where you're wrong. Jack's on the edge, and if we don't do something, he'll end up like my father." His eyes locked with hers. "I might overreact, but in this instance you're under reacting. I won't stand by and do nothing."

Clare opened her mouth to respond, but he stormed in the side door of the garage, slamming it behind him before she could. In all the years they'd been married, he'd never raised his voice to her. Never. Maybe it was a good thing he had now. Maybe it was a sign he cared enough to fight for their marriage. But did she even want him to?

TWO DAYS LATER, Clare walked out of Connaughton and Sons law offices in Coeur d'Alene. Her knees trembled and her stomach churned. She thought initiating divorce proceedings would calm her, but if anything it left her even more overwrought.

She glanced at the manila envelope clutched in her hand and wondered if she'd lost her mind. Would throwing away twenty years of marriage stop the ache inside of her? How could she break up her family, walk away from the man she loved?

Clare shivered and pulled up the hood of her coat. The clack of her boots echoed in the dense fog. Suddenly she felt as alone and isolated as she had when she was lost in the mountains.

She'd hoped after her session with Bruce the other day that she'd feel better, but she didn't. And her fight with Ethan afterward had convinced her she needed to take action.

Heart heavy, she climbed into the Jeep and drove home. She went straight to her office and put the documents in her desk drawer, then crossed over to the window to watch the snowflakes drift from the sky.

She longed for the cold winter mornings where she'd stayed curled in bed, her arms and legs entwined with Ethan's like a bizarre Twister move. She'd felt loved, and wanted, and needed back then, but now she felt—

She wasn't sure what she felt other than trapped in this barren emptiness that sucked the joy from her.

The doorbell rang.

Ben's holler echoed down the stairs. "I'll get it."

His footsteps clomped on the stairs. He skidded across the wood floor and stumbled into the front door with a loud oomph before he yanked it open.

Clare reached the entryway as he launched himself into his grandmother's arms. Dot's eyes misted over a moment before she collected herself.

Clare imagined her mother-in-law missed Grace's exuberant hugs. Even though Grace had been more reserved before she died, it hadn't been until now that Clare understood why. Her daughter had been suffocating.

In their natural instinct to protect their child, had she and Ethan gone too far, kept too tight a reign on her?

Blinking, she focused on Dot. "Would you like a cup of coffee?"

Dot released Ben and he went outside to play.

Her mother-in-law smiled at her. "I'd love some. Thanks."

Clare went to the kitchen, poured the coffee and set the mugs on the small table between a pair of rocking chairs in front of the fire.

Dot picked up her coffee and sipped it, her brow furrowing.

Clare studied her over the rim of her mug. "I get the feeling something is on your mind."

Brushing aside her flyaway curls that had long ago faded from blonde to gray, Dot raised her gaze to Clare's. "Honestly, I'm worried about you and Ethan."

Clare wished she could think of something to say that would reassure Dot, and herself, but she couldn't. Her mother-in-law had good reason to worry, but telling her that would solve nothing.

"What do you mean?"

Dot leveled a glare at Clare, something she'd never seen Dot do in the over twenty years she'd known her. "You know exactly what I mean. You're unhappy and so is Ethan. I've watched it building since Grace died, and I'd hoped the silver lining to your accident would be that it would bring you two closer together. But it's obvious it's done just the opposite."

Clare leaned toward the fire, feeling its warmth on her face, but inside she was frozen solid. Her voice trembled when she spoke. "I can't discuss this with you, Dot."

Dot grabbed her arm and squeezed it tightly. "Don't give up on him, Clare. I know he's stubborn and hardheaded, just like his father, but he's worth fighting for."

The fierceness of Dot's voice startled her. Dot had always been sweet and kind. She'd dedicated her life to cajoling everyone to get along in the fantasy world she'd created where her husband wasn't an alcoholic and they lived an ideal life. The woman sitting beside her now had a depth Clare hadn't seen before.

"You're my daughter, the same as if I gave birth to you. I'm not losing you, not after Grace."

The coffee mug trembled in Clare's hand. "I'm sorry, but I have to move on, which I admit scares the crap out of me."

Dot nodded and clucked her tongue. "Of course you are. Moving forward means leaving some of Grace behind. It might mean leaving Ethan behind."

Clare's gaze shot up to Dot's. Did she know about the divorce papers? "What do you mean?"

Dot lifted her mug, the steam curling up into her face. "I'm saying I know that look in a woman's eyes when she's thinking about calling it quits. I was there once. I even went so far as to have divorce papers drawn after Grace died. I think finally taking a stand drove Ben to change, to be the man I needed him to be."

She didn't ask Clare if she'd made the same move. Instead she stared out the window at Lake Serenity, calm and serene as the Madonna.

"Dot, I don't know what to say."

"There's nothing to say, Clare. Stop stalling and do what you have to do. You need to force yourself and Ethan to become the people you were both meant to be. Just don't give up on yourself or him. That's all I'm asking."

Dot set her mug down. "I need to get home." She pressed a kiss to Clare's cheek, then whispered in her ear. "It will all work out. Just have a little faith."

The sun sank low in the sky as Clare continued to stare into the fire. Her fingers curled into the wooden arms of the chair. Dot wanted her to risk everything. To put all her cards on the table and see if Ethan took the safe bet or went for broke.

And what if he took the safe route and walked away? What if he gave up on them, gave up on her without even trying? Could she bear to start over? Could she bear to live without Ethan?

The real question was, could she continue to exist in the lonely, empty life she was living?

25

Ethan collected the homework assignments he'd forgotten the day before and headed home to grade them. He rarely worked on Saturday any more, but he needed something to relieve his agitation. Since his last fight with Clare, Ethan had felt a sense of doom hanging over him that he couldn't shake.

He locked his classroom door. His heart heavy, he crossed the parking lot to his truck. His relationship with Clare had deteriorated to the point they scarcely spoke to each other. They behaved like a couple on the brink of divorce.

Ethan climbed into his truck and tossed the sheath of papers on the seat beside him. He rested his head on the steering wheel and fought the urge to start the truck and drive away. Leave his problems behind. Leave Clare behind. He was tired of fighting, tired of being alone.

Instead, he put the truck in gear and pulled out of the parking lot. He turned onto Pine Ridge Street and a deer leapt out in front of him.

He slammed on the brakes. Papers flew.

He narrowly missed the doe and her two fawns. Heart pounding, he watched them bound into the forest and disappear. He pulled to the curb and began collecting the papers. He reached under the seat for the rest of them and a bottle of whiskey rolled out from underneath. He picked up the half-empty bottle. His hand trembled as his life did a rapid rewind.

Suddenly the son he cherished had transformed into his alcoholic father. Jack had left this bottle in his truck. He didn't have to ask him to know it was a fact.

Did it make him a horrible father to want to pretend he hadn't seen the bottle?

Jack needs you.

Ethan whipped his head toward the window and searched the wooded area hoping to catch a glimpse of his daughter.

Her whispered words these last two years had been the bridge between despair and insanity.

An image of Jack mimicking his grandfather's drinking made Ethan's heart shudder. He couldn't walk away from his family no matter how tempting the idea. Clare might not need him, but Jack and Ben did. And he wouldn't let them down.

Ethan emptied the bottle, then put the truck into drive, and set off for home.

The house was silent when he arrived ten minutes later.

Find Jack.

He took the stairs two at a time and found his firstborn sprawled across the bed, hung-over and pale. An empty bottle of Jack Daniels lay on the floor next to his nightstand.

Ethan picked up the bottle and hurled it into the garbage can, venting his anger and frustration.

Jack's eyes rolled open. "What did you do that for?"

"To get your attention."

Jack sat up and leaned over the edge of the bed, cradling his head in his hands. "I don't really feel like talking right now, Dad."

"I'm sure you don't, but we're going to. Get dressed. We'll walk around the lake and talk. The fresh air will make you feel better."

Jack's face contorted in rage. "I don't want any goddamned fresh air."

Ethan threw a tee-shirt at him. "Too bad. It wasn't a request. Now get some clothes on, or go naked."

The fact that he rarely raised his voice to his children was probably the reason Jack responded. Ethan didn't care why he obeyed, only that he did.

They walked in silence, the packed snow crunching beneath their feet. The biting wind whistled through the thick grouping of pine trees and cut through Ethan, the same as his fear for Jack.

When they were out of earshot of the house, Ethan motioned to a fallen log. "Sit down."

Jack remained standing, belligerence oozing from him. "If this is going to be a lecture about how your Dad started drinking when he was in high school, and how he became an alcoholic, and how that means I could have the genes for it, too, don't bother."

Jack's words so similar to Clare's brought him up short. He thought back to all the times he'd reigned in his temper and calmly explained his feelings to his children, and he'd seen their eyes roll. Maybe Clare was right. Maybe certain situations called for an emotional approach.

"Sit!"

Jack blinked, then sat.

Ethan inhaled and stared off in the distance. He picked up a rock and skipped the glassy water, while he collected himself. When the ripples faded away, he braced a foot on the log beside Jack and looked him directly in the eye.

"I'm not here to debate whether or not you're an alcoholic or to lecture you."

Jack glared up at him. "Then why are you here?"

Ethan clenched his hands to keep from grabbing Jack and shaking him. Why was it so difficult to talk to his son? They used to talk all the time, but since the accident they'd become virtual strangers, not unlike his relationship with Clare. He had to find a way to reach his son. He wouldn't fail him like he had Clare. Maybe the place to start was from his gut as Clare had suggested. It worked a moment ago. Maybe it would work now.

"I'm here because I'm your father, and I am going to stop you from making your grandfather's mistakes. Mistakes that he may never be able to atone for."

"This sounds like a lecture to me."

Ethan scowled at Jack, his temper ratcheting up a notch. "Stop your wisecracking and listen."

Jack glared at him, but he remained silent. It wasn't much, but Ethan was grateful for it. He exhaled and prayed for a little help from above.

"Why you drink is more important than the fact you drink, whether you're seventeen or seventy-five. My father started drinking when he was just a little younger than you. He didn't do it to be cool or fit in. He did it to forget his mother was dying. He said it numbed him, and he liked that feeling, so he kept doing it."

The hollowness inside that had never completely left, haunted Ethan again. No matter how many times he heard his father's story, resentment stirred rather than empathy. He pushed away the feelings and focused on his son.

"I'm not drinking my problems away."

"Then why are you drinking?"

Jack shrugged, his eyes sliding away. "I dunno."

"That's not an answer. Tell me why you feel the need to drink."

Jack jumped to his feet. He paced along the shore, the water lapping against his shoes. "I said I don't know, now leave it alone, will you?"

"No, I won't leave it alone. I don't want you to end up like your grandfather. I want you to have a better life."

"I'm not him. I'm not an alcoholic."

"I didn't say you were. But that doesn't mean you don't need help."

"What, like rehab?"

"Not necessarily."

"I've heard enough of this shit." Jack tried to elbow past him.

Ethan stood firm, blocking his exit. Jack was testing him to see if he cared enough to break through his bravado. "The only way you're leaving here is through me."

Defiance burned in Jack's eyes, but he remained silent.

"I won't let you mess up your life. Your grandfather lost three decades that he can never get back. When Grace died he got worse. He was drunk day and night. It was so bad the doctor said if he didn't stop it would kill him, but he didn't care because I think the truth was he wanted to die. If he hadn't gotten help I think he would have died. I don't want you to get to that point. I'm here to help you. To be by your side."

Scorn twisted Jack's features. "You're here for me? That's crap."

"What's that mean?"

"It means talking to you does about as much good as talking to Grace. You're both ghosts. At least with Grace I know she's dead. You're here, but you don't see or hear me. You're more concerned with how to fix things with Mom than listening to me."

Ethan wanted to deny his words, but couldn't. "I'm listening now."

"Yeah right."

"I will do whatever it takes to get you the help you need. Your mother and I will do an intervention if that's what it takes."

Jack snorted. "Good luck with that. Like you two can't agree on anything right now."

Ethan flinched and absorbed the words like physical blows. "You can either cooperate with me, or I'll talk to the school counselor. If need be, I'll involve the police. But one thing is for certain, I won't stop until you get the help you need."

Jack's fists clenched and fury burned deep in his eyes. "I don't need your help."

Ethan considered backing down, but he stayed firm. "Yes, you do. You're afraid I'll let you down, and I don't blame you. Honestly, I have let you down. I haven't been much of a father since Grace's death, but this time I'll be there for you."

He grabbed Jack and hugged him tight, ignoring his struggles. "I know you don't believe me, but I will be here for you. You won't know this until it's all over, but you can count on me. I'm not leaving you. I'm here for the long haul."

Jack's struggles gradually subsided, and his arms closed around his father. "I'm scared, Dad. I don't know what to do, where to turn."

"I've got a plan. You just leave it all to me."

ETHAN SEARCHED Clare's desk two days later for a pad of paper.

Nothing.

He opened the middle drawer.

Pens and pencils.

He opened the lower drawer and found a white spiral notebook. He grabbed it, then froze when he read Connaughton and Sons on the outside of a manila envelope. He pulled it out.

Divorce papers.

He slammed his palm on the desk. She'd finally given up on him. Why was he surprised after the fight they'd had a few days ago?

How would he go on without Clare by his side? Since Grace's death she'd kept him functioning. Given him a reason to breathe in and out.

The door slammed, and Clare's voice echoed down the hallway. "Ethan."

He turned as she stepped into the room. Her gaze dropped to the divorce papers scattered over her desk, then up at him. "You found the papers."

"Yes."

Clare folded her arms over her chest, her expression blank. "Aren't you going to say something?"

"What's there to say? You've made your decision."

Anger pinched her lips and narrowed her eyes. "So you're just going to give up? Walk away?"

"Is this some kind of test?"

"No!"

"Then what is it?"

"It's me searching for happiness."

"So, I'm making you unhappy."

"At this moment you're a big contributor."

"What do you want from me, Clare?"

She threw up her hands. "I want to talk, to share what we're feeling. I feel abandoned, alone, even though we live in the same house, share the same bedroom. I can't go on the way we've been. At my last session with Bruce I realized nothing will change unless we do something to change our situation. This is my something."

She paced the length of the room, then spun and faced him. "Have you got anything to say?"

They stared at one another a long minute, then Clare shoved open the glass door and walked out onto the deck.

Anger sent Ethan chasing after her. "That's it? You get to spill your guts then walk away?"

Clare faced him, her eyes alight like a Fourth of July fireworks display. "Do you have something to say?"

He exhaled, his anger replaced with fear. He studied the icy path that led to the lake and felt a similar trail of ice threading around his heart. The thing he cherished most was slipping through his fingers. He might as well go for broke and tell her everything.

"I'll concede I've spent my whole life searching for respectability. Craving it like my father craved a drink. I've gone the extra mile not to become my father."

"You—"

Ethan threw up a hand. "You just told me you wanted me to share my feelings. So listen."

Clare pursed her lips, then tucked her hands in her pockets and nodded for him to continue.

"I may have gone too far, and I will make every effort to change." Ethan exhaled heavily. "After the accident I was certain I'd let you down. That I'd failed you. That I'd become my father. Rather than admit this, I shut you out. You became the scapegoat for all my inadequacies. I told myself I could live with the distance between us, but what I couldn't live with was your loathing.

"I didn't realize how much my actions hurt you, but I promise you things will be different. I can't swear perfection. I can't promise I won't worry when you go out on photo shoots alone, or that I won't bury my feelings about my childhood, or continue to try and be the perfect parent. I want to change, but you have to stop lying to me. You have to help by being more vocal about your needs."

Clare's eyes went wide with surprise. "I don't hide my feelings from you."

Ethan arched a brow at her. "Don't you?"

She kicked the toe of her shoe in the hard-packed snow. "I've tried talking to you."

"You'll talk about anything except what's really bothering you. I think you keep distance between us to avoid controversy. You need to tell me what you're feeling. I'm not a mind reader."

Clare stared out at Lake Serenity, her fingers curled around the railing. "When we lost Grace, I wasn't sure you'd live. I didn't realize until now that to protect myself from losing you, I held back. That I've always held a little bit back. I did it when I was a child, so that my parents' rejection didn't hurt as much. I can see now I didn't tell you things about my past because that would mean baring everything, taking a risk. I withheld information about the kids because maybe I wanted to have the perfect family that never fought, never had problems and blamed you." She faced him. "I'm sorry."

Ethan threaded his fingers through hers. "I'm sorry, too. We have to let go, Clare."

"Let go of what?"

"Of our pasts. Of Grace. I've seen you in Grace's room, heard you talking to her at night when you thought I was asleep."

"I can't forget her if that's what you're suggesting."

He shook his head, the sadness in her eyes slicing him through and through. "You couldn't do that any more than I could. What I'm asking you to do is not to be afraid to live. To embrace the life we have without her."

"I know you're right. I know we need to make a life without Grace. She would want us to be happy." Tears trembled on Clare's lashes. "I just wish Grace was going to be a part of that future."

Ethan caught her tear on his fingertip. "Me too, but if we're going to survive this, we have to move forward—together."

The tears fell freely as she stared into his eyes. "It feels wrong to find joy when our daughter's dead."

"I know." Ethan blinked back the moisture from his own eyes.

"Do you still blame yourself for her death?"

Ethan clasped her hand as he thought over her question. "There will always be a part of me that feels responsible, that will never get over losing her."

"Is it—" Clare paused, her eyes probed his before she continued. "Is it possible your guilt is actually regret that you'll never have a chance to know her after she grew up?"

Ethan considered her observation. "Yeah, that's possible. Bruce said something similar." He swallowed back the lump of emotion in his throat. "It was so hard when she stopped idolizing me."

Clare's eyes mirrored the ache inside him that never quite went away. Before him stood the one person who felt his pain. Lived with it day in and day out. Why had he turned away from her?

His arms went around her, and he pressed his face into her hair, absorbing her warmth and the comfort of her body. "Do you think Grace forgives me for all the arguments we had before she died?"

Clare pulled back and cupped his face in her hands. Her voice turned warrior-woman fierce when she spoke. "Grace was not the kind of person to hold a grudge. Your daughter loved you, worshipped the ground you walked on."

Grace's shimmering image appeared beside them. Her warmth, her sweet cinnamon and sugar scent radiated over them.

Ethan's fingers tightened around Clare's as he reached out his other hand to his daughter. His fingers passed through her, but he felt her warmth, her presence envelop him.

Grace's voice whispered over them. "I don't blame you. Always remember how much I love both of you."

She smiled and waved, then vanished.

Ethan looked down at Clare, her eyes wide and filled with hope, then sorrow.

"Did you see her?" Clare asked.

Ethan tightened his hold on her shoulders. "I did. You've seen her before, haven't you?"

"Yes. I-I was afraid I was losing my mind."

"Me too. But I never saw her. I've only heard her voice. This is the first time I've actually seen her. She was real, wasn't she?"

"Yes! I've been afraid that if I move forward she'll stop coming. Is that crazy?"

Ethan shook his head. "Not crazy no, but we can't put our lives on hold to catch a glimpse of our girl. I don't think that's why she came to us or what she'd want, do you?"

"N-n-no, I suppose not, but I'm scared that without her I'll be alone in my grief. I can't go it alone."

Her voice broke, and so did Ethan's heart. "You have me."

"Do I?"

"You can tell me anything, and I'll be there for you."

Moisture gathered in her eyes again. "I'm not sure that's enough."

Ethan's heart thumped violently. He'd offered her everything and it wasn't enough. "What more do you want?"

Those glacial blue eyes seared into his soul. "It has to go both ways. You have to confide in me. Share your grief with me, too."

The strain across his shoulders eased. "I can do that." He had Clare to confide in when there was no one else to listen.

Clare's finger brushed over his lips. "You are the only man I will ever love."

Ethan looked down at the face he cherished and pressed his forehead against hers. "I love you, too, Clare. The thought of life without you is unbearable. Don't leave me. Stay with me and let's make our marriage work."

"Yes, yes, emphatically yes, but we have to keep talking to each other even if it hurts."

Ethan tilted her face to his, and kissed her long, and thoroughly, and with all the pent up passion he'd been holding inside. "I will move heaven and earth to keep us together."

He pressed his cheek to hers and turned them so they could see the quarter slice of moon that rose in the eastern sky. "I have this crazy thought our daughter is sitting in that quarter moon swinging her leg and watching over us."

He felt Clare's smile against his cheek. "I like that image."

"Me too."

A wolf howled in the distance and one of the kids turned on the radio. A Mark Dinning melody from the sixties drifted outside.

Clare held out her hand to him. "Dance with me."

Ethan slipped his arms around her, and they swayed to the music as Dinning's voice wailed on about his teen angel while Clare and Ethan's own teen angel took her place in their hearts.

"Do you think Grace is okay?" Clare asked.

Ethan stroked his hands over her back. "I do, and I think she's smiling down on us right now. I also think that's why she came to both of us. To reassure us."

"That eases the ache in my heart."

Ethan rested his chin on the top of her head, his voice was garbled when he spoke. "Mine, too. Mine, too."

The song ended and Bob Seger blasted out of the stereo. A vision of Tom Cruise dancing in his underwear made Ethan smile. A good life was indeed risky business and just what he and Clare needed. It was time they lived, and loved, and danced to all the wonderful things life had in store for them.

Ethan swung Clare high into the air.

Her laughter caught on the breeze, and sent it whispering across the lake. A laugh identical to their daughter's. Ethan allowed the bittersweet memory to fill him, and in turn, he was graced with a memory of dancing with his daughter.

He dipped Clare low as he embraced life, and love, and the woman who'd taken him out of the darkness and into the light. He knew with certainty this was their turning point, and they would make it through. But most importantly there was hope that they could build a life without Grace.

Life wouldn't always be easy, but it wouldn't always be hard. Through it all they would be together. And in the end that's all that really mattered.

EPILOGUE

Eleven months later…

Clare clutched her purse to her chest determined she wouldn't cry. It wasn't like Jack would be living a continent away while he went to college. He was only an hour from home, and he would easily be able to visit, but still leaving him with Matty was a huge step for her and Ethan.

There was also the pain of knowing they would never do this with Grace, but that pain wasn't as sharp as it had been in the past. With the help of their counselor, she and Ethan were coming to terms with Grace's death and learning to live with it.

They'd learned there was no escaping their grief, but that it didn't have to consume them. And that being happy didn't mean they'd forgotten their daughter, that they didn't still love her. Nothing could ever do that, but they could lead happy, productive lives without her. They had to for Jack and Ben's sakes as well as their own.

They'd also learned to talk again—something they'd lost. It was a gift Clare cherished each and every day, and it had enriched their lives beyond Clare's wildest dreams.

A hand squeezed her shoulder and Clare looked up expecting it to be Ethan, but it was her father. "It's not easy letting them go, is it?"

Clare shook her head, unable to speak for a moment as she struggled to contain her emotions.

"It was unbearably hard when you left home," he said, his eyes misting. "I wished we'd dealt with it differently, but your mother and I buried ourselves in activities to keep from missing you so much. Unfortunately, our actions came across as if we didn't care about you. Didn't have time for you. And then as time went on, the strain deepened, and it was just easier to keep up our schedules than try and break through the barriers you'd erected."

Clare slid her arm through her father's and leaned her head on his shoulder. "I'm sorry, Dad. I didn't know."

"I'm not blaming you. I just want you to know we always loved you and wanted to be part of your life. When Grace died, we were lost. We didn't cope well, and we weren't there for you. I'm sorry for that, too."

Clare pressed a kiss to his cheek. "It's okay. What's important is that you and Mom are here now. That we're rising from the ashes and starting over."

He kissed the top of her head. "I suppose I had better go find your mother before she starts trying to redecorate this place."

Clare laughed as she watched him walk away. Ethan waylaid her father and was no doubt thanking him for paying for Jack's college.

Not only had she and Ethan learned to deal with Grace's death, but they'd also learned that accepting help from her parents wasn't a sign of weakness or failure, but a way of bringing them all closer together. Clare had also discovered her father had changed his business practices over the years, improving working conditions and pay for his employees.

Dot and Ben stood near the door speaking with Jack. Ethan laughed at something his father said. Her father-in-law continued to struggle with his alcoholism, would always struggle with it, but he was making a real effort to change.

Ethan came over to her and swept her into his arms, kissing her soundly in front of everyone.

Jack made a gagging sound. "Hey, knock that off. You're ruining my appetite."

"Yeah," Ben chimed in. "I thought we were going to get pizza. I'm starving."

"I want ham and pineapple," Jack said.

Ben wrinkled his nose. "Gross. I want a meat combo."

Jack lightly punched Ben's stomach. "You're going to have a heart attack before you get into high school with all the junk you eat."

Ben shoved him. "Shut up."

Jack grabbed him by the waistband.

Ben swung at him and missed. "Let me go."

Before Ethan released her, he leaned down and whispered in her ear. "There are some advantages to having children go off to college."

"A few," she agreed. A break from Jack and Ben's bickering was certainly a plus, but she suspected she might even miss that, too, at some point.

She looked up at Ethan and her heart swelled with love. Since the day she'd torn up the divorce papers, they'd learned their love went far deeper than either of them realized. She knew with certainty that no matter what life threw at them, they would make it, because their love would always and forever tie them together.

The End

If you enjoyed **The Murphy Clan** in *Falling in Love...Again*, here's a sneak peek of book two in the Falling in Love series, Falling in Love With You.

PREGNANT.

Impossible.

Abby Sullivan stared at the twin pink lines on the pregnancy test, willing them to disappear. It had to be wrong. It had to be a horrible mistake.

"Well?" Her grandmother's sharp demand penetrated the thick oak door.

"Well, what?"

"Don't play games with me, Abigail. I've been pregnant six times, and I know the signs like I do my shoe size."

Abby groaned. How could this have happened?

She knew *exactly* how it had happened, and she was elated and dejected at the same time. She stared at the test strip in her hand, then her pale reflection in the mirror. The scattering of freckles across her nose was more pronounced.

She swept her normally lustrous auburn hair into a ponytail, blew out a breath, and pulled open the door.

She held up the pregnancy stick, and her grandmother peered through her wire-rimmed glasses at the results. She grunted and nodded.

"Good." Maureen O'Hara, *not* Maureen O'Hara the actress, spun around with surprising agility for her seventy-two years and started back to the kitchen, leaving Abby to scurry after her.

"What do you mean, good?" How could being widowed and pregnant be a good thing to her staunchly religious Catholic grandmother?

The tea kettle screamed. Her grandmother turned it off, filled the teapot with practiced ease, and settled the lid in place. She carried it to the tiny table covered with a hand embroidered damask tablecloth pressed within an inch of its life.

Hand-painted china tea cups with matching saucers were neatly set on the table—all part of her grandmother's dowry, brought with her from Ireland fifty years ago when she'd married Abby's grandfather.

Her grandmother belonged to an era that had virtually vanished from the twenty-first century. She still ironed everything—sheets, underwear, towels, jeans—anything she could put an iron to was wrinkleless.

Gram believed in meals at tables, afternoon tea with tea cups, saucers, and brewed tea—never from a bag—all seeped in tradition just like Gram. Growing up, Abby had desperately wanted to leave tradition behind, at least a little, but at thirty-eight she'd come to appreciate all the special touches her grandmother clung to.

Abby took the clotted cream and her grandmother's homemade black currant jam from the refrigerator and placed them on the table, alongside the fresh-from-the-oven drop scones.

When the tea was brewed to perfection, her grandmother poured them each a cup, then took her seat in the breakfast nook that overlooked the snow-covered garden. After blowing on her tea, she sipped exactly as she'd done the day Abby came to live with her after her father died. At ten Abby had thought teatime silly, but now she appreciated the regularity, the stability, it had given her when everything in her life had been turned upside down.

"So, when are you going to tell Noah?"

Abby rattled her cup on the saucer. "What makes you think Noah is the father?"

Her grandmother placed a scone on her plate and delicately broke it open. "Who else could it be? You've always been in love with him."

That wasn't true. She'd loved Jon. Had always loved Jon. Noah had been—why could she never define what Noah meant to her? Dependable, trustworthy, kind, caring. That sounded more like a description of Cujo, his dog, than the man she'd made love to less than six weeks after her husband died.

What kind of woman did that? A lonely, desperate woman in need of comfort.

It's more than that and you know it, Abby.

Her grandmother continued, not allowing Abby an opportunity to respond to her comment or the voice in her head. "Are you worried Noah won't be happy to learn he's going to be a father again? When I found out I was pregnant with your uncle Adin, I raced over to the lumberyard to tell your grandfather, who was ecstatic about the news."

"That's different. You were married."

Her grandmother lifted a narrow shoulder. "So, you go to confession and Father Flannigan will have you do penance. I'll admit I'd prefer you'd married him first, but it's a little late for that. We'll have a small service and—"

Abby held up a hand. "Hold on. I never said anything about marriage." But having a baby...That was a dream come true, and one that she had never expected to happen. Picturing her baby replaced the emptiness inside and filled her with warmth and tenderness.

A fierce determination built inside her to be the parent her father hadn't been.

Her grandmother paused, the china cup against her lips, her sharp blue eyes piercing Abby. She set her cup down and folded her hands in her lap. "This baby needs two parents."

"This baby has me." And she would cherish this child and lavish it with love and stability, something she'd never had until she'd come to live with Gram.

"You'll make a fine mother, but a child needs her father."

Gram didn't add "As you well know," but she might as well have. Even though her father had severely lacked in the parenting department, Abby had missed him desperately. He'd been the only parent she'd ever known since her mother had died days after her birth. How could she deny the truth in her grandmother's words? A child needed a father, but a sober one who took care of his child.

Noah would be that and more, but would he want the job? Would he even want her?

She'd married a man who'd loved her like a sister. She refused to do that again. *If*, and it was a big if she married again, it would be with a man who cherished her, loved her beyond reason, couldn't imagine life without her at his side.

Her grandmother reached across the table and squeezed her hand. "Why are you hesitating?"

As a child, Abby had been certain Gram could read her mind, and her grandmother's insight now reinforced her belief. Telling her would mean admitting Gram had been right all those years ago when she'd told Abby it was a mistake to marry Jon.

Abby looked down into the tea cup. "I shouldn't have married Jon."

Her grandmother grunted, then patted her hand. "You know I

wasn't totally right. You did a good thing marrying him. I just didn't want you to sacrifice being loved."

Abby's throat clogged with emotion, and her voice came out in a strangled whisper. "I loved Jon."

Once upon a time, she'd loved him so fiercely it caused a physical pain in her chest. But fifteen years of marriage had changed her from a dewy-eyed college student to a pragmatic widow whose rose-colored glasses had been replaced with a hearty dose of reality.

Gram's eyes softened. "I know you did."

A tear slid down Abby's cheek. "I miss him."

"I do too, but it was time for him to go. His life stopped being a good one a long time ago. I sometimes think he hung on as long as he did for you. He may not have loved you passionately, but he loved you as deeply as he could. You know I loved that boy, too."

Abby could only nod. She'd admitted to no one, not even Gram, her conflicted emotions. She missed Jon, wanted so much to see him, touch him, and at the same time was relieved to have her freedom.

"He'd be pleased about this baby."

Abby stared at her grandmother in disbelief. "You don't know that."

"I do. His one regret was never giving you a child."

"He gave me so much else."

"That he did."

"Why him?"

Her grandmother squeezed her arm. "I don't know. I've never met a more selfless soul. Maybe all his work to raise money for research will find a cure for ALS. Maybe that was his purpose on this earth."

Abby thought it more a cruel twist of fate gave Jon that disease. She'd questioned God and her faith when Jon told her he had ALS.

Abby's stomach rumbled.

"Drink your tea. You'll feel better."

Abby sipped her tea and wondered how to tell a man with two grown children he was going to be a father again. As much as that thought made her stomach churn, the gloom that had hung over her since Jon died eased. Whether or not Noah wanted this baby, she did. And no matter what happened, she would cherish this child.

ORDER FALLING in Love With You now!

Need another Falling in Love book right now? Download a rivals to lovers Falling in Love For The First Time here!

ALSO BY KATHY COATNEY

Thank you for reading *Falling for You...Again,* part of *The Murphy Clan. The Murphy Clan* can all be read as stand alone books, but there are also three series within the Clan—*Falling in Love, Return to Hope's Crossing, Crooked Halo Christmas Chronicles,* and a *Vermont Christmas Romance.* If you enjoyed the characters of Paradise Falls, be sure and check out the Falling in Love series and the entire Murphy Clan.

If you liked this book, I'd love it if you'd leave a review at Goodreads and BookBub.

I love hearing from my fans. You can contact me through my website, newsletter, or join my Facebook group Kathy Coatney's The Beauty Bowl. I share information about my books, excerpts, and other fun information. If you like free books come join Kathy Coatney's Review Team by sending me an email kathy@kathycoatney.com.

All my books are small town, contemporary romances with uplifting stories of hope, a sprinkling of quirky characters and a happily ever after.

Contact me at:

Website

Kathy Coatney's The Beauty Bowl

The Murphy Clan

Falling in Love series

Falling For You...Again

Falling in Love With You

Falling in Love For The First Time

Falling in Love With Him

Return to Hope's Crossing series

Forever His

Forever Mine

Forever Yours

Crooked Halo Christmas Chronicles

Be My Santa Tonight

Her Christmas Wish

Under the Mistletoe

A Vermont Christmas Romance

Santa Comes to Snowside

Box Set

Falling in Love Box Set

Crooked Halo Christmas Chronicles Box Set

ABOUT THE AUTHOR

I've spent long hours behind the lens of a camera, wading through cow manure, rice paddies and orchards over my thirty-year career as a photojournalist specializing in agriculture.

I also love—and write—deeply emotional, small-town contemporary romance. Ironically, some of my books carry an agriculture thread in them, some more than others. Please note I used to write these books under Kate Curran, but now I write all books under Kathy Coatney.

I also writes a series of nonfiction children's books, From the Farm to the Table and Dad's Girls.

When I'm not writing, you'll find me mountain biking, cross-country skiing, or running—a really, really slow jog that's been compared to a pace slower than a tortoise.